Taken by a Dragon

Felicity Heaton

ETERNAL MATES SERIES

Kissed by a Dark Prince
Claimed by a Demon King
Tempted by a Rogue Prince
Hunted by a Jaguar
Craved by an Alpha
Bitten by a Hellcat
Taken by a Dragon

Find out more at: www.felicityheaton.co.uk

CHAPTER 1

She had passed out at some point.

It might have been shortly after the dragon shifter who had abducted her had hit a height that had made her vision do strange things, zooming in and out as she had stared wide-eyed at the thousand-foot-plus drop to the forbidding black lands below. She had certainly lost the contents of her stomach at that point.

Anais lay with her eyes closed, feigning unconsciousness, keeping her breathing light and even and her heart rate steady and slow. She wasn't alone. She could feel the piercing gaze of the man who had snatched her from the midst of the battle.

A battle where they had been enemies, fighting on opposite sides. Her in the army of the Third Realm of the demons, and him on the side of the Fifth Realm.

When she had set eyes on him, laying in the middle of the mad fray, staring at her and Sable as if they were goddesses or something born of myth and legend, the last thing she had expected was him to transform into an incredible and enormous blue dragon, and she definitely hadn't expected him to snatch her and fly off with her.

Anais breathed slowly, biding her time, waiting for her faculties to all come back. Years of training cycled through her mind, everything she had learned as a huntress for Archangel coming to the fore now that she needed it. Calm flowed through her and she clung to it, using it as a shield as she told herself on repeat that fear wasn't an emotion she was going to allow herself to feel.

She was going to remain calm because she needed a clear head, one not clouded by panic, if she was going to find a way out of this mess. That same head ached as she tried to think, throbbing behind her eyes and around her temples. Maybe she had passed out from lack of oxygen. It was possible. Anything seemed possible in this insane realm.

Hell.

When she had been told to assemble as part of Sable's team that would be venturing into Hell on Archangel's first mission to that new land, she hadn't known what to expect. It was black and grim, and filled with creatures straight out of the nightmares of most normal people.

She was far from normal though.

She had fought vampires, werewolves, warlocks and demons. Even some fae and cat shifters. All in the name of protecting the unsuspecting humans and the good non-humans who shared the mortal realm from those who would do them harm.

She had never met a dragon shifter though.

Anais slowly opened her eyes.

They settled on a black-dust-covered pair of bare feet and tracked upwards, over smooth blue leather encased legs and a honed naked torso to the shifter who had abducted her.

He crouched beside her, his aquamarine eyes stunning in the weak light from the fire she could feel near her feet and hear as its crackles and pops filled the thick silence. That same golden light played on sculpted cheekbones and profane lips, a mouth made for wicked things. She quickly reminded herself that he had a killer set of teeth behind those sensual lips. Twin rows of tiny white daggers that he had flashed at Sable when her superior had talked about studying him.

He canted his head, causing a hank of wild blue hair to slip down and caress his brow. His dark blue eyebrows dipped low, causing his striking eyes to narrow. Curious. He had looked that way back in the battle. He had stared at her with a strange mixture of fascination, awe, and desire.

That final emotion combined with a sudden thought that she was alone with him and tapped into her deepest female instincts. They overruled the logical part of her that attempted to point out that she was unmolested despite being unconscious and at his mercy for God only knew how long and hijacked control of her body and mind.

Her calm shattered and her pulse spiked in response. She immediately went on the defensive, scrambling backwards across the pebbly black ground, her eyes swiftly darting around to take in her surroundings but never leaving him for longer than a second. Rock walls arched upwards to meet in a ceiling, forming a cave around thirty feet across. She hit one of those walls a few metres into her attempt to flee him and banged the back of her head against the jagged rock.

Her flinch of pain drew a darker look from the man and he rose to his feet and took fluid, silent steps towards her. Danger and sensuality rolled off him with each graceful stride, each shift of his lean hips that had her gaze lowering to his body before she could stop it, taking in how the muscles of his torso flexed beneath his pale skin as he moved. Her heart pounded harder. Her mouth went dry.

Anais shot to her feet and held her hand out. It was a feeble attempt to stop him when she had lost her only weapon, her favourite dagger, during the flight to wherever they were, but it seemed to work.

He halted a short distance away and even backed off a step.

He was incredibly tall.

The demons she had worked with, and the elves, had all been tall, and this man rivalled them. He stood at least as tall as King Thorne of the demons, an impressive six-foot-seven, but where the demon was broadly built, hewn with thick muscles, this male was more athletic, his build slighter but equally as honed.

2

Anais shook herself and pressed her back against the wall. She was meant to be escaping, not admiring her abductor.

She drew in a deep breath to calm herself and tried to remember all her training. It was hard when he was staring at her, his piercing blue gaze fixed on her with an intensity that shook her. She briefly closed her eyes, sucked down another slow breath, and then nodded as she finally found a sliver of calm, enough to allow her to look objectively at her predicament and search for a way out of it again.

Her gaze flitted to the fire off to her right, where it illuminated the opening of a dark tunnel, and then the cave mouth off to her left. It was dark out there too, a barely discernible difference between the black mountains and the near-black sky of Hell. Either looked like a good option over remaining in the cave with the shifter, but she would take the exit from the cave rather than risking heading deeper into it where she might end up trapped.

Her eyes drifted back to the beautiful male standing before her, his back straight and shoulders squared, and feet noticeably braced apart. He was a warrior all right. He had cut through the battle with ease, taking down demons with one blow of his curved blade. Now he stood in readiness, prepared to defend or attack if she made a move, his fierce gaze tracking her every action.

She knew from his interaction with Sable on the battlefield that he understood English, although she had a feeling she was about to test the limits of his knowledge.

She schooled her expression, steadied her heart, and shifted her feet further apart. His gaze dropped to them and his left eyebrow rose. She used his momentary distraction to assess him. He was far stronger than she was, probably faster too, and he had a weapon. A knife. Sheathed at his waist.

That was her target.

Somehow, she would get her hands on that knife. It wouldn't level the playing field, but it would make her feel a whole damned lot better about her situation.

His aquamarine eyes lifted back to hers and narrowed again, shimmering with curiosity. Why was he so fascinated with her?

"Amazon," he husked in a voice so deep and smooth it was like taking a pure hit of the finest chocolate, more than most girls could handle without melting into a puddle of bliss.

Anais shook herself again, forcing herself to focus.

On the battlefield, he had called her and her fellow huntresses Amazons. Sable had responded to that by pressing her boot against his throat and correcting him. He had to know she was a demon-hunter. Unless he hadn't understood that part.

"I'm not an Amazon. I'm a demon-hunter. I work for Archangel."

He frowned. "An angel?"

Anais resisted the overwhelming temptation to sigh. "No. *Archangel*. A hunter organisation. I work for them and believe me when I say that they'll be coming to get me."

He snarled, flashing white teeth.

That weren't all tiny daggers.

She made a mental note of that. It seemed that like vampires, elves and demons, the fangs were under his control. She would have to tell Olivia when she got out of this hellhole and back to Archangel.

But they weren't at Archangel right now. Her team were back in the Third Realm, fighting against demons, bear shifters and dragons. Her heart started a hard thumping against her chest and she looked back towards the mouth of the cave.

"Take me back," she said and when he didn't respond, she turned her focus to him, giving him her best glare. She didn't dare hope he would do as she asked, but she had to try. He hadn't laid a hand on her since taking her and he had kept his distance when she had warned him away. If there was a chance she could convince him to return her to her friends, she had to take it. "Take me back to the battle. I have to go back."

His frown deepened, pinching his blue eyebrows together. Didn't he understand? She spat a curse at him and his handsome face blackened into a scowl. Apparently he understood that perfectly well.

"Why?" he murmured with a glance towards the cave mouth.

Anais looked there too, heart aching as she thought about the why of it. "Because my friends are there. Fighting. They need me."

Were they alright? Was Sable okay? Emelia and the others? Her team of hunters had been small and no match for the enemies the Fifth Realm had thrown at them, but the demons of the Third Realm and the elves had been helping them. She had to have faith that her friends were strong enough to survive to fight another day and that the Third Realm would win the war.

The dragon's steady gaze bore into the side of her face, heating her skin, sucking all of her awareness away from the world and her friends and narrowing it down to only him.

She slid her eyes back to him and found him frowning at her, a confused edge to his expression.

"You fight... as a... unit?" His stilted manner of speaking confirmed that he knew his way around her language but it was limited, not his mother tongue.

She nodded. "Of course."

"Strange." He glanced towards the cave mouth again and then back at her.

Anais frowned this time and spoke slowly in the hope he would understand her. "I saw you with the other dragon warriors. You were fighting as a unit."

His lips quirked into a half-smile that lit up his eyes with sparks of gold fire and heated her insides even when she tried not to let it affect her. "They were heading… in the similar… no, same… direction as me. Dragon warriors do not fight as a unit. Only weak species do."

Anais folded her arms across her chest and glared at him. Her species weren't weak. They were strong because they fought together. Only idiots refused to aid each other on the battlefield.

"Take me back."

He didn't look inclined to agree to that demand. "What species?"

Her eyebrows dipped together until it dawned on her that he was trying to find out what species she was. He moved on before she could answer.

"What realm?"

"The mortal one." She looked up at the roof of the cave, trying to emphasise her point, even though she wasn't sure that Hell was beneath her realm like the traditional interpretation of its position.

Sable had tried to explain to her and a few of their team that Hell was like a separate plane, connected to their one via a series of portals. It was beneath their world but not at the same time. Anais had been inclined to agree with her leader when she had called it a 'mind fuck'.

"Impossible." He canted his head to one side again and narrowed his eyes on her, giving her a look that part questioned her sanity and part demanded she tell him the truth. "What realm?"

She did sigh now. "The mortal one. I'm not from here. I'm human."

He shook his head and advanced a step, and she swiftly raised her hands again, hoping he would halt as he had last time. He didn't. He moved another step closer, narrowing the distance between them down to under ten feet, and ran his gaze over her, scrutinising every inch of her.

"An Amazon." His expression was resolute, challenging her to deny what he had evidently decided was the truth about her.

Anais muttered a prayer for strength. "I'm not a damned Amazon! Look… just take me back. If you take me back, I'm sure Sable and Archangel will let you off with a warning."

He just stared at her.

Her temper frayed despite her best attempts to maintain her calm air as per her training. Enraging an immortal was never a good move, and was definitely number one on the list of things not to do when faced with an enemy, but her emotions and her nerves were shot and she was beginning to feel a little enraged herself.

She was sure there was a saying about pissing women off but clearly this man had never heard it.

She straightened and looked him right in the eyes, refusing to let how beautiful they were distract her.

"Take me back."

His eyes darkened and his lips compressed into a thin line. "No."

Fine. He wanted to do things the hard way and she was good with that. If he wouldn't take her back out of the kindness of his black dead heart, she would force him to do it at knifepoint.

Anais slowly shifted away from the wall of the cave, heading into the open area between the dragon and the fire. He countered her, turning on the spot, keeping his front to hers. A darker edge flickered in his eyes, one that warned he was on to her and knew she intended to attack now.

"Last chance. Take me back." She was fairly certain that he wasn't going to take her up on her offer. She knew stubborn when she saw it. She looked at it in the mirror each day. In a battle of stubbornness, he wouldn't win.

He took a step towards her.

Anais kicked off, lunging towards him, her eyes on the knife sheathed against his left hip.

He snatched her wrist before she could reach it, his strong grip sending a hot bolt of electricity arcing along her bones. She twisted her arm in his grip, turning her back to him and coming around on his left side. She made another grab for the knife with her free hand and he whipped the arm he held her with forwards, shoving her away from him and making her miss her target.

His growl echoed around the cave and she ducked beneath his other hand as he tried to grab her.

She broke free of his grip but didn't back off. She didn't know what he wanted with her, but she wasn't going to stick around to find out. He'd had his chance to play nice. Now she was going to play rough.

He stepped into her and she brought her knee up hard, slamming it straight into his balls.

He grunted and doubled over and victory flashed through her as he cupped himself, leaving his knife wide open.

Anais made a grab for it.

He reacted in an instant, his head coming up and his hands leaving his groin. In a lightning fast move, he had blocked her attempt, knocking her hand away. She unleashed a short noise of frustration and attacked him, swinging her fist at his face. He blocked again, and again, stopping every punch she threw or kick she swung at him. Her anger rose with each failed attempt to hit him, her temper fraying at the same time.

The bastard was humouring her.

It was there in his eyes as he blocked her, always defending and never attacking. Their bright jewel-blue depths shimmered with amusement. He knew he could stop her any time he wanted because he was far stronger and quicker than she was.

Son of a bitch.

She growled and went to kick him between his legs again, and he caught her shin with both hands, stopping her. She tried to take her leg back but he refused to let go.

Anais launched a solid right hook at him, lost her balance and almost fell. His hand on her upper arm stopped her. What the hell? She would have thought he would be pleased if she had landed face first on the black ground, humiliating herself, but he had saved her.

She had the strangest notion as she pulled free of his grip and faced him. He didn't want to hurt her.

His self-assuredness wasn't the reason why he was only defending. He wasn't doing it to amuse himself either. He was doing it because any other course of action might hurt her.

He cemented that feeling when she made another lunge for the knife and he grabbed her right upper arm. The cut beneath the sleeve of her black t-shirt burned and she flinched, biting her tongue to muffle the cry of pain that blazed up her throat.

He quickly released her and backed off, distancing himself.

"I am sorry." He lowered his hands to his sides.

Anais wasn't sure what to make of him, but she refused to let his behaviour sway her. He probably wanted that. He wanted her to lower her guard.

She rubbed her arm and he looked away from her, glancing down at the ground beside his bare feet.

Giving her one hell of a golden opportunity she wasn't about to waste.

She made a break for it, her boots eating up the black ground between her and the cave mouth.

"No!" His roar deafened her and echoed around the cave and the mountains beyond.

Strong arms banded around her waist from behind before she could reach the exit of the cave. She caught a glimpse of a green-black world as he lifted her off the ground—a swath of thick forest that covered the valley below the side of the mountain she was in and the forbidding black mountains all around her. That view disappeared as he turned her in his powerful arms, twisting her to face him, and shocked her by pinning her to his very solid chest.

"Do not go that way, Little Amazon," he husked, his deep voice strained and thick with emotion.

Anais shoved at his chest as panic burst through her, sending her pulse racing, and her mind screamed at her to escape his hold.

He didn't fight her. He turned so she was closest to the fire and set her down. The moment he released her, she backed off, placing some distance between them again and breathing hard to quell the dizzying rush of her heart.

He remained where he was as she slowly pulled herself back together, towering over her, and she found herself staring up at his handsome face. He looked as raw with emotion as his voice had sounded. Why?

As much as she wanted to know the answer to that question, she wanted her freedom even more.

She tried to get around him again but he countered her each time, moving left or right to block her path, keeping her contained in the back half of the cave, away from the mouth.

"You cannot leave."

Those three words chilled her to her bones and panic and fear surged back to the surface, an unstoppable force that she could no longer control. They shook her and she couldn't stop them from chipping away at her strength, breaking down her courage and filling her mind with a thousand horrific scenarios she didn't want to entertain but was powerless to shut out.

"What do you want with me?" she whispered, unable to find her voice as she stilled and stared at him, her heart hammering against her chest and her hands shaking. She curled her fingers into fists and drew down a deep breath, trying to steady herself when all she really wanted to do was collapse onto her knees and maybe even cry. "Why won't you let me leave?"

"Others cannot see you." He looked back over his bare shoulder, towards the cave mouth. "It is not safe for you out there, Little Amazon."

"It's not safe for me in here either." She clenched her fists and narrowed her eyes on him.

He turned back to face her, his expression soft and a touch wounded. Bloody hell, she wasn't sure what to make of him.

"What do you want with me?" She tried again, needing an answer this time, because she feared he intended to do something terrible to her, even when there was a part of her heart that said it was never going to happen.

He had been upset and had apologised when he had hurt her, and that reaction had been genuine. She had met enough good guys and enough bastards in her life to know them apart. A man who reacted in such a manner as he had wasn't the sort of man who would then resort to physical abuse.

"I want to keep you safe."

Of course, men who didn't want to hurt women could also be dangerously possessive of them. He might be the type who was acting out an obsession, a deep need to nurture and take care of another person, despite how much it terrified that person or how little they wanted to be there with them.

"It's hard for me to believe that when you kidnapped me." She backed off another step and did a quick scan of the cave again, checking her options.

He had left the back of the cave open to her, which meant he didn't think she could escape that way. Her only option was getting past him. Her hope tried to deflate but she refused to let it happen. She would get out of here and away from him.

It just might not be this instant.

His face softened again and he held his right hand out to her as his blue eyebrows furrowed. Like hell she was going to take it. He could want to comfort her all he liked, but she didn't have to let him fulfil that need.

A flicker of resignation crossed his expression and he looked at his hand, smiled briefly, and lowered it to his side. "I had to. If I had not—"

Dread went through her like shards of ice.

"If you hadn't… what?" Anais couldn't stop herself from advancing a step towards him. She didn't like how he had cut himself off or the flash of fear that had touched his face.

He dropped his gaze to the patch of ground between them and it turned distant. "Dragons have the gift of foresight. What I saw…"

A chill ran through her as she remembered how he had looked at her on the battlefield and how she had felt in that moment. A deep sense of connection had bloomed inside her and he had looked as if he had shared it, and then he had changed. The heat in his eyes had turned to darkness that had coloured his expression, making it grim. She had felt that same sharp stab of dread in that moment, a sickening sensation of her life draining from her.

A heartbeat later, he had grabbed her. No longer a man. He had been an enormous, and breathtakingly beautiful, blue dragon. He had tucked her against the paler blue plates of his chest, holding her gently in both huge front paws, as if he had wanted to shield her, and then he had attacked everyone.

Her side.

His.

He had driven them all away from her.

Because of what he had seen?

"I cannot let you leave. Please, Little Amazon." His blue eyes implored her to listen to him, flooded with sincerity, hope and a dash of fear. "I will return you… when I am sure you will be safe."

Anais shook her head, reeling and trying to make sense of everything. It crashed over her, muddling her feelings and leaving her shaken.

"We were in a battle," she said and shook her head again. "I knew the risks. You had no reason to save me. I wasn't a damsel in distress. I was there to fight. Why save me? I was… am… your enemy."

He stared at her, blinking slowly, unmoving as silence stretched between them. She couldn't read him at all. She had no clue about how he felt or what he might say. His expression gave nothing away.

He held her gaze, his blue eyes locked with hers. "I did it because I had to."

"That isn't an answer." She took another step towards him, growing frustrated with him and with herself. What was she doing? Did she want him to give her an answer that would sway her? Did she want him to say something that would make her trust him?

Hell, maybe she had been right on coming around. She had passed out from lack of oxygen and her brain had been starved of it, because nothing she was thinking or feeling was making any sense to her logical mind.

Something about the man standing before her had her throwing logic and all of her training out of the window, and listening to her heart over her head.

Anais shut down the softer part of herself and forced herself to focus again. She needed to get away from the dragon and this cave, but he was right. It was probably more dangerous out there. She needed to know what she would be up against and where she was in Hell. She needed a plan, or she would end up in an even worse position than she was now.

"It is the only answer I have," he whispered and he looked as if it didn't make sense to him either, but he had been unable to find another one to give to her. "I had a vision, and I responded to it. I had no choice. It was instinct. I wanted to protect you."

Another sensation went through Anais, this one not altogether pleasant either, and it frightened her a lot more than the thought of dying.

She had seen how King Thorne of the demons had acted around Sable, driven by instinct to protect her at any cost because she was his fated mate. Some of the species of Hell had such mates, a person fated for them.

One in a lifetime.

She stared at the dragon where he stood with his back to the cave mouth, cragged black mountains as his backdrop and the light from the fire behind her shining on him, turning his skin golden as it flickered across his honed bare chest and arms, and his blue-leather-clad legs.

He was every bit as stunning as he had been on the battlefield.

A dark and alluring warrior who spoke to her on a deep and primal level.

The sense of fierce attraction and connection returned.

This time it filled her head with flashes of Sable and Thorne, of how they behaved around each other, driven by a possessive need of each other, a hunger that went beyond mere attraction and desire, defying all logic and reason.

Bloody hell.

She refused to allow herself to believe that the man standing before her, a dragon shifter, was such a thing for her. He was a means to an end. A source of information. She would bide her time, gather knowledge, and once she was ready she would escape and return to her world, the one that made sense to her. The one filled with logic and reason, just how she liked it.

"Swear you won't hurt me and that you'll return me to my people." It never hurt to have a few assurances that she could use to quell her fears. He was a warrior. He wasn't a team player by his own admission, but warriors always had a code. He would keep his vows.

He pressed his left hand to his bare chest and bowed his head. "You have my word. In return, you will swear you will not attempt to leave."

Anais nodded. "You have my word."

His hand drifted downwards, drawing her gaze with it, over honed muscles that delighted her eyes and heated her insides. His voice was rich and warm, as deep as an ocean as he spoke to her, cranking her temperature up another few degrees and making her forget she was meant to be afraid of him not attracted to him.

"Will you stay, Little Amazon?"

Anais raised her eyes back to his. They were bright, spotted with gold fire, entrancing her as much as his voice and his body.

She nodded, and for some reason it wasn't as reluctant as it should have been.

Heaven help her.

She wasn't sure it was such a great idea after all, because she was certain there wasn't enough willpower in the entire planet that she could draw on to stop herself from succumbing to the desire that swept through her whenever she looked at him.

CHAPTER 2

Taking the little Amazon from the battlefield might not have been the best decision he had ever made, but Loke couldn't change it now. He could only regret it, and even then he couldn't manage to bring himself to truly feel bad about what he had done. He only regretted frightening her. It hadn't been his intention.

He'd had only a split-second in which to absorb the vision he had seen of her blood-soaked and dying on that grim demonic land and consider what path to take in response.

Leaving her to die hadn't even crossed his mind.

That troubled him.

As she had stated so vehemently, they were enemies. Enemies fought and died on battlefields all the time in this realm, hundreds of them marching to their deaths each day. He had stormed into the midst of the war between the Third and Fifth Realms knowing that fate might await him, just as she had.

Yet he hadn't been able to see her die without reacting to it on a visceral level, one that had seized control of him and demanded he do whatever it took to stop her death from happening.

That same primal reaction flooded him whenever he recounted what he had seen, seeing flashes of her covered with blood overlaid onto her where she stood just metres from him, her pretty face set in grim dark lines that warned she was considering kicking him in a most delicate place again. His balls throbbed with the memory and he decided to keep his distance from her, at least until she had calmed down and felt more comfortable with her surroundings and situation.

Another thing he should have considered before snatching her.

Females didn't like it when males seized hold of them and took them somewhere against their will. They had a tendency to think the vilest things of the male who had taken them, presuming they meant them harm. It was a reasonable assumption, he supposed, but one he wished she hadn't pinned on him.

He had no intention of harming her.

He only wanted to protect her.

Once he was certain that whatever he had witnessed couldn't come to pass, something that depended on him receiving word that the war was over between the Third and Fifth Realms of the demons, he would keep his vow and return her to her people.

Mortals.

He still refused to believe that she belonged to that race. She was too strong and brave to be a mortal.

He had never met one, but he had been told through the tales of the elders and his parents that mortals were a weak species without any redeeming qualities. Fodder for the dragons who had been old enough to walk the mortal realm and fly in their blue skies.

Loke looked up at the black ceiling of his cave, seeing beyond it to the dark grey sky of Hell, and then beyond that to imagine how blue and clear those skies would be.

Would they be spotted with white cloud as his mother had told him? She had heard the tales from her parents, dragons who had been to that world. They had flown in those skies. They had spoken to her of wondrous things. Thunderstorms. Rain. Sunsets.

The moonrise over a glittering sea.

A shiver ran down his spine and he reluctantly dragged his focus away from fantasising about a place he could never see with his own eyes. The little Amazon was watching him again, no doubt studying him for an opening she could use to reach his knife. They had struck a bargain, but he wasn't about to lower his guard around her.

He wanted to believe she would keep her word, but she had yet to trust him and therefore he couldn't trust her. Until she felt certain he wouldn't harm her, she would keep attempting to escape.

He couldn't blame her.

He didn't see her as a captive, but he knew that was how she viewed herself and her situation. He wasn't sure how to convince her otherwise either. Would making her more comfortable go some way towards assuaging her fears?

"Hungry?" he said and she lifted her head, causing the rogue strands of her blonde hair to brush her cheeks.

Her dark blue eyes held his, no trace of fear in them now. They assessed him, pierced him, leaving no part of him untouched by her scrutiny. She was sceptical of his offer.

"I will not poison you." Her tongue was difficult for him, but he had studied it as all good dragons did, although he hadn't needed to use it in a long time. It had been many centuries since he had bothered to trade with the people of the free realm or the elves. He had kept himself up to date with her language though, in case he needed it to communicate with others who didn't speak dragon or demon.

"I was more concerned about you drugging me." She pinned him with a glare he supposed was meant to be threatening.

It just made her look more beautiful.

His fierce little Amazon.

Definitely not a mere mortal.

A flash of her covered in blood and bleeding out overlaid onto her and hit him hard, knocking him back a step.

She scowled at him, but didn't ask what was wrong, even though he could see that she wanted to voice that question.

He pressed his right hand to his forehead and cursed the aftershocks of the vision. Normally they died down by now, leaving him with only a memory of what he had seen. Almost a day had passed since he had witnessed her death. Something was wrong.

"I do not intend to drug you," he muttered and grimaced as a swift hot stab pierced his head like a burning needle. It had been a long time since the visions had given him pain. His concern grew. "Sit."

He waved to the pile of dark furs near the fire and she folded her arms across her chest and tipped her chin up. Perhaps he had been a little blunt and commanding, but the ache in his head and the aftershocks of his vision were wearing his patience down and his temper was getting the better of him. He drew in a slow breath and blew it out, attempting to ease his frustration and clear his mind so he could proceed without upsetting the female further or giving her reason to attack him again.

She eyed him, her blue eyes narrowed and her rosy lips compressed into a thin hard line.

He would have to learn to tread carefully around her. He wasn't used to company, or females outside of his kind. Female dragons could be stubborn, but often deferred to the males.

He had a feeling that his little Amazon wouldn't be submitting to him.

"Please, make yourself comfortable." He gestured to the furs again, hoping she would do as he had asked this time.

She huffed and looked away from him, towards the back of the cave. "Is this your home?"

He looked around the wide cave. "Yes."

Her blue gaze roamed it, sweeping over everything in it, which didn't take her long. She looked at the fire in the middle of the widest section of the cave, at the stack of wood he kept against the wall behind him, his meagre stack of books beside it and then at the furs on her side.

"It's not very comfortable. How can you live in such a basic place?"

Basic?

He studied his belongings again, a frown etching itself on his brow as he realised that she thought his home was far below her standard of comfortable. *Basic*. It grated on him. He had never considered his home lacking before, not in all the centuries he had lived here, but in only a handful of seconds she had made him feel it was and had made him question it. He didn't like that.

He had everything he needed in his home.

Yet she had made him feel it was lacking, and therefore he was lacking too.

She pointed to the furs. "I'm guessing that's your bed *and* your seating area?"

He growled now, flashing his teeth at her, but kept them from changing as they wanted to. He wanted her quiet, not frightened.

"Touchy." She meandered around his scant belongings, curling her lip at the furs, as if the thought of sitting on them disgusted her.

"Sit or do not sit. I do not care." He folded his arms across his bare chest and glared at her.

She shot him a smile that was victorious and rubbed him the wrong way. She meant to provoke him. An unwise course of action. Provoking a dragon was not a clever thing to do.

"I'll stand, thanks." She nudged one of the rocks that surrounded the fire with her black boot.

She wore clothing as the others of her kind had. Black trousers, boots and a top that hugged her curves and her breasts. He kept his gaze away from them, unwilling to give her more reasons to prod and poke at him.

Her sigh filled the silence.

He had never heard one more overwhelmingly and intentionally dissatisfied sounding.

Loke scowled at her. He had no modern comforts to offer her, but she didn't need to rub it in his face and make him feel he was a lesser male because of it. He had nothing he could give her that would satisfy her. He felt sure of that. No downy bed in a separate room. No bathing facilities other than the thermal pools he kept stocked with water.

Her blue gaze flitted to him and then skipped beyond him, towards the mouth of the cave.

He moved on instinct, blocking her view of the outside world, driven by the deep possessiveness that lived within him. Her eyes lifted to his face, locking with his again, stirring that possessiveness and breathing more life into it, making it grow stronger. It was his nature speaking, that was all. It had nothing to do with her beguiling beauty.

He was a dragon.

Dragons were all possessive creatures.

They were highly territorial too, and that was the reason he didn't want her to venture near the cave mouth.

She couldn't get down from the ledge, but another dragon might see her. That dragon might fight him for her or take her from him. He growled under his breath at the thought, his teeth all sharpening in response to the intense wave of emotions that rocked him—rage, fear, possessiveness.

The female looked at him, her blue eyes a little wider than normal as they met his, captivating him. Quelling his anger and fear. Those emotions instantly evaporated, leaving only the raw sense of possessiveness behind. She had looked at him that way on the battlefield. Right into his eyes. She had seen him. He had felt it then. She had really seen him. Not a glance or a fleeting look that only touched the surface.

She had looked right down into his soul, just as she was now.

She was a brave little female. He had never met a braver one.

Not even the female dragons at the village could contend with her.

"What do they call you?" he said, his voice distant to his ears as he stared deep into her eyes, picking out every fleck of black that marred deepest blue.

Would the skies of her world look like that? Would they be so deep and rich, or lighter?

Was she really mortal?

Could she answer his countless questions about her world and sate his desire to know more about the land his people had left behind, never to return?

"Anais." She offered it with a slight smile that barely curved her rosy lips but added a touch of warmth to her expression, softening the harder edges of her eyes and entrancing him.

Not a trace of fear touched her gaze or her scent now. She flitted from afraid to calm, dancing between the emotions so quickly that he couldn't keep up. He wasn't sure how long this calm phase would last, but he meant to do all in his power to make it remain. He wanted her to feel at ease and to begin to trust him.

"They call me Loke." He offered it with a smile of his own, one that felt foreign to him. He couldn't remember the last time he had smiled.

"Like the mischievous Norse god?"

His smile stretched a little wider and he shook his head. "My name ends with an E in your tongue."

She raked her eyes up him, from his bare feet, over his legs to his torso. It slowed from there, drifting at a leisurely pace, one that stirred heat within him. He couldn't remember the last time he had experienced that either. What was it about this female that had him quick to smile and even quicker to hunger for her touch?

Her gaze finally reached his face and narrowed. "You are definitely mischievous."

Before he could gather his wits to respond by saying that if he was mischievous then she was mysterious because he couldn't get a firm grasp on her when she bounced so swiftly between polar emotions, she turned away and headed towards the back of the cave, her boots loud on the black rocky ground.

"Where do you go?" He started to follow her when she made it past the fire and didn't stop walking.

She looked back over her slender shoulder at him, a wicked twinkle in her eyes. "You only forbade me from going near the mouth of the cave. You didn't set out any ground rules about the back of it. I'm going to see where the tunnel goes."

"It goes to chambers. Some where I store meats and things I have gathered, others where I bathe, and some go deep into the mountain to places where dangerous things lurk." He frowned when she pouted, as if he had spoiled her fun.

Perhaps he had.

Perhaps he had also ruined a chance for her to become more comfortable in his home, and around him.

Would she like to see the rest of the cave?

He could join her in her adventure, although he supposed that would make it more like a tour. He didn't want her to go alone though. He hadn't lied about the dangerous things that lurked in the tunnels. They ran deep into the mountain and sometimes fissures opened where creatures could get into them. He had disturbed a nest of Hell beasts down one of the paths before and had barely come away with his life. The tunnels were too small for him to transform in, placing him at a disadvantage against the vicious creatures in close quarters combat.

"So none lead to a big hoard of treasure then?" The wickedness was back in her blue eyes and she flicked her blonde ponytail over her other shoulder as she came to face him.

She toyed with the ends of her hair as he frowned at her, trying to unravel the riddle of her, distracting him with a sudden desire to do that. He wanted to feel the strands wrapping around his fingers before slipping from them. Would they feel silky? He bit back a groan at the jolt of pleasure that ran through him as he imagined they would and brought his focus back to her and what she had said.

She meant to mock him again.

Loke huffed and grudgingly admitted it. "I have a little gold."

He didn't like how she smiled, as if he was predictable and she knew him. She knew nothing about him.

"Can I see it?" she said.

He shook his head, flatly refusing her.

Her smile dropped off her face. "Why not?"

"I have decided it is off limits." Mostly because he had weapons there too. She still eyed his knife from time to time when she thought he wasn't paying attention to her. She wanted a weapon she could use against him. He wasn't about to show her where he kept his, issuing an open invite to her to take one and try to stick him with it.

She crossed her arms over her breasts again. "You can't add rules now. I make no promises that I won't go back there while you're sleeping."

Loke cursed himself. She had just pointed out a major flaw in his plan to keep her safe. She was liable to move around while he was resting and might even attack him, or attempt to leave. She was a warrior. A little Amazon. One of a legendary race known for their cunning. She would take whatever chances he gave to her, whether it was kill him and escape, or just escape.

But she kept telling him that she wasn't an Amazon, and the longer he was around her, the more he believed she was telling the truth, even when it seemed impossible. He would try to force a confession from her again. If she stayed true to her story, then he would somehow convince himself that she was mortal, even when all the evidence suggested otherwise.

"Are all Amazons as strong as you are?"

She rolled her eyes at him. "I'm not an Amazon."

She lifted the right sleeve of her black top, revealing a thick red gash across her upper arm. The scent of her blood hit him and he took a step towards her, his eyebrows dipping low as he stared at the wound darting across her pale skin.

"You are hurt." He realised that she had flinched when he had grabbed her because he had pressed down on the wound, not because he had used too much of his strength on her and his grip had been too tight.

How had he failed to notice her injury?

Loke was closing in on her before he was aware of what he was doing. She didn't back away. She stood her ground and it pleased him. She was beginning to trust him.

He slowly reached for her arm, giving her time to adjust to his proximity, and she didn't resist as he carefully curled his fingers around the underside of her upper arm. He gently raised it and frowned at the deep gash. It required attention, but he wasn't sure how she would react.

This close to her, it would be easy for her to land another blow on his balls if she didn't like what he was about to suggest.

"It requires healing." He lifted his gaze to hers.

She seemed so small when he was close to her, standing almost a foot shorter than he was and her frame tiny in comparison. It ramped up his need to protect her. Such a small female shouldn't be on a battlefield. It was suicide.

She surprised him by nodding and lowering her eyes to the wound.

He dipped his head and swiftly ran his tongue across the wound. She gasped and pulled free of his grip, her shock rippling through him and mingling with his own.

"Your blood is weak." He stared at her as it sank in. "You are mortal."

She threw her hands up in the air. "Hallelujah! He finally gets it. I'm mortal. Mortal! This cut might get infected. It's ragged and I'm filthy. Heaven only knows I'm behind on my tetanus shots. If it doesn't get proper medical attention, it could kill me."

Loke wasn't sure what tetanus or shots were, or what hallelujah meant, but he knew what infected and death were.

"Die?" A vision of her splattered with blood and gasping for air as she stared at him with wide fearful eyes blasted across his mind and he growled as he shoved it away and shook it off. "It is merely a scratch."

"I'm not like you, or any of the insane things that live in this world. Where I come from, even a scratch can turn septic. A scratch can kill me."

His lips flattened as he took that in. He had heard mortals were weak but he hadn't known just how weak they were. She seemed so strong, but perhaps he was mistaken. Perhaps she was weak and this cut was the reason he kept seeing her death on repeat. He needed to heal it, and not only to see if it would halt the visions.

Her confession that mortals were weak enough to die from a mere scratch had cranked up his need to protect her. While she was in his care, he would ensure that she didn't gain another scratch. Not even a prick on a sharp rock.

Loke gently took hold of her arm and marched her over to the furs. He piled them in a way that would stop any rocks from jabbing her and pressed on her left shoulder until she huffed and sat down in the centre of them. Satisfied that she couldn't pick up another injury, he set about tending to the one she had already gained.

He kneeled before her, keeping hold of her right arm as she wriggled and tried to escape him.

"Be still. You want the injury seen to and that is what I will do." He grabbed the hem of her black top and pulled it up.

Her fist connected hard with his right cheek, knocking his head around and making his teeth clack together.

He growled at her, flashing those teeth. "What was that for?"

"Keep your damned paws to yourself, Buddy," she snapped and shoved at his other hand, trying to get it off her top.

He released it and sat back, waiting for her to calm down. When she switched to attacking the hand he had kept on her arm, he realised he would be waiting a long time and gave up.

"I only desire to help you. I need to heal the wound... and your garment appears to be flammable." He pointed to it and her eyes shot wide at the same time as the scent of her fear swept over him.

"I don't like the sound of that." She began clawing at his hand again, attempting to prise his fingers off her. "You're bloody well not going to breathe fire on me!"

A reasonable assumption, but wrong again. Well, he was going to attempt to not breathe fire on her anyway. There was a slim chance he might accidentally do it. It was difficult to control and there was such a fine line between heat and fire.

He wouldn't tell her that though. "Only a little heat. No fire. I swear. It will kill any bad things that might be at the wound site."

She stilled and stared at the cut on her arm, her expression shifting constantly. He couldn't decipher what she was thinking, but he guessed she was considering the pros and cons of his offer.

Finally, she pulled her gaze away from the cut and looked right at him again. She didn't speak or nod. She just grabbed the hem of her top and began pulling it up, flashing a toned flat stomach.

He released her arm so she could remove the garment, doing his best to keep his eyes off what she was revealing to him. He could understand her reluctance to strip. It placed her in what she probably imagined to be a precarious position, and that was the reason he was going to keep his eyes off her body.

And the fascinating garment she wore over her breasts.

19

He had never seen anything like it.

She laid her black top across the equally dark garment, covering herself, and held it there with her good arm.

"Do it." Her voice was steel and determination, confidence that he couldn't sense in her. He could only detect fear.

She was good at concealing her feelings in her voice and expression, but she couldn't hide them from him when his senses were so acute and her scent gave them away.

Loke leaned in and focused on the gash on her arm, refusing to let his gaze stray to her body. He licked the cut and then drew in a deep breath. She tensed, the scent of her fear growing stronger. He murmured a quiet reassurance in his native tongue and then pursed his lips and blew on the wound, careful to hold back the fire and give only enough heat to seal the cut.

She cried out, the sharp sound echoing around the cave and stabbing through him. He whispered softly to her, driven to comfort and soothe her, and then blew another wave of heat along the length of the cut. It drew a whimper from her that hurt him worse than her cry of pain. It made him want to stop and he had to battle that urge, forcing himself to continue. It was for her own good. Just one more and he would be done.

She reached for him and made it as far as grabbing his bare shoulder to shove him back when he blew on the cut again and she clutched him instead, digging her short nails into his flesh. She grunted and tensed, every inch of her stiffening. Her top fell away from her breasts and he had to close his eyes to keep himself from looking at them.

He swiftly licked the wound to cool it and then pulled back, breaking free of her grip and settling on his heels.

She breathed hard, her chest rising and falling, tempting his gaze. He kept it pinned on her face, trying to discern whether she was angry with him, or afraid, or perhaps both. He wasn't sure he would ever come to understand her when the rapid shifting of her emotions had him constantly on his toes, but he studied her anyway, attempting to decipher her mood. He wanted to learn about her. He wanted to understand her.

He felt sure that if he gained that understanding of her that he would finally be able to set her mind at ease and make her feel more comfortable around him.

She scowled at him and then looked down at the cut.

After a full minute's silence, a flicker of gratitude coloured her eyes and sent an unsettling sensation through him, and she opened her mouth to speak.

He looked away from her, not wanting her to thank him, because he didn't deserve it. She'd had no injuries he could see or smell when he had met her on the battlefield, which meant he must have caused her wound when he had grabbed her or during their flight to his home.

He had vowed he wouldn't hurt her, but he already had, without even knowing it.

He would have to be more careful if he was going to keep his promises.

The heat of her gaze burned into the side of his face, the softness of her skin was branded on his, and the taste of her coated his tongue. He had a sinking feeling that he had to be more careful in general when around her. She was temptation incarnate, a beauty who stole his breath and had him thinking dangerous things, the sort that would only give her more reason to believe him a monster capable of hurting her.

She roused the deepest dragon instincts he held, the most primal of needs.

The need to protect her.

The need to possess her.

CHAPTER 3

Loke stared off to his right at the mouth of the cave, searching for a way to improve the relationship between him and his ward, and stop himself from surrendering to the darker instincts that were beginning to wake inside him. He wanted her and had done since first setting eyes on her, he would never deny that, but he would also never seek to possess her in the traditional ways of a dragon. She wasn't an object to be owned or a slave to be taken against her will.

She was beautiful and fierce. She was a little Amazon. A warrior.

That side of her both fascinated and concerned him. It drew him to her but pushed him away at the same time. He had to keep reminding himself that she wasn't strong. She was mortal. A weak species. He had proven that by hurting her without ever realising it.

He cursed himself and swiftly stood, intending to apologise to her. When he risked looking back down at her, her deep blue eyes were on the tunnels to his left again. Maybe there was a way to make her feel more comfortable in his home. She did seem very interested in the tunnels.

"Come. You must be hungry. I will show you the larder." He held his hand out to her but she didn't take it.

She rose to her feet and he looked back at the cave mouth while she dressed, giving her some privacy.

"It's probably just because you think I'll run off the moment you turn your back," she muttered.

Loke smiled. "It had crossed my mind."

She swept her arm out towards the tunnels. "Lead the way."

He decided that would also be unwise, so he opted for walking beside her. On her left. So she couldn't grab his knife he had sheathed against his left hip.

When he reached the fire, he picked up the wooden torch he kept near it, lit it and held it ahead of them, illuminating the path.

"In my world, we have things called torches… but they're powered by batteries."

"Batteries?" He looked down at her and caught her staring at his bare chest. His heart missed a beat as fire swept through his veins and he had to battle to bring it back under control.

Her gaze leaped away from him and her cheeks darkened. "Tiny power cells. We use them to run all kinds of electronic equipment."

"Electronic?" He tried to focus on their conversation and his curiosity about her world, using it to shut out the temptation to shift closer to her. He wouldn't cross that line. No matter how fiercely he desired her. She was under his protection only until the time came when he received word that the battle was over and she could return to her people. He meant to keep his promises.

Perhaps his desire to understand her was too dangerous to indulge. He feared that if he came to understand the sylph beside him, he would be done for, no longer able to keep his distance from her. It was better she remained a mystery then and he interacted with her as little as possible.

His dragon instincts roared to the fore, pushing back against that idea. Leaving her as a mystery meant denying his curiosity about her. It meant not learning about her world and her life as a mortal. She was his chance to gain knowledge about a world he could never venture into, no matter how fiercely he wanted to see it. He needed to hear her tales, her first-hand accounts of everything the mortal world had to offer.

Loke scrubbed his free hand through his hair, grasping the longer lengths and tugging them back until his scalp stung.

Everything about her was impossible.

She was impossible to understand as she leaped between polar emotions in a heartbeat. Impossible to comprehend as he pitted the fact she was mortal against the knowledge she was a warrior. Impossible to ignore as she huffed beside him and he felt her gaze briefly touch on his body again.

Impossible to resist.

Loke glanced down at her, his eyes straying to her despite his attempt to keep them locked on the tunnels ahead of them.

She looked unimpressed and he was coming to hate seeing that expression on her face because it made him feel inadequate.

"You seriously don't know what electricity is?" She rolled her eyes and sighed emphatically again. "Heaven help me."

"I do not think the angels will help you, Little Amazon. They cannot venture into Hell as far as I know."

She stopped dead and he walked a few steps, her gaze boring into his back, before halting too and looking over his shoulder at her. Her stunned expression drew a smile from him and lightened his mood, chasing away the ache in his head and lifting him out of the mire of his conflicting desires.

"Angels?" she whispered, a touch of fascination in her voice.

He grinned now. "Ah, it would seem it is my turn to sigh ever so dramatically."

Her face darkened into a scowl. "Whatever. I'm sure if there were angels, Archangel would know about them."

She had mentioned Archangel before, when she had called herself a demon-hunter. The other female he had met in the battle, the one with black hair, had called herself such a thing too. It made sense for that female. She had been powerful.

His little Amazon was not.

Yet she apparently hunted immortals. A foolish venture for a mortal. He was surprised she had survived to her current age.

23

He wasn't sure what age that was, or how many cycles of the earth around the sun it took for a mortal to grow to adulthood, and he wasn't about to ask her. She would sigh again and right now he had the upper hand and he was enjoying it.

"Angels exist." He made it a statement, so she didn't question it.

It didn't stop her. "So where are they? Why haven't I met one? I've been hunting for years and I've never met one."

"You would most likely be dead if you met one of the breed who make Hell their home. Fallen angels are dangerous prey, Little Amazon. You must not approach or engage them."

He must have looked serious because she didn't argue. Instead, her eyes took on a shimmer of curiosity.

"You've met a fallen angel?"

He nodded. "And barely escaped with my life... but it was long ago and I am stronger now. I am confident I could hold my own against one if I ever meet another."

She ran her gaze over him, a wave of heat following it, scalding him wherever she lingered, and then raised her eyes back to his. "How long ago?"

Loke thought about that as he began walking again, leading the way towards the tunnel. He gave up searching for a definite answer and shrugged as he made a guess. "Around four thousand years ago. Give or take a few centuries. It is difficult to remember."

She stopped again and he sighed. If she kept stopping whenever he said something that astounded her, they were going to take hours to reach the larder.

"Four thousand years. Blimey. Prince Loren is around five thousand years old or something like that according to—"

"Prince Loren... of the elves?" Loke ignored her scowl but noted she didn't like being interrupted. "You know him?"

She nodded and his eyebrow quirked.

He had known they had fought on the same side in the battle between the Third and Fifth realms of the demons, but he hadn't expected her to know royalty. It surprised him that the prince of elves had worked directly with her people rather than allowing one of his commanders to do such a low and menial task in his place.

"He's getting married to one of our scientists," she said with a smile. "Something about Olivia being his mate."

Olivia. He frowned at that name. The black-haired female had mentioned it, stating how Olivia would love to study him. A scientist. He knew of science in the sense they meant it. Studying. Cutting open creatures to see their insides and gain knowledge of them. He curled his lip at his little Amazon, flashing a hint of fang.

She planted her hands on her hips. "I don't recall saying or doing anything to deserve that sort of look."

"Speak not of scientists and mates. It is a ridiculous notion that the prince of elves would find a mate in such a weak species."

"Well, it happened… like Sable is probably going to get hitched to King Thorne." She stormed past him and he was the one standing still and staring at her in astonishment now.

"King Thorne has a mate too?"

She nodded and looked over her shoulder at him. "You met her. She trod on your throat."

He rubbed the front of it and pinned her with a black look as he recalled the dark-haired huntress. "She was strong. A worthy mate for a demon king."

Her pretty face darkened, her fair eyebrows dropping low above her deep blue eyes, and she turned on him. "Strength comes from more than the body, you know? It comes from in here too."

She pressed her hand between her breasts.

"Strength of heart does not make you strong, Little Amazon. It does not stop a blade from slicing your throat open." He stepped towards her, closing the gap between them, and swept his fingers in a straight line just inches from her delicate throat as he stared down into her eyes. "It does not make you a match for one of our kind. Physical weakness cannot be overcome by emotional strength. A mortal is a poor match for an immortal. It would be far too easy to harm you by mistake."

He swept past her, leaving her to follow, and paused only when he reached the mouth of the tunnel that led to the larder.

She stood where he had left her, staring at him, a myriad of emotions crossing her face and colouring her eyes, clashing and colliding, but through them all one rose.

Defiance.

She straightened her spine, tilted her chin up, and clenched her fists at her sides as her lips compressed into a mulish line.

"You know nothing about mortals. Physical strength isn't everything. Without emotion… without heart… you're nothing but barbarians. But I should've known that you were a barbarian… after all… you act like one." She stormed past him again and didn't slow this time.

She marched ahead of him into the darkness and he let her, even though he wanted to argue with her. He scrubbed his free hand over his face and held back his sigh. Perhaps he had been too hard on her kind. He wasn't sure what had possessed him to say those things to her, pointing out the differences between mortals and immortals. The thought that the prince of elves had been given a mortal female as a fated mate, and that King Thorne of the Third Realm had also received one, had set him on edge for some reason.

Loke watched her stomping towards the edge of the reach of the light from his torch.

If she kept marching blind as she was now, she was going to trip over something and hurt herself. He quickened his pace, eating up the distance between them with long-legged strides, and only slowed when he was within a few feet of her. She muttered things beneath her breath and he caught his name from time to time.

The larder came into view ahead of them and she finally slowed down, her head turning this way and that as she took it in. He had carved shelves into the black walls of the small round cave many centuries ago, allowing him to keep his food off the floor, where bugs were prone to nibble on it.

He placed the wooden torch in the diagonal shaft he had hacked into the rock near the entrance of the larder and picked up the iron cauldron he had traded from a witch in the free realm. He placed his only metal bowl and a wooden spoon down inside it, and then set about gathering the items he needed for their meal.

"Eww, what is that. Tell me you don't eat that."

He turned to find Anais pointing at a lump of white fat he had carved off an old Hell beast, one of the kind with horns and talons. It had been a difficult battle. He could have easily won if he had resorted to using his dragon form, but his kind preferred to hunt in their mortal appearance. They relished the challenge and the chance to test their skills against a larger foe.

Loke shook his head. "I do not eat that. I use it for fuel."

"For the fire?" She looked back towards the exit. "And the torches I guess?"

He nodded this time. "It helps. I eat this."

He picked up a skinned side of Hell beast, around a quarter of the original carcass, with the front left limb and ribs intact, and she looked as if she might vomit.

She swiftly covered her mouth and turned away from him.

Would he ever understand her?

She claimed to be strong, but when faced with a butchered creature, she paled and looked ready to flee. He was beginning to wonder whether she had ever taken a life during her battles. Surely a female who couldn't look at a piece of meat was incapable of taking a life?

"I think I might be vegetarian," she muttered into her palm.

Loke wasn't sure what that meant but he didn't like the sound of it. "I will make a stew from the leg."

"What does it taste like?" She peeked over her shoulder at it. "Does it taste like beef or maybe lamb? I'm not big on lamb."

Beef. Lamb. He presumed these were creatures of the mortal world.

He shrugged. "I am afraid I cannot compare it with something from your realm as I have never been there."

She frowned and shifted to face him, her fear of the carcass evidently forgotten. "You haven't left Hell?"

He shook his head. "No dragons leave Hell... so you see I cannot offer you a comparison to ease your mind... but it tastes good."

26

"I think I'll have to be the judge of that. If it does, I'll tell the world… there's a bachelor in Hell who can cook." She paused and ran another glance over him, rekindling the fire in his veins. "You are a bachelor? I figured you were since this cave doesn't look like the sort of place where a lady dragon would live. It lacks a female's touch."

Loke bit back a groan.

His cave wasn't the only thing that lacked a female's touch. He had been lacking that for a long time.

His gaze fell to her hands and he was wondering what her touch would feel like before he could stop himself. He tried to shake away the image of her running her palms over his bare chest, making him burn with a soft caress, but it was impossible. He had invited the images into his mind, had opened himself to them, and they flooded him, refusing to go away.

He was vaguely aware that he was standing in the larder, staring at her like a complete dolt and asking for another kick to the groin.

Anais snapped her fingers in front of his face and he jerked backwards, blinking at her.

"I don't want to know what you were thinking, but your eyes were being weird." She shuffled away from him, to such a distance that it was clear she had lied and knew what he had been thinking about and knew the reason his eyes had brightened, verging on glowing.

He was hungry, but not for food.

He wanted a taste of something far more dangerous and alluring.

The fascinating little Amazon diligently keeping her eyes off him.

As if that would stop him from desiring her.

Perhaps that desire was part of the reason he had taken her from the battlefield. He had been drawn to her then, powerless to resist her beauty as she had stood over him. She had enslaved him with nothing more than a look into his eyes, a moment where something had passed between them. A silent understanding.

A mutual attraction.

"I am a bachelor," he said, his voice low at first but gaining strength as he locked his gaze on her and allowed it to drift down her back, taking in her curves and how her black top and trousers hugged them. "I have no female… and it has been that way for a very long time."

She whirled to face him, a touch of rose on her cheeks. Her mouth flapped but no words came out. When he risked a step towards her, she bolted, slipping past him and rushing down the corridor. She grunted and he switched his senses to her, concerned that she had hurt herself by running into the darkness.

She had stopped a short distance into the tunnel.

He sighed when her voice rang along it.

"Bloody buggery son of a bitch." Those words held venom that had disappeared when she next spoke, her voice far softer and weaker. "It's a bit dark. Are you coming?"

Loke smiled and finished gathering what he needed for their meal.

He hacked the leg off the carcass with his knife and set it into the pot, and wiped the blood off the blade with a cloth that he tossed into the pot too. He grabbed the torch from the wall and strolled along the corridor, making Anais wait. The firelight danced ahead of him, reaching her first, slowly running up her legs to her torso and then illuminating her face.

She stared at her knees and muttered to herself as she dusted them down.

"Are you hurt?" He looked at her knees and then her hands, not seeing any scratches or smelling any blood on her.

She shook her head. "For the record, I've decided to add another rule. You have to swear not to look at me like that again."

"Like what?" He stepped closer to her, staring down into her eyes, holding her gaze and challenging her to look away.

She truly was beautiful. The Amazons would have been proud to have her as one of their race.

"Like that." She managed to hold his gaze but he could see she was teetering on the brink of losing her nerve and looking away.

"Like what?" he husked again, inching closer to her. "Tell me how I look at you."

She did look away now. "Like you're a beast and I'm your damned prey… like a barbarian who took someone captive and thinks they can do whatever they please with them."

He dropped the pot and had her wrist in his hand before she could run away from him. She fought him as he pulled her around to face him, and he held the torch higher, afraid of hurting her with the fire. He released her wrist and had his arm around her waist a split-second later, pinning her against his front. She rained blows down on his bare chest and he let her vent her frustration, because he had more important matters to focus on than mere physical pain.

"Look at me, Little Amazon." He waited for her to do as he had asked and when she didn't, he dropped the torch behind him and captured her cheek. She instantly stilled and he cursed when she began to tremble, her fear an acrid note in her soft scent. He slowly skimmed his fingers down to her jaw and tilted her head up. She closed her eyes and he huffed. "Look at me, Anais."

Using her name seemed to be the key to making her listen because she opened her eyes. Their rich sapphire depths drew him in, leaving him aware of only her.

"I am no beast or barbarian," he murmured and wished she could believe him. "I have no intention of using you in that manner. I have sworn not to hurt you… have I not?"

She nodded.

"Then why persist with this nonsense?"

She tried to look away but he held her firm. "Because… just because. I don't have to give you a reason."

Because she feared the reason she had to give.

She didn't want to voice it and tell him that he wasn't the only one who felt desire, who was drawn to her and powerless against the ferocity of his need of such a delicate little female. She wanted him too, and for her it was infinitely more difficult to comprehend and cope with. She viewed herself as a captive and he her abductor. That alone was reason enough for her to fight her feelings.

But she had other reasons too, just as he did.

A mortal was no match for an immortal.

He brushed his fingers across her soft cheek and reluctantly released her, stepping back to give her room to gather herself. He picked up the torch and grabbed the handle of the cauldron.

"Come. I need water." He waited for her to finish smoothing her clothes before moving.

She followed him, a silent shadow in the low light.

He searched for something to say to dispel the tension between them but nothing came to him. It had been a long time since he'd had female company, had desired one as he desired her, and he wasn't sure how to go about things. He didn't know how to charm females of her world, and wasn't sure he should be charming her at all. He was trying to keep his distance, but the moment he let his guard down, he found himself close to her, seeking a way of touching her or winning a smile from her.

He banked left when they reached the end of the tunnel and led her along another one. The path sloped downwards and the air grew moist as he approached the area deep in the heart of the mountain where he had created a bathing pool and one for his store of water.

Anais busied herself with touring the large cave, her fingers drifting over the stalagmites that rose from the ground, forming jagged black spikes.

"Why live in the front of the cave when you have all these rooms?" She glanced across at him.

He dipped the small wooden pail he had made into the well near the entrance and pulled it out, setting it down on the rocky side. "The fire."

She frowned. "What about it?"

He lifted the torch and wafted it around, making it smoke. That smoke rose up to the top of the cavern and stayed there.

Her eyes lit up with understanding. "I get it. Smoke accumulates back here."

"It is safer at the mouth of the cave too. I can sense intruders and it is a bigger space. I can shift if I need to." He held the pail out to her and she crossed the room to him and took it.

Perhaps she was finally settling in and becoming more comfortable with him. He wasn't going to hold his breath though. Whenever he thought she was becoming accustomed to being around him, she revolted and turned on him again.

"What's it like to shift?" she said to the pail.

Loke shrugged. "It is difficult to explain. It does not hurt, and it is over so quickly for me that I barely notice it. It is as natural to me as breathing or walking."

She frowned at the water, her nose wrinkling with it. "I've met wolf and cat shifters. It always looks like it hurts when they shift."

"I suspect that is because you are hunting those creatures." He looked across at her and tried to imagine her fighting people from those species. Perhaps she was strong enough to battle cats and wolves, maybe even vampires with the right weaponry, but she was too weak to fight dragons or bears, and he definitely couldn't imagine her surviving a fight against an elf or a demon. "They are forced to shift quickly. I have heard that it causes them great pain… but then I suppose the death you wish to deal will hurt them worse… giving them to others to butcher in the name of science."

She raised her eyes to his, narrowing them at the same time. He had offended her again, but this time he didn't care. Fighting with honour in a battle was one thing. Both parties knew what to expect—death if they failed. Hunting prey for handing them over to others to study was another. The losing side was expecting death, not an agonising torture at the hands of scientists.

He curled his lip again.

She huffed. "I don't do that… so get it out of your damned head. Archangel doesn't slice and dice. It studies, but using modern technology. Scans… machines… bloodwork. That sort of thing."

It didn't make him change his opinion of this Archangel she was always quick to defend.

"You do not deny that you hand over some of your prey to them though." He began walking again, heading back towards the fire.

She didn't respond.

He wasn't surprised.

She worked for people who made a business of hunting and studying creatures, and he suspected that what she had been told about those studies differed greatly from what really happened.

He led her back to the cave mouth and she placed the pail on the ground near the fire and sat on the furs without him asking her to make herself comfortable.

Loke wasn't going to read into that either.

He kneeled on the black ground by the fire in the middle of the cave and focused on making their meal. She was silent the whole time, studying him. He stopped several times, on the verge of asking her what she was thinking, before continuing with his work.

She spoke once, during her meal when she mentioned that the meat tasted like beef. He still wasn't sure what kind of animal beef was. He had taken the empty bowl from her and served himself some stew, and by the time he had gathered the courage to ask and risk her mocking him, she had fallen asleep.

Loke set the bowl down, rose to his feet and crossed the short stretch of ground between them. He kneeled beside her and canted his head as he studied her. She lay on her left side, her back to the wall of the cave, the firelight playing over her soft features and making her fair hair shimmer like gold.

What was it about this little female that drew him to her? She had spoken about strength of heart to him, her belief shining in her words for him to hear. Was emotional strength really a match for physical strength? Did it really make a mortal capable of mating with a strong immortal?

He didn't believe that.

He brushed a rogue strand of golden hair from her face and settled the tips of his middle and index fingers against her temple. His eyes slipped shut and he breathed deeply and evenly as he focused on her.

Dragons had limited magic born of their connection to the earth and nature. Every generation born in Hell had weaker powers than the last. He was born of the generation before the final one to bear magic.

His magic was weak and he could only use it sparingly. It would drain him and leave him vulnerable for the next few hours, but he had no choice. He couldn't risk her waking and attempting to escape.

He funnelled a little magic into her, enough to bind her sleep to his.

If she woke, he would too.

When he woke, she would.

It was safer this way.

He hadn't lied to her. Beyond the cave were other dragons, ones who would live up to her fears.

Barbarians.

They wouldn't treat her with respect as he did. They wouldn't seek to take care of her. They wouldn't want to protect her for no other reason than her safety meant something to them. They would only protect her because she would be theirs and dragons defended what they owned.

She would be nothing but a possession to them.

Loke stroked his fingers down her cheek.

What was she to him?

He wasn't sure, but the longer he was around her, the more he was coming to fear he knew the reason why the thought of a prince of elves and a demon king finding their mate in a mortal female concerned him.

He had a feeling that their meeting on the battlefield had been more than chance.

It had been fate.

CHAPTER 4

Steaming water lapped at her bare breasts, rippling with each move Anais made. She washed on instinct, her focus elsewhere, around one hundred metres behind her in the main area of the cave.

With Loke.

Her fingers skimmed up and down her arms and she shivered from the light touch, a fuzzy memory of masculine fingers stroking her cheek with the same gentleness bubbling to the surface of her mind only to sink within the mire of her thoughts.

Loke.

He confused her at every turn, muddled her feelings and stirred her thoughts, until she wasn't sure what to make of him. He had snatched her from the battlefield, but not to enslave her or abuse her. He had done it to protect her. She firmly believed that. She had offended him enough times in the few hours they had been together to gather enough evidence to support his case. He wanted to protect her from whatever danger he had witnessed in a vision.

She had never met a species capable of seeing the future before.

It fascinated her.

He fascinated her.

When he had offered to allow her to bathe, she had expected him to be present while she used his thermal pools. She had expected him to stand sentinel and ensure she didn't attempt to escape.

He had escorted her to the cavern, using a torch to light the way. When they had arrived, he had placed the torch into a holder near the pool, and had offered her a bar of what she imagined to be homemade soap, a small scrap of cloth, and a larger piece that looked like a rustic sort of towel. Watching him instruct her on his method of cleaning had been amusing, drawing a smile from her.

When he had caught it, he had muttered something in his strange tongue, his words holding a lyrical and soft quality, and had left her alone.

Anais had been stuck thinking about him ever since.

She had sat on the rock near the pool and washed herself using the small towel, soap and a pail of water. It all felt terribly Japanese to her. The thermal vents that heated the pool kept the room warm and moist, but the water she had used to wash the suds off onto the black ground had been cold. She had literally jumped into the pool.

The moment she had sunk beneath the water, letting it lap around her shoulders, her thoughts had turned to Loke, to wondering what he was doing while she bathed.

She leaned her back against one set of the stalagmites that enclosed the pool, cupped her hand and drew the water up over her arm and shoulder again, sighing as the heat of it soothed her weary bones but failed to settle her thoughts.

It felt as if everything Loke did waged war on her, confusing her feelings and weakening her defences.

He had healed her wound for her, not once looking at her body, had taken care of her, had fed her, and had allowed her to take his bed.

She hadn't meant to sleep. She had meant to pretend to nod off, wait for him to settle into a deep sleep, and then investigate the cave and check out the mouth of it. She knew that Loke would have been angry with her if he had caught her, but she needed to get a good look at the outside world. She would have to try again later. She felt more relaxed now. Stress and too much good food had to have been the reason she had fallen asleep. Tonight she would make sure she didn't eat as much, and would fight the lure of sleep so she could continue with her plan.

She stared ahead of her, watching the golden light from the torch set into the wall behind her as it danced across the black rocks, casting shifting shadows from the stalagmites across the wall on the opposite side of the cavern.

Anais ran her hand down her right arm and frowned as her fingers brushed the wound that darted across it. She turned her arm towards her and peered at it. There was little more than a faint scar. Magic. How had Loke healed it? She knew vampires had healing saliva and believed elves did too. Did dragons also have it, or was there magic in his breath?

A flash of him as a majestic blue dragon ran across her eyes and she let the memory wash over her, invading her heart and her mind. He had been beautiful. She hadn't been afraid of him, not until he had grabbed her. She had been too entranced to fear him, but then she had been in his front paw and instinct had driven her to fight him.

Even though he had been holding her carefully.

He could have easily crushed her.

But he hadn't wanted to hurt her.

Anais pushed him out of her mind and focused on bathing and planning. She needed to survey her surroundings, find out if there was anything she could use as a weapon in case she needed to fight, and pull her plan together so she could put it into action.

A tiny fragment of her heart hurt at the thought of breaking her vow to Loke. He had kept his, and she was planning to break hers. She wasn't sure what that made her, but she couldn't afford to think about it or let her feelings rule her. She needed to get away and get back to her team somehow.

Even when that small part of her still wanted to stay here, trusting that Loke would keep his other vow and would return her. It would be easier than trying to make her way back to the Third Realm when she didn't know the topography of Hell or where she was in it.

She would need to draw Loke into telling her about the area.

She only hoped he wouldn't grow suspicious of her.

Anais stood and let the water run off her. The air felt chilly on her damp skin, instantly sucking the heat from it. She stepped out of the pool, quickly dried off and dressed in her black combats and t-shirt. She would kill for a change of clothes, but she hadn't spotted anything resembling a wardrobe in Loke's cave. She had a suspicion he owned a pair of blue leather trousers and that was all.

Those trousers had disappeared when he had shifted.

Like magic.

She found herself stuck on that word. Archangel knew nothing about dragons except for their existence. It was entirely possible that they could use magic. The elves used something akin to it. They could teleport things and had telekinesis. Witches used magic. It wouldn't surprise her if Loke could too.

Anais shoved her feet into her boots, picked up the wooden torch, and started back towards the cave mouth, following the black rock tunnel. It forked a short distance from the main cave and she glanced down the tunnel to her left, her steps slowing.

Loke had treasure.

Was it down that tunnel?

He had also warned her that he sometimes had unexpected visitors. The thought of running into something when she wasn't armed sent a cold shiver tumbling down her spine and she turned away from the tunnel, unwilling to live up to the old adage of curiosity killing the cat.

Her steps slowed for a different reason as she entered the main area of the cave.

Loke stood with his gaze on the fire, skilfully running the edge of his knife over his cheek, scraping away dark blue stubble and leaving clean smooth skin behind. She watched him in silence, admiring his skill with the knife as he tipped his chin up and shaved his neck, never once cutting himself. Not even the tiniest of nicks.

She admired him for a different reason as he swallowed, his Adam's apple bobbing, drawing her gaze there. Masculine. Everything about this man screamed masculine. He was powerful. Honed. Intelligent. Beautiful.

Dangerous.

She shoved against those dangerous thoughts about him and scuffed her boot on the gritty black ground so he noticed her and stopped tempting her with something she shouldn't want.

Desire.

She couldn't pretend that she was experiencing simple want born of not having been with a man for over a year. It was desire. Full-blown, no-holes-barred, deep and dangerous desire.

The sort of desire she had never experienced before.

He flicked her a glance, his dazzling jewel-blue eyes bright in the light from the fire, and then finished shaving. When he was done, he lowered the knife, twirled it in his palm and sheathed it in one fluid move.

She stared at it. "That's a dangerous method of shaving."

He shrugged perfect muscular bare shoulders. "There is no other method of grooming."

She recalled him being astounded when she had spoken of electronic goods, but she hadn't expected his limit of technology to be a knife. She hadn't thought about the basic necessities of life at all. No shaver. Not even a razor.

Heavens, she could kill for a razor. If her plan failed or wasn't viable and she had to stay in the cave, she was going to need at least a razor, some perfume or deodorant, toothpaste and a toothbrush. That was the bare minimum. A change of clothes was up there, but she could wash what she had.

She was damned if she was going to shave with a knife.

She eyed Loke. He probably wouldn't let her near it anyway. It was clear that he used that one knife for everything. Shaving. Cutting his incredible blue hair. Cooking. Everything revolved around that knife.

It was obviously quite precious to him.

If she stole it, would he let her go in exchange for having it returned?

"It's a nice knife." She nodded towards it and his left hand came down, settling on the spiralling metal grip.

He drew it from the sheath and stared at it for long seconds, his handsome face turning pensive and his blue eyes filling with emotions she couldn't decipher, ones he decoded for her when he spoke, his deep voice echoing around the cave.

"It was my father's."

"I can see it means a lot to you." She hadn't expected it to mean so much though or that just mentioning the knife would affect him so dramatically. He looked lost as he stared at it, and a little broken, no longer the strong and determined male he had been just a moment ago. "Have you lost your father?"

He nodded and his expression shifted, turning even more sorrowful. "I lost my mother at the same time. The dragon wars took them both when I was two hundred. My aunt too."

Anais's heart went out to him. She couldn't imagine what it must have been like to lose so many people who were close to him at the same time. It must have devastated him. She didn't know whether two hundred was young or old for a dragon, but she guessed from his look that he had been young and that those two hundred years hadn't been enough time with his parents.

"I lost my sister." Those words slipped quietly from her lips, spoken from her heart to his, born of a need that seized control of her.

A need to connect with him and show him that he wasn't alone in his pain.

They had both experienced loss.

35

He lifted his head and looked across at her, a softness in his eyes and his expression that touched her and felt dangerous. She looked away, unable to keep her gaze on him, because he was tearing down her defences again. Or maybe she was the one to blame. She had reached out to him after all. She fought the fierce gravity that tried to pull her to him and cursed herself for seeking a deeper connection with him. She didn't want to get closer to him. She needed to focus on escaping.

Even though she felt certain it was more dangerous for her out there than it was in the cave with him.

"How?" he whispered and slowly sheathed the blade.

Anais focused on it, mentally cursing herself again for raising her sister's death. She should have known he would ask about it and would want to know the particulars. It had been a long time since she had thought about it and even longer since she had spoken to anyone about what had happened, but it still hurt. The pain of grief was still raw even after all these years.

"I lost her nine years ago." She kept her eyes on the blade sheathed against his left hip, afraid to look at him while she told him about her sister, letting him into her heart. She didn't want to see how he would be looking at her. She didn't want to see the sympathy in his rich blue eyes. She didn't think she could bear it. "I never knew that she was a member of Archangel. I only found out after she had died. I didn't even know the man she had married was a light fae. Christ, I had been so happy for her when she had brought him to meet me. They had been so in love."

She closed her eyes and suppressed the sigh that wanted to leave her lips. Her sister really had been in love with him, the sort that rarely came around. True love. One that would have lasted forever. Literally in her case.

"They had a kid… a little girl." Her throat closed and she swallowed hard, fighting the tears as she thought about Annabelle and how she was growing up in a world without her mother. "She was only a baby when Suzanne, my sister, was killed in an attack on their family home. Suzy's husband's enemies targeted her and the baby. He managed to save Annabelle, my niece… but my sister… the injuries… he couldn't—"

She cut herself off as tears filled her eyes and she couldn't breathe. Pain consumed her, tearing her heart to pieces all over again, so strong that it felt as if the attack had happened only yesterday. It had killed her when she had discovered what had happened to Suzy, and that they had almost lost Annabelle too.

She had been so angry with Aevys. She had blamed him for what had happened to her sister. He had come to her and explained, and she had wanted to hate him, but she hadn't been able to bring herself to feel that emotion towards him. He had been devastated by the loss of his mate. He had been broken.

And he had never recovered.

Whenever she visited him and Annabelle, he slowly gained a look, one that told her that seeing her pained him, even when it gave him pleasure too. He had told her once that she looked too much like Suzy. She didn't want to hurt him, and she had told him so. She had even offered to meet with Annabelle elsewhere. He had refused, had hugged her, and told her that she was always welcome before confessing that he liked seeing her, because it reminded him of his mate.

Archangel constantly pressed her about him and she constantly lied and said she had no contact with him or her niece. She protected them. She had to, in honour of her sister's memory, and for the sake of her niece and Aevys.

She wouldn't let Archangel hurt them and she feared they would if they found them, shattering her fragile and carefully constructed image of the organisation that had become like family to her and was now her home.

"Anais?" Loke whispered softly and she lifted her head, a little gasp escaping her when she found him standing just inches from her, his handsome face etched with concern.

"Sorry… I was just thinking about Annabelle and Aevys." She scrubbed her hands across her eyes and drew down a deep breath to steady herself.

"Do you still see them?" he said and she nodded.

"I pretend not to know where they live though."

Loke's deep blue eyebrows dipped low. "Why?"

Anais sighed. "Because of Archangel. They want to study him because he's one of a rare breed of fae that they don't have documented. Annabelle is just like him too."

He backed off a step and his face darkened. "Study. It is a nice way of saying capturing, torturing and dissecting."

She wanted to reassure him that Archangel wasn't like that, but she couldn't bring herself to lie to him again. Her earlier words to him still haunted her. She had been so quick to defend Archangel, spouting the lie without flinching, even when she knew they did bad things as well as good. They actively studied species and he was right, it did mean capturing them, holding them in cells, and often forcing them to reveal their abilities. She didn't condone it, but she couldn't pretend it didn't happen.

Archangel were her family though. It was her home and it meant the world to her. She couldn't stop herself from defending it, even when she knew deep in her heart that they did terrible things to some of the people they captured, and not all of those people were guilty of committing a crime against a human or good non-human. There was a shadier side of Archangel that many of their hunters didn't know existed anymore, or perhaps they were like her and turned a blind eye to it because Archangel was the only family they had and the only place they could call home.

It was the only place where they belonged and fitted in, a part of something that made sense to them in a world that was no longer the one they had grown up in. She was sure many hunters felt as she did, as if Archangel was the only place for her now because she couldn't turn back the clock and return to the time when she had been unaware of the dangerous fae and demons who shared her world.

It was a place where she could be with others like her, others whose eyes had been opened and whose heart beat with a need to protect the innocent and unsuspecting humans from the dangerous world around them.

The light from the fire faded and she glanced at it. The branches were black, nothing more than ash, threaded with glowing orange cracks. Loke looked there too and moved away from her. He gathered more wood from a stack against the side of the cave, placed it onto the dying fire, and crouched in front of it.

He leaned closer to the stack of wood, shut his eyes and frowned as he opened his mouth.

Shock rippled through her as he breathed fire.

It ceased and he raised his head, his eyes opening and locking on her. "You are surprised. Why?"

She shook herself and shrugged. "I just didn't think you'd be able to do such a thing in your current form. Yesterday, you said you wouldn't breathe fire… and I sort of figured that meant you couldn't… not when you're not a dragon."

"You think strangely." He sat back on his heels and prodded the fire with a stick, encouraging it to spread to the other branches. "There is no dragon and no man. There is only me. I am both. Both are one. I merely have two forms and I am comfortable with both. I do not think, feel or act any differently depending on my form. My mind and my heart remain the same. However… it is more difficult to breathe fire as I am now."

Anais supposed that made sense, even when her mind rebelled against it. "Archangel teaches us to view the animal separately from the other form. The animal is always the more dangerous form."

Loke's lips curled into a smile that held no warmth. "From what you have told me, and what I know of your kind, it would appear the other form is the more dangerous one… the person and not the animal."

Anais fell silent and sat down on the furs near the fire, on the opposite side of it to him. She couldn't argue with him. Humans were dangerous. Animals tended to live in a sort of harmony with each other and their environment. People tried to control their environment and each other.

She frowned at her knees and then at Loke. "Your kind are no different though. You mentioned a war."

"Wars." He loosed a sigh and tossed the stick onto the fire, his blue eyes fixed on it as it caught and burned. The golden light played across his bare torso, highlighting his honed muscles with accents and shadows, and danced across his face as his expression turned pensive.

"That's even worse then." She didn't flinch away when he raised intense eyes to meet hers. She weathered his dark look, not heeding the warning. She wasn't going to sit in silence and let him make her species out to be the more dangerous one when his kind had gone to war many times. "Your species didn't learn their lessons. Humans don't either. We fight over everything."

Loke shook his head, causing a slender thread of blue hair to fall down across his brow. He swept it back into place and ran his fingers through his hair. "Mortals fight over one thing. Land. The same as dragons. The wars did their work. Entire clans were wiped out. Our numbers are few now and our lands no longer crowded. Mortals will end up the same way if they are not careful."

Anais couldn't argue with that either. It was only a matter of time before humans unleashed Hell on Earth, killing vast numbers of the world's population with weapons of mass destruction.

"So dragon numbers are low now?" She leaned back against the rough black wall of the cave and resisted looking off to her left towards the huge arched entrance to it. "How many dragons remain?"

Loke shrugged again. "I do not know. In my clan... perhaps no more than fifty when once there were over three hundred."

"Does your clan live near here... in another cave?" Maybe a bigger one. She couldn't imagine fifty people sharing a cave like Loke's one.

He shook his head and shifted position. He sat on his backside, crossed his legs and leaned back, bracing his palms on the black ground and showing off his torso. Anais did her best to keep her eyes off him, but it was difficult. She didn't want to appear rude, or as if she was avoiding looking at him. She also didn't want to end up blatantly staring at his chest either, and she knew she would if she dared to look at him longer than a few seconds at a time.

"They live in the village. I have not been there in many weeks. I prefer it here."

He looked around his cave and she had to wonder why he liked it here more than he did down in the village.

"How long have you lived here?" She took in the cave again. Sparse. Grim. Far from comfortable. The word village conjured images of homes, structures with roofs and furniture. Maybe even more modern conveniences.

Like a razor. Perfume. Clean clothes.

Loke tipped his head back and stared at the ceiling of the cave, his blue gaze distant.

She fought the urge to run her gaze over him while he was distracted and failed. Her eyes drifted down the strong line of his neck, lingering on his pronounced Adam's apple again as he swallowed, and then wandered over the square slabs of his defined chest and down the thick ropes of his stomach. Eight pack. She had never seen a man with an eight pack before. She lost herself in counting each muscle, only stopping when she reached below his navel. A dusting of dark blue hair led down from it, into the tight waist of his rich blue leather trousers.

They were laced over the crotch.

Anais's cheeks heated and a wave of desire crashed over her, ratcheting her temperature up and making her heart beat harder.

The intense sensation of Loke's eyes on her caused the blush on her cheeks to darken and she dragged her eyes away, pinning them on the fire instead. She fought for her voice, needing to say something to dispel the tension in the air, the thick buzz of desire and passion that stemmed not only from her, but from him too.

"Eight centuries." His deep voice curled around her, and her body reacted as if he was speaking low words of seduction rather than stating facts.

She heated inside, heart fluttering weakly against her chest, skin prickling with awareness and need, a yearning to feel his strong callused hands skimming over it and maybe pressing in a little to give her a glimpse of how powerful he was.

She coughed to clear her throat, battled her out of control emotions, and focused on what he had said, trying to use it to distract herself enough that she could rein in her desire.

Eight hundred years.

Anais raised her chin and looked across the fire at him.

There was heat in his eyes, but something else too, a feeling that struck a chord within her. Loneliness. He had lived in a cave, high in a mountain, for eight centuries, and he looked as if it had taken its toll on him, whether he knew it or not. He was lonely.

A dragon in his mountain.

But he was no longer alone.

She was here with him.

But for how long?

CHAPTER 5

Anais kept her eyes closed, feigning sleep and struggling with her thoughts. She had to do this. It didn't matter that she was beginning to feel she really was safe here, in this cave with Loke. It didn't matter that she felt as if she was growing closer to her dragon companion, or that they had opened up to each other to a degree. All that mattered was returning to her world.

She didn't belong here.

She needed to get back to Sable and the others and find out what had happened to them.

She needed to know they were all okay.

Even though the thought of leaving Loke made a recess of her heart ache.

She listened to Loke moving around the cave. He had already started the fire again. That had roused her from sleep. She mentally cursed herself for falling asleep when she had meant to just pretend. She had a faint sensation that she had been pretending, and that Loke had come to her, and then she had been dreaming.

Maybe she had dreamed it all.

The light touch of his fingers on her face. The way they gently stroked her cheek. The soft words he had murmured in his unfamiliar tongue.

It had all been a dream.

She felt sure of it.

He moved away and she cracked an eye open, watching him heading into the tunnels with his wooden torch. When the light from it disappeared, she made her move.

Anais sprang to her bare feet and ran to the mouth of the cave, flinching every time she trod on a pebble. She had taken her boots off last night to aid her in her recon mission. She had to move silently to avoid rousing Loke. Every non-human species she had met had heightened senses. Hearing being the most sensitive. She couldn't have moved quietly enough in her boots. She was having enough trouble moving quietly with bare feet. Another pebble bit into the sole of her left one and she grimaced and hopped a few steps, giving it time to recover.

The ledge came into view and her heart rocketed, thundering against her chest. She was just going to have a look. That was all. There was no need to get nervous. Her palms sweated and she rubbed them on her black t-shirt. Just a glimpse and then she would go back to the fire. She just wanted to see what was out there.

She glanced back into the cave, afraid of Loke finding her gone. She didn't want him to see what she was doing. She didn't want him to be upset with her and she knew he would be. He would feel as if she had betrayed him by breaking her vow, and that didn't sit right with her. Not anymore.

She slowed to a halt at the edge of the ledge and stared down at the dizzying drop to the sweeping cragged side of the black mountain below. It was at least three hundred feet. She swung her gaze left, studying the mountains that formed a wall around the valley.

Harsh black rock as far as her eyes could see.

Bleak against the dark grey sky of Hell

It was incredible. Formidable.

There was no way she was going to be able to climb up the mountain. It rose sharply from the cave's ledge, rising up into a jagged peak. Other obsidian peaks met it further down, blending into the most dangerous set of mountains she had ever seen. Not even the world's best climbers could scale them. She would have to go down into the valley.

Even that looked as if it was going to be easier said than done. Around a thousand feet down the mountain, the dark green trees began. They were strange and gnarled, with only a bare covering of leaves. Anais couldn't help thinking that they looked like something right out of a movie, liable to come alive and capture her with their branches. Those branches were tangled together, forming a thick canopy. She couldn't tell how tall the trees were from this height, or what the ground looked like.

Or whether there was ground down there and not a swamp filled with dangerous creatures just waiting to eat an unsuspecting mortal like her.

The trees seemed endless too. They covered the valley floor, from the furthest point she could see off to her left, to the end of her vision off to her right.

Anais realised something as she looked at the trees.

The valley had no open ends.

The black mountains rose to block it on all sides.

If she was going to leave, she was going to have to ascend one of the peaks and hope that she chose the right one. If she chose wrong, she could be faced with another valley, or worse.

Anais let thoughts of escape drift away.

There was no way to escape.

No need either.

She knew Loke better now and she felt sure that he would keep his promise. He would take her back to the Third Realm. If he didn't, she would try her luck with the mountains and the forest that looked as if it might try to eat her. Until then, she would trust that he was going to fulfil his vow to her.

She stepped back from the ledge, determined to return to the fire before Loke found her gone.

A sudden rush of air swept down the mountainside, pushing her forwards. She grabbed her hair as it covered her face, wrestling the tangled golden ribbons back so she could see where she was going and wouldn't fall off the ledge. Another blast of wind came.

Something clamped around her waist.

Anais gasped and tried to turn, sure that it was Loke behind her.

The black ground dropped away and she looked down instead, her eyes widening and a bolt of fear piercing her heart. Huge red scaly talons held her around her waist and legs, each thicker than her body. Glossy black claws pressed dangerously close to her skin and she did the only thing she could think of as her mind shut down and she realised with horror that it wasn't Loke who had her.

She screamed.

The dragon bellowed in response to her shriek and shook her, rattling her right down to her bones and making her ache all over. She bit her tongue to stop herself from crying out and tried to prise the beast's claws off her as her survival instincts kicked in. She would take a long drop to a swift death over being stolen by another dragon.

Anais attacked as best she could, alternating between punching the dragon's talons and trying to get her fingers under its scales. She was going to yank the damned things off and make it hurt. The dragon kept flying, enormous dark red leathery wings beating the air, carrying them higher above the mountains.

The world beyond them came into view and Anais's heart plummeted.

Nothing but more mountains and valleys for hundreds of miles.

If she had run away from Loke, she would have died out there. She never would have reached Sable and the others.

She wasn't going to reach them now either.

She looked up at the huge red dragon that held her. The great beast kept its large golden eyes on the distance but opened its crocodilian jaw, revealing rows of deadly long white fangs as it roared again.

An answering roar came this time.

Loke.

Anais looked back towards the cave but saw only the barbed tip of the red dragon's tail. The valley was so far away already, too distant for her to make anything out, but not far enough for her not to realise with disappointment that Loke wasn't coming after her.

There was no blue dragon chasing them.

Anais ignored how her heart stung and went back to hitting the dragon's paw, using both of her fists this time. She didn't let up until the dragon dropped lower in the air as they swept over another mountain range.

Her hands fell to resting on the dragon's talon as she stared down at the clearing below. Round stone huts filled most of the space, with what looked like an arena carved into the mountain beyond them and a large flat tract of land left open at the end of the village closest to her. Anais realised it was the dragon equivalent of a landing strip when the red beast holding her touched down there.

The second it set her down and released her, she turned on it, launching punches against anything she could reach. Two bare-chested men rushed forwards from a broad path between the thatched black stone huts and grabbed hold of her, pulling her away from the dragon. She fought them too, wrestling against their hold, even when she knew it was futile. They were far too strong for her.

The one to her left, a man with silver hair, muttered something in their language and his companion, a green-haired younger male, responded, a grin curving his lips and revealing sharp white teeth.

She stared at the dragon as it began to transform, waiting for it to turn into a red-haired man.

It was a woman.

A very beautiful woman with flame red hair.

Mahogany leather trousers formed over her legs and she twirled her hair up, tying it in a knot at the back of her head. Anais waited for another garment to appear over her ample breasts but nothing happened.

A golden dragon circled lazily above them, bright against the dark sky, and snorted. The woman looked up at the beast, her expression souring, and motioned for the men to follow her.

The men grunted and marched Anais into the village.

The moment they were clear of the landing strip, the golden dragon touched down.

She looked back at it and it stared right at her, its elliptical pupils stretching thin as it eyed her. It wasn't as beautiful as Loke had been.

Her captor stormed ahead of her and her guards, still topless. When they entered the main area of the village, Anais realised that it wasn't just her captor who was flashing her upper body. Every female she could see wore only trousers.

Every male she could see on the broad streets between the rows of huts stared at her, eyeing her in a way that made her skin crawl. She didn't like how they looked at her. Fascinated. Awestruck. Hungry. When Loke looked at her that way, she found it appealing, but with these men, she only felt a deep need to flee.

To escape.

She had the feeling she had made a grave mistake by disobeying Loke and she was going to pay for it.

The men halted, jerking her to a stop with them, and she looked ahead of her, towards a larger round building that stood on a high solid black stone platform at the other end of an open square.

A golden-haired male lounged on an obsidian throne in front of the thatched hut, cragged mountains his grim backdrop. His large hands rested over the ornate ends of the arms of the throne and his deep bronze leathers stretched tight over long powerful legs that were spread, giving him a relaxed and easy-going appearance that his sharp golden gaze contradicted.

This man knew everything that was happening around him without even needing to look to confirm it.

Was he the dragon equivalent of a king?

The woman approached him and he eyed her, a bored edge to his gaze as they spoke. She fawned over him but the male didn't seem impressed with her, not even when she pointed to Anais. His expression only darkened further then, his lips compressing into a thin line of displeasure. What was the woman telling him?

Anais looked at the green-haired and silver-haired men that held her, their strong hands clamped tightly around her upper arms and their faces impassive. Others had gathered around the square too, standing in front of the huts that lined the edges of it, a mixture of men and women.

She gasped when the men holding her began walking with her again, jerking her away from her study of the village and the other dragon shifters. Her eyes leaped to the blond male on the throne ahead of her. The redhead moved to one side, her head bowed as she backed away from the male.

Anais guessed this was Loke's clan's village and this man was the chief.

He looked no older than Loke, but that didn't mean he was the same age. She had to assume he was older and more powerful than Loke, and not nearly as nice. If she did that, she might just survive whatever was about to happen.

The two men released her and backed away too, leaving her standing a short distance from the chief in the middle of the circle. She could feel everyone staring at her and it was hard to fight her nerves and not let them get the better of her. She had faced a lot of powerful enemies in her life as a hunter, but never without a weapon and never in such numbers.

"Where do you hail from?" the man said, his voice silken and smooth, and his English perfect.

Loke could take a few lessons from him. He spoke it as if it was his native tongue, not a second language. Loke still stumbled from time to time. She looked back in the direction they had come, heart sore with a need to see him flying over the mountain range.

Coming for her.

She hated relying on anyone, never wanted to be coddled or have another person fight her battles, but she was also a realist. She wasn't so stubborn that she couldn't recognise when she was in trouble and needed help.

She needed it pretty badly right now.

"I asked you a question."

Anais turned back to face the chief, because not answering him sounded as if it might not end well for her.

"From the mortal realm."

A murmur ran through the crowd around her but she didn't take her eyes off the golden-haired male on the throne. His only reaction was a shift in position. He propped his left ankle on his right knee but kept his hands dangling off the ends of the arms of the throne. His fingers began a slow drumming against the carved black stone as he studied her.

Casual, yet deadly.

She could almost sense it radiating from him. He was dangerous. More powerful than Loke. She got the impression that being the chief of the clan wasn't a role you were born or voted into. She had the feeling that it was a position you won through brute force, determination, and possibly bloodthirstiness.

"A mortal… and how did Loke come across a mortal… may I ask?" He ran golden eyes over her and she felt other men do the same.

Her skin crawled in response and she wanted to rub her hands over herself to wipe away that disgusting sensation, but didn't want to draw their attention to her even more by openly touching herself in front of them.

"He took me from the fight in the Third Realm." She had figured that honesty would be the best policy to adopt, but the way the chief's eyes darkened dangerously warned her that it might have been the worst.

She had the feeling she had just got Loke into a lot of trouble, and possibly herself too.

"You are a prisoner of war and Loke should have notified me, as the others did."

Anais stared at him as those four words ran around her head.

As. The. Others. Did.

Her stomach dropped into her bare feet.

"Others?" she whispered and started to shake her head as that tried to sink in. Other dragons had taken huntresses from the battlefield. They had taken her kin.

The man smiled cruelly. "Our males always have need of spoils of war."

Anger curled through her veins, obliterating her fear, and she clenched her fists and took a step towards the man before she could stop herself. "Spoils of war? Those are my friends… I want to know where they are."

His smile only widened and he pointed beyond her. "I believe Zephyr has one… do you not? You could attempt to take her back from him."

Anais whirled on the spot to face the green-haired male who had marched her to the village. He folded thick arms across his bare chest, causing every muscle to tense, and she swallowed hard.

"Perhaps Zephyr would like a companion for his female?"

The bastard named Zephyr smiled at that suggestion and ran forest-green eyes over her, lingering on her breasts.

"The female has grown tiresome. She constantly cries and whimpers like a mewling bitch. A new female might suit me." He took a step towards her. "You have fire. I should have taken you. Perhaps I shall."

"You bloody bastard," Anais growled, scooped up a small pebble from the black ground and hurled it at him with every drop of her strength. It beaned him in the eye and he snarled at her, flashing sharp teeth. Her heart leaped into her chest as he took a step towards her, menace and dark intent rolling off him.

"Enough." The chief's voice rang out and Zephyr stopped and backed off, settling for glaring at her even though she could see he wanted to get his own back and teach her a lesson she would probably never forget.

She slowly turned back to face the chief.

Her courage failed, immediately disappearing when he rose onto his feet and came to stand at the edge of the stone platform. He glared down at her, his golden eyes bright with fire that warned her to keep her temper in check. She was no match for him, or for the one called Zephyr, or any of the men present. She wasn't even sure that she would be a match for any of the women, not without a weapon.

All she could do was bide her time and hope that Loke would come for her. She wasn't sure that he would. She had broken her promise. She hadn't just broken it, she had shattered it into a million pieces. She didn't deserve to be rescued, but she held on to the hope that he would give chase and save her.

She hadn't been a damsel in distress on the battlefield, but she was one now.

It was ironic that she didn't want a prince to save her from a dragon.

She wanted a dragon to save her from Hell's equivalent of a prince.

A chief who looked as if he was considering killing her or handing her over to Zephyr.

Loke had been right.

He'd had a vision. He had seen something terrible happen to her. He had asked her not to go to the cave mouth and had confessed he hadn't wanted the other dragons to see her.

What if she had just made that vision come true?

Was she about to die here?

No.

Her nightmare wasn't going to end here. She knew it. If Loke didn't come for her, she would end up in the hands of one of the male dragons surrounding her, and she was one hundred percent certain that whichever dragon took her, he wouldn't be taking care of her wounds, cooking for her, and protecting her out of the kindness of his heart.

He wouldn't vow not to hurt her.

He would view her as a spoil of war, a way of satisfying whatever dark urges gripped him, and she would have no way of stopping him.

"What did Loke want with you?" the chief said and she stared up at him, her hands shaking at her sides and her knees on the verge of buckling as the gravity of her situation pressed down on her.

It took her a moment to understand what he was asking and when she did, she knew that the chief was somehow aware that Loke hadn't taken her as a spoil of war.

"He didn't take me prisoner," she whispered, finding it impossible to speak any louder or with confidence. All of her strength was draining from her and nothing she did stopped it from flowing out of her, leaving her weak and trembling.

Zephyr's words haunted her, tearing at that strength, ripping it away from her piece by piece. Whoever he had taken from the war, he had broken her. She rubbed her arms, trying to get the chill off them as fear crawled through her. He would break her in the same way.

Loke.

Her heart called for him, ached with a need to see his face, to look into his clear aquamarine eyes and hear his voice telling her that everything was going to be all right. No dragon would lay a hand on her. No dragon would hurt her.

She pressed her hands to her chest and the chief frowned at them, his eyes narrowing in a way she didn't like. He looked as if he could see straight through her. He knew her inner fears and her thoughts. He knew her heart called for one of his dragons.

"Why did Loke take you?" he said, a commanding edge to his deep voice, one that warned her again not to disobey him or displease him.

Anais looked him right in the eye and opened her mouth to tell him. Her words died on her lips as his eyes left her, lifting towards the dark sky beyond her.

His golden gaze shimmered with fire and narrowed, focusing on something. She looked back towards the mountains but no dragon broke the bleak sky. What was he looking at? She turned back to face him and a quiet murmur ran through the people gathered around them.

"Save your answer." The blond man didn't take his eyes off the horizon as he addressed her. "I shall ask the dragon warrior himself."

His eyes fell to her, intense and fierce, piercing her and leaving her feeling that he knew something she didn't. He stared at her for long seconds before raising his hand.

"Shackle her. Let us see what Loke thinks of that."

Zephyr grabbed her arm and began pulling her towards the edge of the square just as a distant roar shattered the silence. She whipped around to face the mountains and her heart leaped as she saw the majestic blue dragon zooming towards the village.

Loke.

She fought Zephyr and managed to break his hold, but didn't make it two steps towards the landing strip before one of his hands clamped down on the nape of her neck and the other struck her across the back of her head. Her ears rang and her vision wobbled, and the grim colours of Hell whirled together into a single swathe of black as darkness claimed her.

CHAPTER 6

Loke landed hard in the clearing near the village, threw his head back and roared again, unleashing every drop of his anger so all in the clan would know it. He lowered his head and focused on the clan chief, Ren, where he stood at the edge of the platform in the main gathering place of the village. Ren held his gaze, unflinching as Loke snarled at him, baring twin rows of deadly sharp teeth.

Several males rushed towards Loke through the alleys between the huts, some of them with red hair. Which was the one who had taken Anais from him? They would be the first to die.

He growled at them all as they reached the clearing and they backed off, edging towards the circular black stone huts.

When they had moved to a distance that pleased him, he carefully curled his left paw around his knife so he didn't lose it and focused on his body, willing it to change. In the blink of an eye, he was back in his more human form and his blue leathers had appeared over his legs. He twirled his knife and sheathed it beside his left hip as he strode forwards, each determined stride carrying him swiftly through the village.

His gaze locked on the square ahead and Ren and the fire in his veins burned hotter as his chief calmly stared back at him.

Rayna hurried towards him, her bare breasts bouncing with each step, but he paid her no heed. She always singled him out whenever he visited the village. He had no interest in what she wanted to offer him. There were other males more willing than he was to satisfy her.

Female dragons were nothing if not assertive. They never shied away from staking a claim on a male they found attractive and often pursued them until they gave up and gave the female what she wanted, slaking both of their carnal hungers. Sleeping with someone who desired you, even if you didn't particularly desire them, was acceptable behaviour in dragon society.

Loke had never been into that side of life as a dragon. Free sex had no appeal to him, at least not anymore. Females had pursued him and he had slept with some of them when he had been younger and the mood had struck him. Since leaving the village to live in the mountain, he had kept to himself, evading the females who desired a tryst with him.

Most of them had given up and gone after a more willing male.

Not Rayna though.

She persisted and it irritated him. She was part of the reason he rarely visited the village, only coming to it when he was called to battle by Ren.

Or when someone took something from him.

Something he was beginning to feel was precious.

Rayna moved in front of him, a huge smile plastered on her face, as if she couldn't see that he wasn't in the mood to speak with her and it was a dangerous move to hinder him.

She didn't get out of his way when he growled at her, flashing sharp teeth and warning her away. She stood her ground and even went as far as pressing her hands to his chest. He knocked them off him and stepped around her, sparing her little more than a glance before he locked eyes with Ren again.

Rayna grabbed his wrist.

Loke turned on her with a feral snarl and she flinched, drawing back in an instant and bringing her other arm up across her chest to protect herself. Dragons weren't allowed to fight in the village, but she was pushing her luck.

She rallied and smiled at him, fluttering her eyelashes and daring to step closer to him.

"Leave me," he said in their tongue and she frowned at him as he twisted his arm free of her grip and began walking again.

She pursued him and caught up with him near the edge of the circular clearing in the centre of the village. His gaze scanned it and stopped on a small dark form laying on the black ground off to the left of the raised platform where Ren stood waiting for him.

Anais.

Metal shackles linked her ankles and wrists, a thick length of chain between them. He growled at the sight of her laying at the mercy of his kin, unconscious and vulnerable.

Rayna looked from him to his little Amazon and loosed a growl of her own. "You are come for the mortal?"

He nodded and went to enter the square, but Rayna grabbed his arm and pulled on it, stopping him. He flicked her a glance, catching her glare as she directed it at Anais, her golden eyes filled with darkness.

"The mortal is weak and not made for you. A powerful dragon warrior needs a powerful mate."

Loke shook her hold again and continued into the square. Rayna followed him, an irritating shadow that frayed the tethers of his anger. She was risking her neck by refusing to leave him alone. He had warned her enough times.

She slowed and he thought he was rid of her at last.

"If you will not listen to me, perhaps I will ask my brother to have the mortal killed."

A red veil descended and the fire in his veins exploded into an inferno, burning through the tethers holding his anger at bay.

He was on her in an instant, his hands clamped around her upper arms and his claws digging into her flesh. He brought his face close to hers and snarled at her, eliciting a gasp from her as she stared at him through wide eyes.

"You lay a claw on my female, and I will kill you, Rayna," he growled down at her, his claws pressing in harder.

The coppery tang of her blood filled the air around him, goading him into carrying out his threat.

Only the thick silence that descended stopped him.

He knew he had overstepped the mark by threatening her. A male dragon killing a female was unheard of, but she had pushed him too far and he hadn't been able to hold back his fury. The thought of Anais dying turned his blood to fire that burned hotter than dragon's breath and set him on a warpath. If Rayna's brother dared to harm Anais, Loke would take him down too.

Regardless of the fact that he was their clan's chief.

Loke shoved her away from him, sending her crashing into a nearby male, and stormed towards Ren.

Ren flicked a bored glance at Rayna as she spat a vile curse at Loke's back and then settled his fierce golden gaze back on Loke.

"You would think that if my dear sister desired the death of the mortal so much, she would have killed her when she took her from your cave." Ren smiled coldly at him.

Loke's fury flared hotter than ever and he turned back towards Rayna, a growl curling from his lips as his claws extended. He would do more than draw blood this time. He would take her head for daring to steal Anais from him. Rayna edged behind another male.

"Enough. Face me, Loke, and tell me what you seek from the mortal female." Ren's voice rang clearly above the din of the crowd and they fell silent again.

All eyes came to rest on Loke.

His gaze slipped to Anais where she lay at Zephyr's feet. The male wore a sick look of satisfaction, leaving Loke in no doubt that he had been the one to deal with Anais. The warrior would pay for hurting her.

Loke lifted his gaze back to Ren, aware that his chief's patience was in short supply. Anais had probably tested him to his limit already, leaving Loke little room to manoeuvre.

What did he seek from Anais?

He said the only thing that came to him—the only thing these males would understand. He couldn't tell them that he'd had a vision of her. They would want her gone from the area and would view her as a bringer of misfortune. Or worse, Rayna would get her wish and Ren would kill Anais.

"She is a spoil of war. I meant to inform you of her presence in my cave, but she is a handful… as you are probably now aware. She made several attempts to escape, so I was waiting to regain enough magic to send her to sleep before coming to the village." Loke held Ren's golden gaze, his expression schooled in the hope that his chief would believe him.

Ren sat on his black throne and eyed him in silence. Loke held his nerve, unwilling to let his fear show, not in his expression or in his scent. He would find a way to get Anais out of the grip of his kin and back to the cave. He would ensure she was safe again, and then he would have words with her about disobeying him and breaking vows.

"You are a terrible liar, Loke," Ren said and Loke's stomach filled with cold lead. "Your mother was too."

He growled at the mention of his mother, baring his fangs at the blond male. Ren was old enough to have known his mother, a clear thousand years older than Loke, and always brought her up when he wanted to weaken Loke's defences. He wouldn't let it work this time, because he had too much on the line.

He looked to Anais. She was out cold and he hoped she remained that way for at least the next few seconds, because he felt sure she wouldn't be impressed with him if she heard and understood what he was about to say.

She would be furious.

"She is mine," he announced and a murmur ran through the crowd.

Ren's eyes narrowed on him, seeking the truth from his soul.

Loke let him see it, because he meant what he had said. He had never experienced what he felt for her. He had never desired anyone so deeply or needed anyone so completely.

Ren raised his hand to silence the gathered dragons, his eyes remaining locked on Loke.

"She is not yet yours." The blond male stood and approached the edge of the black stone platform again. "You know that and you know the rules, Loke. You kept her a secret, hidden from others, for that reason. A mate must be won. You must prove yourself against the others who might desire her and prove yourself worthy of the female. We will have a contest."

Loke's stomach turned and ice formed in his veins.

He had wanted to avoid this and Ren knew it. The male had twisted the rules and what Loke had said. He hadn't called Anais his mate. He had said that she belonged to him. The noise of the crowd rose, surrounding him and irritating him as he tried to think of a way to avoid having to enter the arena in order to secure Anais's safety.

He didn't want to fight, but the cold look in Ren's eyes said that he had no choice.

He had to fight and he had to win.

If he didn't, another male would take her as his mate. That male would attempt to charm her into surrendering to him and becoming his, and if that failed he would use whatever magic he possessed to manipulate her feelings, making her desire him, until the strain of having her mind repeatedly controlled broke her.

Anais would never willingly submit to a male. They would have to use their magic to control her.

He couldn't bear the thought of her going through that, not when he had been the one to bring her into his world.

"Step forward if you wish to challenge Loke." Those words leaving Ren's lips dragged his focus back to his chief and he sent a silent prayer that no male would challenge him, even when he knew that he would be lucky to end up with only a single adversary.

He had seen contests before and many of them had been one male against five or more.

A large black-haired scarred male called Brink marched across the square and came to stand before Ren. Loke knew little about the dragon warrior other than Brink had come from another clan, an orphan of the wars. He was the last remaining member of that clan and the chief at the time had taken pity on him. Brink had been sent to train and had become one of their fiercest warriors.

Loke doubted Brink actually desired Anais or wanted her as his possession. The male lived to fight. He desired the battle and wanted to spill blood. That was the only reason he had stepped forwards. If he won, he would probably discard Anais, either by letting her go free or killing her.

Zephyr stepped forwards too, a lascivious smile on his face as he looked at Loke, one that made him burn with a need to take the male down. He wouldn't let the sick sadistic male near Anais. He knew the tales of Zephyr.

Most male dragons valued females in any form, be them other dragons, witches, fae or even mortals. They resorted to using their powers only when charming the female failed. Zephyr was a different breed. He had no respect for the females he took from battle. He used no magic on them. He took them whether they were willing or not.

No other males stepped forwards. Loke couldn't blame them. Zephyr and Brink were formidable opponents, likely to kill each other in an attempt to be the victor.

The contest only called for defeat of the other participants, not death.

If Loke could injure them badly enough that they could no longer fight, he would be declared the victor and Anais would be safe.

It was a sound plan, except for the fact that Zephyr and Brink were both stronger than he was and he had a sinking feeling they would work together at first to eliminate him before they turned on each other.

"Very well. Gather at the arena when you are ready." Ren looked at each of them in turn and then lingered on Loke. "You may speak with the female."

Loke nodded his gratitude. It was more than he had expected. Normally, none could speak with the female before a contest. She was kept locked away until the battle was over and the victor decided, unable to see what was happening. Loke knew that wouldn't be the case this time. Ren was making an exception for Anais. He wanted her to witness the fight. Why? Because she was mortal?

Mortals weren't the reason they had been forced to leave that realm, but dragons blamed them for it regardless.

He turned away from Zephyr and Brink, and went to Anais where she lay on the black ground. He could feel Rayna glaring at him from across the square, and could feel the eyes of others on him, but he paid them no heed as he crouched beside Anais, balancing on his bare toes.

Loke canted his head as he brushed strands of her untamed blonde hair from her face.

His beautiful female.

His gut clenched as he checked her over, scanning her face first and then her body for signs of trauma. Not a single scratch marred her. The relief he had wanted to feel didn't come. Someone had rendered her unconscious.

Zephyr.

That male had no qualms about silencing females in such a manner. Anais had probably disobeyed him or fought him. His fierce little mortal. He could well imagine her standing up to the dragons gathered in the village, just as she had stood up to him.

The cuffs around her wrists and ankles were loose, but there was no way she could slip out of them. They would hinder her movements and keep her in check, and that would leave her vulnerable.

He needed to deal with Zephyr and Brink quickly, and free her. He didn't want her to feel fear, expecting the worst from his kin. Most of the males and the females in the village weren't a threat to her. The only ones who would seek to harm her were Rayna, Zephyr and Brink.

And possibly Ren.

Loke didn't trust his chief.

He had followed the male into battle countless times, but he hadn't done it because he respected him and believed him a competent leader. He had done it because Ren was their clan chief, and tradition dictated that Loke obey his commands.

He had his limits though.

If Ren pushed him, he would push back.

Ren had been the leader of their clan for centuries now. Loke was sure there were other males who would like to take his seat of power from him. It wouldn't take much on Loke's part to stir a rebellion, and he would do it if Ren forced his hand by attempting to harm Anais.

He would do anything to protect her.

Even fight to the death.

He swept his fingertips lightly across Anais's cheek, using a sliver of his magic to heal her, and whispered, "Wake now, Little Amazon."

Her eyelids fluttered and he withdrew his hand, rested his elbows on his knees and settled back on his haunches as he waited for her eyes to open. When they did, they immediately sought his face and the fear in them died as she locked gazes with him.

"Loke." His name softly spoken on her lips stirred heat within him, a fierce tempest of need and desire that had his heart pounding.

"I am here, Little Amazon." He brushed his knuckles across her cheek and smiled down at her as her eyebrows drew together, wrinkling her nose, and she groaned. "The pain will cease soon. I swear it."

She closed her eyes and tried to evade his touch, and he sighed as he realised his words had wounded her. He hadn't meant his mention of a vow to be a reminder of the one she had broken. He had only wanted to reassure her.

"Can we go now?" she whispered and slowly opened her eyes as he helped her into a sitting position.

He held her upper arms and drowned in the deep blue of her eyes as they locked with his, every male instinct he possessed commanding him to obey her and take her away from this place so she would feel safe again.

He forced himself to shake his head instead.

"Not yet. There is something I must do first." He silently pleaded her not to ask the question that rose in her eyes because he didn't want to frighten her.

The gods must have heard his prayer because she asked another instead.

"Like break these?" She raised her hands between them, the chain that linked her manacles clanking as she moved. Her hopeful smile wobbled on her lips.

"Soon. I must secure the right to break them." He looked away when she frowned at him, unable to hold her gaze when he knew he was on the verge of making her feel more guilty about what she had done. "I will not be long. You will wait here. No one will hurt you. I swear it, Anais."

She grabbed his wrists before he could move, the tightness of her grip demanding that he look at her. He closed his eyes and sighed as it struck him that she wasn't going to release him until she knew what was happening.

"Why do you need to leave?" Her grip on him tightened, squeezing his bones together. "What is it you're going to do?"

Loke looked over his shoulder at the raised platform where Ren still stood, deep in discussion with Rayna, and then beyond him to Zephyr where he was sharpening his curved blade outside his hut.

He sensed a shift in Anais's feelings. They turned colder, laced with fear that drew him into looking at her again so he could discover the source of it. Her blue gaze was fixed on Zephyr and he growled under his breath as he thought about that male stepping anywhere near her.

"I am going to win a contest."

Her eyes leaped back to him and widened. "You mean you're going to fight."

"I must. It is the way of my kind. I will secure your freedom, Anais."

"No," she barked and dug her short fingernails into his flesh. "You can't fight to the death for me. It's barbaric!"

Loke smiled softly. "And I am a barbarian... remember?"

She shook her head and her fair hair swayed across her breasts and shoulders, strands of it sticking to her black top. "You're not a barbarian... but these men... let's just fly out of here... now... please, Loke?"

Gods, he wanted to do that. He wanted to fulfil that request because he knew that she was scared—for him and for herself.

"I cannot." He twisted his arms free of her grip and then took hold of her hands and looked at them.

They were small in his, dainty, but strong. He turned them both palm up and rubbed his thumbs across the calluses at the base of each finger. She had wielded weapons for many years, had clearly fought in many battles. His fearless little Amazon.

Yet she feared this place. She feared his people. She feared for him.

"You can." She closed her fingers over his thumbs and held them.

He sighed and lifted his eyes to hers. "It will not change anything. It will not make you safe. If I do not fight for you, another male can claim you without a battle. The strongest will be chosen."

"Which one is that? Not the green-haired bastard." She glared across the square at Zephyr and Loke decided that he would take Zephyr's head for upsetting his female so deeply.

He didn't need to know what Zephyr had done to her. Just the fact that she feared him was reason enough for Loke.

He reined in that bloodthirsty desire and put it out of his head. He didn't need to kill either of his opponents to win Anais. He only needed to incapacitate them. He wasn't sure how Anais would react if he killed his fellow dragons in order to save her, but he had a suspicion the guilt she felt would only increase, and he didn't want that to happen.

Loke pointed to Brink where he waited at the entrance of the path to the arena, staring at her through midnight eyes.

Anais paled.

Her blue gaze gradually inched back to Loke and she leaned closer to him. He wanted to open his arms and pull her into them, needed to give her the comfort she craved, but setting his hands on her in that way would only incite Brink and Zephyr. He had been given leave to speak with her. He didn't dare do anything else, not when Ren was watching him so closely too.

"Does anyone die in these contests?" she murmured, her gaze flitting between him and Brink.

She didn't look at Loke for longer than a second, but he could see that she had changed her mind and wanted him to fight and win now that she had seen what male would take possession of her if he defaulted.

Loke risked it and stroked her cheek, running his fingers over it and absorbing how soft and warm her skin was beneath his. She slowly looked back at him and her gaze stayed with him this time, never leaving his, piercing him right down to his soul just as it had that day they had met.

He fell into her eyes and the world around him faded, his awareness narrowing to only her.

"Many fail." He lied.

He didn't want to lie to her, but he couldn't tell her the truth either. He didn't want her to know that most dragons who entered into a contest didn't walk away from it. He was certain she felt nothing for him, other than viewing him as a safer dragon to be around than the others, but he felt compelled to soften the blow.

He didn't want her to feel guilty. He didn't want her to fear for him either. Both of those emotions filled her eyes though, tearing at him, and he wasn't sure what to do to make them go away.

Besides winning a contest.

He searched for something to say to reassure her, but words failed him and shock rippled through him, a startling wave of heat and tingles, when she instead did something that reassured him and made him want to roar.

She moved onto her knees, wedging her hips between his spread thighs, cupped his cheeks and pressed her lips to his.

Fire coursed through him, strength that obliterated his fears and his doubts as her lips gently swept over his in a tender kiss.

Before he could pull together his scattered senses and wrap his arms around her to hold her in place while he kissed her back, she withdrew.

She dropped her gaze to her knees, her cheeks darkening as she whispered, "Good luck."

He didn't need luck. Not anymore. Anais had filled him with the strength he needed to face Zephyr and Brink and emerge the victor. A single kiss had made him feel more powerful than he had ever done. He felt as if he could take on the entire village and win.

Gods, he could take on the world.

Nothing would stand between him and his little Amazon.

CHAPTER 7

Loke trod the path to the arena in silent contemplation, running over every possible scenario that might happen during the battle ahead of him. Zephyr led the group. Brink brought up the rear. The walled corridor cut into the black earth allowed the spectators to follow their progress from above as they too headed towards the arena.

Rayna's gaze constantly sought him, but he kept his fixed ahead, unwilling to allow her to distract him. She could stare all she wanted. He wasn't interested in anything she had to offer him. He was only interested in surviving the fight for Anais, claiming his little Amazon, and leaving with her.

Later, he would return to deal with Rayna. She would pay dearly for what she had done. He curled his fingers into fists at his sides and set his jaw, grinding his teeth as he thought about how the female dragon had snatched Anais, bringing her to the village. She had done it with the intent of eliminating Anais, whether that was through death or through Ren handing her over to another male.

He spared Rayna a glance and caught the flicker of fear in her golden eyes. He growled at her, baring twin rows of sharp teeth, making his anger clear to her. She could fear for him all she wanted. She had placed him in this position. She would pay for that too.

Brink muttered beneath his breath behind Loke, reciting an ancient warrior's prayer. Loke chanted it in his head, using it to give him focus and clarity, to hone his senses and prepare himself for battle. Ahead of him, Zephyr began whispering the same prayer as he entered the arena.

A great cheer went up around the oval coliseum.

Loke entered behind him, his bare feet crushing the black sand as he took swift steps towards the centre of the obsidian stone coliseum where they were to gather before Ren in his private box.

The arena was enormous, a fragment of a time long past, when dragons had been numerous and games had taken place on special days through the cycle of the planet around the sun. In those days, thousands had gathered from far and wide to watch the spectacle of the finest dragon warriors battling the great beasts of Hell. Now, the clan used the arena for contests and training purposes, and their numbers barely filled a single row on one side of the arena. That side was carved from the black mountain that towered above the village, spearing the dark sky.

His gaze tracked up the height of it and fixed on the bleak sky of Hell.

How blue was the sky in Anais's world?

He imagined it to be as blue as her eyes.

How warm would the sun feel on his skin?

He imagined it to be as warm as hers had felt beneath his fingers.

Silence fell as Ren entered and Loke dragged his eyes away from the sky and his thoughts away from the mortal realm, and lowered them to the covered private box in the centre of the side of the coliseum he faced.

His mood blackened and his lips compressed into a thin line as he watched Anais enter, stumbling as Rayna held the chain attached to her manacles and dragged her along behind her. They had removed her ankle shackles when he had requested it, but had refused to take off the ones around her wrists.

Ren smiled coldly and motioned for Anais to take the smaller throne next to his one, much to Rayna's obvious displeasure.

Anais didn't move to take it. She fixed Ren with a dark scowl, her blue eyes filled with hatred that tainted her soft sweet scent. Ren turned on her, a male far taller and more powerful than she was, but she didn't flinch away. She stood her ground and even tipped her chin up.

Defiant.

Loke had seen that look before. He had found it charming then, but he found it concerning now. She was playing with fire. Ren wasn't known for his kindness or patience. When he issued an order, he expected it followed without question or hesitation.

Ren moved a step closer to her, coming to tower over her, and his golden eyes narrowed, filling with fire that warned Loke he was close to losing his temper and forcing Anais to submit to him.

She flicked a nervous glance in Loke's direction and he gave her a pointed look and then glared at the smaller throne, silently willing her to take it. There was a time and a place for defiance, and this wasn't it. He was participating in this contest in order to spare her and stop his kin from hurting her. He didn't need her actively attempting to get herself hurt, or worse.

Anais finally lowered her head and slumped onto the throne, her lips moving as she muttered something. Whatever she said, it drew a black look from Rayna, one that held an equal measure of hatred as the look Anais had given Ren. Rayna's golden eyes slid Loke's way and he bared his fangs in a silent warning to her. She huffed and took the seat on the other side of Ren.

Ren stepped forwards to stand at the low wall that formed the front of the private box and raised his hand. "You all know the rules. No shifting. You may use whatever weapons you have at your disposal or those in the arena. Fight until the last dragon stands."

He dropped his hand.

Brink turned on a pinhead and swept his silver blade upwards in a blurred arc.

Not at Loke.

Zephyr leaped backwards, barely evading the blow, and snarled as he retaliated, lunging forwards and lashing out with his curved blade.

The sword sliced clean across Brink's bare chest and the black-haired male staggered backwards, growled and then roared at Zephyr as he banded one arm across his chest and struck with the blade he gripped in the other.

Loke shifted backwards, moving out of the path of the blow, and quickly scanned the arena for a weapon. Brink lived in the village and Zephyr had a hut there, giving them access to their favoured weapons. All Loke had was his knife.

His gaze zoomed around the arena and a cold weight pressed down on his chest as he found no weapon.

He cursed Ren's name when he caught sight of the male grinning down at him. He must have ordered all the weapons cleared from the arena while Loke had been occupied with speaking with Anais.

His heart accelerated, flooding his veins with adrenaline as he searched for a way out of this unholy mess he had found himself in. He was skilled with it, but his knife was no match for the blades that Zephyr and Brink wielded.

His gaze narrowed and he smiled slowly.

There were two blades in the arena.

He just needed to get his hands on one.

Brink dodged a blow aimed at his throat, sweeping beneath the blade and strafing right, gaining space as Zephyr growled and flashed his fangs. Blood drenched the front of Brink's torso, pumping from the deep gash across his bare chest.

Loke wasn't sure why Brink had decided to attack Zephyr and leave him alone, but he was grateful to the male for the much-needed thinking time. Zephyr pressed forwards with his attacks, clearly bent on removing Brink from the equation and leaving the battle for Anais between him and Loke.

Loke could go along with that.

He pulled his knife from the sheath against his left hip and targeted Brink.

The black-haired male swept around to face him, his expression twisting into grim lines as he saw Loke running at him. Brink said something but Loke couldn't hear the words as he roared and kicked off, launching high into the air. He gripped his knife with both hands above his head and kept his eyes locked on Brink's black ones.

Brink glared and swept his curved blade upwards, on a direct path with Loke's descent.

Zephyr took the bait.

He ran at Brink's back, his blade tucked against his side, ready to thrust. The moment he was within striking distance, he launched the blade forwards, plunging it deep into Brink's right side. Brink staggered forwards with the blow, leaving Zephyr in the path of Loke's strike.

Zephyr's head began to lift and he tried to evade, but he wasn't quick enough.

Loke brought his knife down hard, slicing across the green-haired male's left shoulder and down his chest. Zephyr reacted in a heartbeat, shoving the flat of his palm into Loke's face and sending him stumbling backwards into Brink.

Brink snarled and lashed out at Loke, raking sharp talons down his back. "I was trying to help you, you son of a bitch."

Loke screamed and arched forwards, blistering pain tearing through him, blinding him for a second before his senses came back and blared a warning at him that cut through the guilt that had flared inside him on hearing that Brink had entered the contest to aid him.

He hurled himself to his right and landed hard on the ground there, the impact making him lose his hold on his knife as he narrowly avoided the thrust Zephyr had aimed at his gut. Zephyr's blade skewered Brink's stomach instead and the black-haired male stared down at the curved silver sword that stuck out of him.

Zephyr grinned as he pulled the blade out and Brink collapsed to his knees.

Loke barely had time to check on Brink and make sure the wound wasn't fatal before Zephyr turned on him and attacked.

He rolled to his right as Zephyr brought his blade down in a swift arc. It struck the black sand and Zephyr growled, his face contorting with the anger and frustration that Loke could sense in him. Zephyr struck again, driving Loke further away from his knife where it lay on the ground near Brink.

Loke swung his left leg at the male's hand as he stopped rolling. His bare foot connected hard with it and sent Zephyr's blade tumbling from his grip. It didn't stop the male. He leaped onto Loke and clawed at his chest, slicing deep grooves into his skin and tearing an agonised howl from Loke's lips.

"Loke!" Anais's voice rang out around the arena and he growled as he sensed her fear.

She feared Zephyr.

She feared for Loke.

He would take away her fear and make her feel safe again.

He snarled and slammed his right fist into Zephyr's face, following it with a swift left hook and knocking the male to one side. The moment Zephyr's weight lifted from him, he was on the male, shoving him onto his back and dealing his own round of punishing blows. He sliced his emerging claws down Zephyr's chest, from the top of his left pectoral down to his navel, adding to the scars that already littered the male's body.

Zephyr tipped his head back into the sand and roared in agony, and Loke could sense his intent to attack.

He grabbed Zephyr by the throat and pressed forwards to hold him down.

Brink grunted something and Loke's knife tumbled into view at the edge of his vision, landing close to Zephyr and him. He would have to apologise to the male later and thank him for his assistance, and perhaps find out what had possessed Brink to help him in the first place. Brink had always kept to himself, ever since he had been found wandering through the dead after a battle, covered in blood but otherwise unharmed.

Loke was sure they hadn't exchanged more than a handful of words in the millennia they had known each other.

He reached for his knife, the fingers of his right hand groping around for it as he struggled to keep Zephyr pinned. He found it and had managed to get it into his hand when Zephyr spotted it and doubled his efforts, bringing both hands up and slamming his palms over Loke's ears.

They rang, his head spinning from the sudden pressure in his ears, and he tried to shake it off.

Zephyr grabbed Loke's wrist and panic prickled down his spine as the male twisted the knife he held towards him. He quickly clutched the spiralling hilt of the short blade with both hands and fought Zephyr, struggling against him as he tried to force Loke to stab himself. Zephyr pressed the flat of one hand against the end of the hilt and shoved forwards.

The tip of the blade pierced Loke's stomach above his left hip.

He gritted his teeth against the pain and Zephyr grimaced as he drove forwards with the knife.

Fire burned through Loke's side and he cried out as Zephyr roared, the victorious sound filling the arena and setting Loke's temper aflame, making him forget his foolish desire to win this fight without taking the life of a fellow dragon.

He wouldn't let Zephyr have Anais.

Anais was his.

He bared his fangs at the green-haired male and used the sudden burst of strength that blasted through him to yank the blade free of his side.

Zephyr froze and Loke was quick to seize the chance he offered him. He plunged the blade down towards Zephyr's chest. The male bucked just as it was about to pierce the centre of his chest, throwing Loke backwards and off him.

Loke rolled onto his feet and sprang at Zephyr as he was getting onto his, taking the male back down onto the black sand. Zephyr threw a punch at him and Loke reared backwards to evade it. The male's hand struck his arm, the force of the blow sending pain splintering along his bones and knocking his knife from his grip.

A wave of dizziness rocked him, the fire burning in his side blazing hotter as blood pumped from the deep wound above his left hip. He growled through the pain and punched Zephyr, knocking his head to one side. He followed it with another blow, splitting the green-haired male's lip and spilling his blood. Zephyr fought back, landing a solid right hook on Loke's jaw and sending his head spinning faster.

Zephyr unleashed a feral snarl and jabbed his thumb into Loke's stab wound, tearing at it.

He threw his head back and roared in agony, the harsh sound echoing around the mountains and eliciting a soft feminine gasp from Anais's direction. The scent of her fear grew stronger.

The urge to shift blazed through him and he barely held it back, retaining his mortal form by sheer force of will. He couldn't break the rules. If he did, Zephyr would be declared the winner. He would never allow the male to lay his filthy claws on Anais.

The thought of her being at Zephyr's mercy drove the pain from his mind and the agony from his body, replacing it with a deep hunger to spill blood and ensure her safety by destroying Zephyr.

Zephyr pressed his thumb deeper and Loke grabbed his wrist, holding him fast.

He unleashed a fierce snarl of his own as he punched the male beneath him, pounding his face with his right fist. Blood burst from Zephyr's nose and the male retaliated, blocking Loke's next punch and landing one of his own. Loke rocked to his left but refused to release Zephyr.

He weathered the male's wild blows as Zephyr struck hard, alternating between slashing with his claws and punching him. Loke dealt blows of his own, raking his talons over the male's flesh as he struggled to pull Zephyr's other hand away from him. He ground his teeth and grunted as the male dug his claws into Loke's flesh, locking himself in place.

The black world twirled around Loke and his grip loosened as he fought the devastating wave of nausea that crashed over him. He could feel the wet heat of blood as it slid down his side and his chest, his life force draining from him. Zephyr bled too, but not to the dangerous degree that Loke was. He needed to end the fight soon, or he was going to pass out and Zephyr would be the last dragon standing.

He would win Anais.

A feeble growl curled from his lips and victory flashed in Zephyr's green eyes again.

The male knew he was close to winning.

Never.

Loke would never give up.

He would never let anyone else have Anais.

She was his little Amazon and no one else's.

He threw his head back and roared as he gave up on trying to pull Zephyr's thumb from his wound and threw everything he had left into defeating him before darkness claimed him. He pushed himself past his limit, gathered his strength and threw it into one last blow.

His fist struck hard. His aim true.

Zephyr grunted as Loke punched the front of his throat and immediately released him, both hands coming up to clutch at his neck as Loke withdrew. The male wheezed as he tried to breathe through his crushed windpipe, his face reddening and a wild look filling his eyes.

Loke rolled off him and collapsed onto the ground beside him, breathing hard and fighting the pain as it tried to swallow him.

Ren's disappointed huff reaching his ears was like the sweetest music to Loke, easing his heart and his fears.

He rolled over onto his front, shoved his hands into the black dirt and forced himself onto his knees. An inferno burned white-hot in his side and he clutched it, his fingers slipping around in the thick flow of blood as he tried to stem it. He lumbered onto his feet and struggled to stay there, his knees wobbling beneath him as his head turned, spinning the world around him.

Loke frowned at the private box, trying to bring it into focus. It wobbled and distorted, but eventually he caught a glimpse of Anais. She was on her feet at the wall, her face pale and blue eyes enormous as she stared down at him. He took an unsteady step towards her and the faintest of smiles trembled on her lips.

Ren tossed a disappointed look off to Loke's left and then beyond him. Loke looked there too. Brink lay unconscious, his arms still wrapped around his stomach and his skin ashen. Loke was glad the male wasn't dead. He could hear Brink's heart beating slowly but steadily. When he was strong enough, he would return to the village to thank him.

Behind him, Zephyr had lost his fight against the darkness and lay still, barely breathing.

Loke had half a mind to join them and pass out for a while, but he couldn't give in to that need.

Anais was waiting for him, her manacles gone and a look on her face that warned she was considering clambering over the wall of the private box to reach him and escape his clan's chief.

Loke called on the last shreds of his strength, tapping into the deepest well inside him, and roared as he transformed, unleashing his dragon form. The world shrank below him, Anais becoming smaller and more fragile looking as he gained height. The wound in his side opened wider, a great gash that spilled dark blood onto the ground as he settled all four blue paws onto the black sand. He beat his blue wings, preparing for flight, and reached for Anais.

She didn't shrink away.

She reached for him.

Rayna went to round her brother, dark intent in her eyes, and Ren held his arm out, blocking her path to Anais.

"He has won her fair and square, by the way of our people."

Rayna glared at her brother but Ren didn't relent.

Loke carefully curled his talons around Anais and lifted her off the platform. She sat in his palm when he opened it, a small and fragile thing, but one that imbued him with great strength. He went to curl his other paw around her but she held her hand up.

He cocked his head, his long curved dark blue horns brushing his wing muscles as he wondered what she wanted.

"Your knife." She pointed to it and he made a mental note to thank her later for being so thoughtful and aware of how much it meant to him, and how upset he would have been on discovering he had left it behind.

He carefully lowered her, fighting another wave of dizziness as he did so, and she hopped off his palm, picked up the knife, and clutched it. He scooped her back up again and carefully tucked her against his chest as he beat his wings. Black sand swirled around the arena as he lifted off, each powerful beat of his wings sending a gust of wind against the side where Ren stood watching him with a dark look in his eyes.

He was sure they would come to blows one day, but not today.

Today he had more important matters that required his attention.

He turned towards the mountains beyond the village and brought his other paw up, curling it around Anais, ensuring she was safe as he tucked his hind legs against his body and flew back towards his cave.

Each beat of his wings was agony, but he endured it, fighting to remain conscious as he carried his prize back to his home. He could feel one of her hands stroking the palm of his paw, brushing over his blue scales in a tender caress that he felt sure was meant to soothe him. It did. It warmed him right down to his bones and gave him the strength to keep fighting to remain airborne.

He flew over the peak of the mountains that stood between the village and his cave and faltered as a gust of wind swept up off them, battering him. He dropped several hundred feet and Anais clutched him, a startled gasp escaping her. He cursed himself for rushing and placing her in danger, but he hadn't been able to ignore the deep need to take her away from the village. He had needed to take her away from the males who wanted her and meant her harm. She was his and he would let no other male near her.

Loke levelled out and stretched his blue wings wide, catching the air currents to conserve the last shreds of his strength and letting them carry him across the thick forest. He steadily glided over the trees and waited until the last minute to beat his wings and twist his body so he shot upwards, skimming the cragged sloping side of the mountain he called home.

He overshot the ledge and spread his wings again, stopping his ascent and drifting down to land.

Hard.

His left hind leg gave out beneath him and he crashed onto the black rock, thrusting Anais forwards so she rolled into the cave and out of his path. His chest struck the ledge and his jaw cracked off the top of the arch above the cave entrance. Loke grunted and collapsed in a tangled heap, his wings draped across the mountainside on either side of the cave.

Anais regained her feet and ran to him, fear painted across her pretty face as she reached for him.

The sweetest sight he had ever seen.

His hind legs dropped off the ledge as he began to transform back into his mortal form, the weight of them and his tail dangling above the sheer drop pulling him backwards, and she swam out of focus as oblivion swallowed him.

The last thing he saw was the dark sky.

The last thing he felt was a sensation of dropping.

The last thing he heard was Anais screaming his name.

CHAPTER 8

"Loke!" Anais hurled herself towards the edge of the platform as Loke finished transforming back and slipped over it.

She caught his arm and grunted as the weight of him pulled down on her, pressing her into the hard ground, and her muscles burned from the sudden exertion. She grimaced, gritted her teeth, and pulled with all of her might, clinging to his arm. It was wet with his blood and slippery in her grip. He fell several more inches, sliding through her grasp and sending her heart pounding and adrenaline flooding her veins, until her fist reached his wrist and butted up against his hand.

"Bloody heavy bastard," she muttered and growled as she pulled and manoeuvred into a better position at the same time, slowly edging around until she was sitting with her feet braced against the black ground and could see the whole of his arm. "Please wake up. You're too heavy."

She wasn't sure whether he could survive the enormous drop to the side of the mountain either.

He showed no signs of stirring so she did the only thing she could. She heaved, leaning backwards and pulling on his arm. Each inch she gained tore at her muscles, sending pain blistering across her bones, but she refused to give up. Loke had saved her and now she would save him.

She grunted as she shuffled backwards, her bare feet slipping on the harsh rock surface. It scraped across her skin but she didn't feel the pain as she focused on hauling Loke onto the ledge. His head appeared in view and she leaned backwards, yelling out her agony as she fought his dead weight, dragging him up.

When his upper body was on the ledge, she put her feet beneath his arms, hooking him. She worked her hands down his arm and held it near his elbow, and reached for his other arm. He loosed a muffled grunt as she grabbed hold of it and she stilled, checking his face.

He was still out cold.

"Come on, Loke," she whispered and pulled him, issuing a silent apology at the same time as she dragged him across the rough ground. His injuries were already extensive. He didn't need her adding a multitude of scrapes and grazes to them, but he was far too heavy for her to lift.

When his entire top half was on the ledge, she rolled him over onto his back, hooked her hands under his arms and stood on trembling legs. She raised him off the ground as much as she could manage and pulled him backwards with her, towards the cave.

Christ, he was heavy.

She set him down a short distance from the edge of the ledge and struggled to catch her breath. She needed to get him inside the cave, but she also needed to do it without hurting him. She looked back into the cave and her eyes fell on the furs. She hurried over to them, grabbed the biggest one from the pile, and raced back to him. She laid it out beside him and gently rolled him onto it, so he lay on his back in the thick black fur.

Anais kneeled beside him and checked him over. The wound in his side was the worst, still spilling blood over his left hip. She needed to bind it, but she wasn't sure he had anything she could use. The furs were too thick and she hadn't seen any other material lying around.

She looked down at her t-shirt and hesitated for only a second before pulling it off over her head. She found his knife a short distance away and used it to cut her top open down one of the seams, and then sliced it into two pieces around the middle, so it formed long strips. She wrapped one around his waist as tight as she could get it and placed the other beside him on the fur for later.

Satisfied that she had slowed the bleeding, she moved around to his head, grabbed the fur and began hauling him deeper into the cave. She diligently kept her eyes off his lower half. He hadn't sustained any injuries there, so she had no reason to look at him below the waist.

Especially when he was completely naked.

Apparently, his trousers didn't magically appear by themselves when he transformed back.

She stopped when they were close enough to the fire and looked around her, trying to get her mind to stop racing so she could figure out everything that she needed to do. She had to be quick, but it was hard when fear and panic were colliding inside her, sending her thoughts spinning together.

Anais sucked down a deep breath and closed her eyes, seeking some calm among the storm of her emotions.

She needed to focus.

What did she need?

Water. The pool.

Cloths. Hell, she wished she had remembered the ones he had given her to use when she had bathed before she had ripped her only top in half.

Warmth. The fire.

He had all those things. It was a start anyway.

She burst into action, throwing more branches onto the fire and leaving them to catch as she took the torch and raced towards the bathing pool. She skidded on the black pebbly ground as she ran at full pelt into the cavern and gasped as one bit into her bare right foot. Ignoring the pain, she grabbed the pail and filled it with the cool water from the well, and checked the two cloths she had left laid out over the rocks after she had bathed. They were dry.

Anais ran back to the cave and straight over to Loke.

She set the torch down by the fire, put the pail beside him and let the cloths fall from her arms. Her gaze ran over him, assessing his injuries. The grooves in his chest where he had been clawed were deep and weeping blood. She wasn't sure how quickly dragons could heal. The slashes weren't pouring blood as they had been before, but she wouldn't know whether they needed her assistance to heal well until she cleaned him off.

She couldn't do that until she had addressed the stab wound above his left hip though.

She went to his knife where it lay on the ground a short distance away and drew down a deep breath, mentally preparing herself for what she had to do. There were no needles and no thread on hand. She would have to seal Loke's worst wound in a more ancient way.

Anais toyed with the knife as she built up the courage she needed. It was going to hurt him and he was already weak, badly injured because of her, but she had no choice. If she didn't seal the wound, he might bleed out.

She took another of the furs and laid it over his hips, giving him some warmth and dignity, and then kneeled beside him, between him and the fire. She set the knife down, took up the smaller cloth, and plunged it into the pail.

Anais focused on Loke, slipping into a detached and methodical state as she worked to remove her makeshift bandage from around his waist, wring out the cloth and use it to clean his stab wound.

It was ragged.

She tentatively prised it open, stopping when she reached a point where his flesh was already knitting back together. Blood rose like a tide, filling the wound and spilling across his pale skin again. She mopped it up and applied pressure to the wound while she picked up the knife with her other hand. He was healing, but not quickly enough. She needed to seal the jagged cut for him.

She held the knife over the fire, waiting for the blade to glow red-hot before pulling it out, lifting the cloth from the wound and pressing the blunt edge of the knife against the gash.

Loke arched upwards, his bellow deafening her and making her ears ring long after he had fallen silent and still again.

"Sorry," Anais whispered and peeled the blade off him, revealing angry red raw skin. She bathed it in cool water, her hands shaking.

In the quiet, alone with him, it all threatened to overwhelm her.

She was safe now because of him. He had fought for her, had taken blows meant to kill him, in order to stop another male from being able to claim her. It was all her fault. She was the reason he was in this state, fighting for his life. He had saved her. Again.

Tears filled her eyes and she scrubbed them away, refusing to let them come.

What he had done was noble and kind, and she had realised something as she had watched him fighting for her, being clawed and beaten.

She felt something for him.

Perhaps that wasn't entirely the truth.

Perhaps she had realised it before that moment, when she had seen the way the female dragon had looked at Loke and it had dawned on her that the female wanted him. That bitch had taken Anais from him with the intention of handing her over to another male so she could have Loke for herself.

But Loke had looked at her with only hatred glowing in his eyes.

And he had looked at Anais with a wealth of tenderness and heat.

That tenderness and heat, and the feelings she felt for him in return, had been the reason she had foolishly kissed him. She hadn't meant it as a good luck kiss. Hell, she had intended it to be far from that when she had pressed her lips against his, but her courage had failed her, even when he had begun to respond.

She had feared what she had done, so she had covered it up by pretending she had done it purely to wish him luck.

Was it so wrong of her to desire him?

She stroked her fingers across his brow and looked down at his face, studying the strong line of his jaw and his straight nose. His dark lashes and wild blue hair. His sensual lips. Lips that had felt right against hers. Heat curled through her, stirred by the memory of their kiss.

He was handsome, noble and kind. He was gracious and tender, and attentive. He was brave and strong. A warrior who spoke to the one within her. He didn't coddle her in a way that made her feel weak or belittle her. He was everything she had ever wanted in a man.

But had never expected to find in a dragon.

Anais leaned over him and pressed a long kiss to his brow. It was damp beneath her lips, dotted with sweat, and cold. Those two things drove her concerns about herself and what she was doing out of her mind, replacing them with concern for him. He needed her now and she would take care of him.

She focused on washing him, bathing him from head to toe and tending to every one of his wounds. She carefully cleaned the claw marks on his chest and inspected them. Beads of blood broke the surface in a few places down each red line, but the slashes were already closing so she left them alone, allowing them to heal naturally.

When she was done with washing him, she covered him with the furs and then rolled one and placed it beneath his head, raising it off the ground. She kneeled beside him and watched over him as he slept, determined to stay awake and on hand in case he needed her.

Behind her, wind whistled across the cave mouth.

A quiet voice pointed out that this was the perfect opportunity to escape and she pretended not to hear it. She didn't feel like escaping anymore, and her change of heart had nothing to do with the other dragons or any fear that they might grab her again. The desire to stay came from Loke alone. He had fought for her and now she honestly believed that he had meant every word that he had said to her.

70

He wanted to keep her safe.

He had done just that.

Now it was her turn to keep him safe.

Anais brushed her fingers across his brow, smoothing strands of his rich blue hair from it, her gaze fixed on his face as he slumbered.

She had been so afraid when she had watched him fighting for her. She had felt on the verge of losing him and it had filled her with dread, with a deep consuming need to call his name and somehow convince him to break with his warrior's code and fly away with her.

Far away.

She no longer wanted to run away from him.

She wanted to run away *with* him.

But he was right. They couldn't run.

They couldn't run because Loke wasn't the only one who needed her now.

She frowned down at him as anger burned through her veins, setting her blood aflame.

Her friends needed her too.

She didn't know how many huntresses the other dragons had taken from the battle, but she was going to find out. She wasn't going to let them suffer anymore.

She would find a way to save them just as Loke had saved her.

CHAPTER 9

Darkness pulsed around him like a living thing. It seared like fire and burned like ice. It thickened and closed in on him, and then thinned and swept away, growing transparent in places, granting him a glimpse of Heaven from the blackest pits of Hell.

His little Amazon.

Anais.

She danced into view and then disappeared again, twirling out of existence.

Loke reached for her, stretching towards his elusive female, desperate to grasp hold of her slender wrist and pull her close to him.

Where she would be safe.

Forever.

She appeared again. A brief smile. A flash of warmth in her eyes. A laugh that echoed around them. His fingers brushed hers and he tried to curl them around to lock her to him, but she faded away, leaving only emptiness behind, a cold that swept over him and numbed him to his soul.

The darkness closed in again. Cloying. Choking. He shoved at it and fought like a wild thing, swatting at it and pushing his palms into it, trying to drive it away from him so he could catch another glimpse of Anais.

When it faded this time, he saw her standing in the middle of the village and his heart stopped dead before rocketing into action, thundering against his chest. Ren struck her hard, sending her staggering backwards across the black ground, and a cheer went up around Loke.

He growled and tried to run towards her, driven by a fierce need to pull her into his arms and shield her from the male's blows, but his feet refused to move. He grabbed his bare legs and tugged at them, desperate to pull them free of the dark earth that covered his feet.

Ren struck again, dealing a blow that sent her crashing to the ground, and Loke's heart lurched into his throat.

He reached for her, calling her name even though no sound left his lips.

Anais rolled onto her front and struggled onto her hands and knees. She shook her head, causing her long blonde hair to sway and brush the ground, and then pushed herself up onto her feet. She swayed on the spot as she turned to face Ren and something flashed silver in her hand. Loke's eyes darted down to it and widened.

His knife.

She roared a battle cry and launched herself at Ren.

Ren's golden eyes flashed like fire.

Loke bellowed a cry of his own, trying to call her back and stop her.

Too late.

The dragon male lashed out at her with long talons, cutting her across her chest. She stumbled a few steps, her hand coming up to her chest as her face tilted downwards towards it, and then wavered and collapsed in a heap.

Loke snarled and pulled on his legs again, filled with a need to reach her.

The village swirled into darkness, drifting away from him as he flew backwards through the air, still reaching for Anais.

The abyss swallowed him. It crashed over him and then receded, revealing his cave.

Anais stood on the ledge with her back to him, her golden hair streaming behind her in the breeze and her arms wrapped around herself. Her hands clutched the sides of her black top, tightly gripping the soft material. The wind buffeted her, whipping her hair around, but she didn't move away from the edge.

He called her name and she turned as if she had heard him. The sorrowful look in her eyes faded and a smile curled her lips, filling her face with warmth that he felt deep in the pit of his soul.

Loke held his hand out to her and she mirrored him, stretching her right hand out to him, her lips moving silently.

He took a step towards her, forever drawn to her by her beauty and grace, and all that was kind and good in her.

His little Amazon.

Her smile widened and she opened her arms to him as he approached.

A great dark shadow loomed behind her.

Gusts of wind sent Anais staggering forwards and drove Loke backwards, away from her. He leaned into them, fighting them as his heart set off at a pace again and the shadow took form.

A dragon.

It landed behind Anais and she turned towards it, her hands coming up to press against her chest as her eyes landed on it. It transformed into the black shape of a male and Loke roared as he kicked off. Anais shook her head and turned back towards him, her hands stretching for him.

The immense male seized her by the back of her neck.

A sharp sense of dread pierced Loke's heart.

He tried to call her name again.

"Anais!" Loke screamed at the top of his lungs, not stopping even when they burned and his head spun from the lack of air.

He saw the cave and the fire. Felt the breeze on his bare damp skin. Scented Anais.

His heart beat hard against his chest as he shoved the furs off him, flipped onto his front and collapsed. He growled and forced himself to move. His arms and legs shook beneath him, trembling with the fear that ruled him as he crawled towards the mouth of the cave.

His little Amazon stood there with the wretched male's hand around her throat.

He had to reach her.

Arms clamped around his waist and he snarled as he fought his enemy, driving his elbow into their side and battling their hold as they tried to pull him backwards, away from Anais. No. He needed to reach her. The male was shoving her backwards now, towards the cave wall, and fear tainted her beautiful face.

The male was going to kill her.

He roared and tried to shift, but the arms holding him tightened like bands of steel, inhibiting him and stopping him from moving.

He needed to reach her before the male killed her.

"Loke."

He paid no attention to that voice as it breathed a sweet melody against his ear. He had to reach Anais. She needed him. She was going to die if he didn't tear the male away from her.

"Loke... please."

The voice came again, edged with desperation and a touch of fear.

Fear that tainted the owner's soft scent.

A scent that curled around him and comforted him.

Warm hands pressed against his chest and a body pressed against his back. The satin caress of a cheek on his shoulder made him still for a heartbeat of time.

"Please, Loke. Stop."

He blinked and the Anais on the ledge flickered and disappeared, leaving only ragged black mountains and dark grey sky behind.

And the female clinging to him, her soft body pressing against his, her breath warm on his skin.

"Stop," she whispered, stirring the hair at the back of his neck and sending a shiver through him.

He did as she asked as he realised he was dragging her towards the ledge.

"You screamed my name. Was it another vision?" She slowly released him and he sat back on his heels.

A powerful need to see her and see that she was all right consumed him and he looked to his right, towards where she knelt. Her blue gaze was resolutely locked on her knees and a trace of rose coloured her cheeks. He looked down at himself, saw that he was naked, and covered himself with his hands so she would no longer feel embarrassed to be around him and would look at him.

As predicted, her eyes lifted to meet his and relief swept through him, chasing away his fears. She was with him. Safe. Well. Unharmed.

But also partially undressed.

Her top was gone, leaving her in only the black garment over her breasts and her trousers.

He looked back down at himself as he recalled seeing black on him and frowned at the bandage around his waist. She had tended to him and had sacrificed her top for his sake, using it to bind his deepest wound.

It touched him. So did the fact that she had taken care of him and she hadn't left him.

"Was it a vision?" she said again.

He nodded.

"Of me?" she whispered, the warmth in her eyes faltering and a trickle of fear showing in them.

He didn't respond to that question. He couldn't bring himself to tell her about them because he didn't want to frighten her. He had thought the visions would end after he had removed her from the battlefield, but they had only changed. He still kept seeing her dying, but he couldn't make out who killed her. The visions were always fuzzy and disjointed and they tormented him.

The sequence of events between Ren and Anais in the village had been nothing more than a nightmare, but it had paved the way for the vision that had come afterwards.

A vision that had her dying in his own cave.

Who was destined to kill her? It was a dragon. He knew that much now. Perhaps she would be safer away from this place, but he couldn't bring himself to part from her and he would have to if she returned to her world.

"You screamed my name, Loke."

He looked away from her and drew in a deep breath, seeking a sense of calm even when he felt sure he would never feel that way again, not until he had figured out what the visions meant and put an end to them.

Not until Anais was safe.

"Loke?" she murmured softly.

He closed his eyes, heaved a sigh, and then lifted his gaze to meet hers. Her blue eyes challenged him, demanding he tell her what he had seen in his vision. He didn't want to hurt her, so he held his tongue and stared at her instead, giving himself a moment to absorb that she was safe and with him. It wasn't enough.

He needed to feel her. Only then would he be able to believe that she was with him and she was safe again.

That need was a force he couldn't fight. It was too powerful to deny.

He reached out and snagged her wrist, and she gasped as he pulled her into his arms and banded them around her. She tilted her head back and looked up at him, her hands pressing against his bare chest. Her eyes widened and her lips parted, and a different need filled him.

A fiercer one that ruled him.

He needed to kiss her, and he didn't care if she struck him for it.

He just needed her.

CHAPTER 10

Anais wasn't sure how to respond when Loke slid his hand around the back of her neck and dragged her up to him, claiming her lips with his in a kiss that drove every thought out of her mind and left only feeling behind.

His mouth fused with hers, the hard press of his lips as they swept over hers enticing her into opening for him. She did it without hesitation, her lips parting to welcome his invasion and a kiss that rocked her right down to her soul.

It had been too long since she had been kissed like this.

Thoroughly. Passionately.

Wildly.

It burned away every shred of reservation and shattered her inhibitions. It destroyed every thread of resistance.

She melted into him, her palms pressing harder against his bare chest. His heart thundered against them, the wild beat matching the one in her ears and against her breast. His arm tightened around her and his groan made her shake inside, trembling with a need for more.

She shoved her hands up his chest and broke free of the confines of the small gap between their bodies. His hold on her tightened further, squashing her breasts against his chest, and she moaned as she clutched his shoulders, drowning in the heat and passion of his kiss.

Fire burned through her, as if he breathed it into her with each sweep of his lips across hers. His fingers tangled in her hair and tugged at it, forcing her head back and making her open further for him. He plundered her mouth and all she could do was cling to him and ride the storm of his passion, as lost in her own need and desire as he was.

Loke moaned against her lips and the fire blazing in her veins burned hotter, stirred into an inferno by the sound of the pleasure he took from their kiss. She responded by pressing her fingertips into his shoulders and unleashing a soft gasp of pleasure. Need swirled within her, growing more intense and powerful by the second, with every brush of their mouths and every touch of their tongues.

That need consumed her. It owned her. She could do nothing but surrender to it.

Anais pressed against his shoulders and rose onto her knees, bringing her face up level with his and seizing control of the kiss.

He groaned and grabbed her backside, hauling her closer to him, and grunted as he fell backwards. She landed on top of him and immediately pushed herself up, speared by awareness of his injuries and how her weight would hurt him. He didn't seem to give a damn. He growled, a sound born of pure frustration, and pulled her back down on top of him.

She tried to edge her weight away from his left hip at least, but he refused to let her move. He wrapped both arms around her, settling one hand between her shoulders and the other on her backside, and pinned her to him. His mouth claimed hers again and pleasure blasted through her, obliterating her concerns for a heartbeat of time before they came rushing back.

"Loke," she breathed against his lips and he kissed her again, as if he could silence her that way.

Hell, she wished that he could, but the concerned voice in the back of her head wasn't going anywhere and it was ruining her mood.

"Let me move," she whispered and he snarled this time, the feral sound shocking her and making her heart skip a beat. She pressed against his shoulders and fought his hold. "Loke, let me move!"

His answering growl made her go still but she braced her hands against his chest, stopping him from pulling her back down to him.

"Loke." She softened her tone and he finally gave up trying to tug her back down to him and loosened his hold on her.

Displeasure etched darkness onto his handsome face as she raised herself off him and his aquamarine eyes were as stormy as a violent ocean. She hadn't meant to upset him, or make him feel she was going to run away from him and what was happening between them. She wanted—needed—him to know that.

Anais lifted one hand to his face and swept her fingers across his brow first, feeling his temperature without alerting him to what she was doing. She traced those two fingers downwards, over the sculpted curve of his cheek and then down the straight strong line of his jaw. Dark blue whiskers dusted it, scraping against the sensitive tips of her fingers. She smiled as she stroked his lower lip and his mouth opened, revealing a hint of white teeth. His gaze bore into her but she refused to look at him as she explored his face, feeling as if she was looking at him with clear eyes at last and seeing him properly for the first time.

He was more than handsome.

He was beautiful.

She had never liked it when men dyed their hair outrageous colours, but the bright cerulean of his suited him and she couldn't imagine him with dull brown, black or blond instead. It was a trace of his dragon showing through, a reminder that he had another form, a majestic and incredible one that still seemed more fantasy than reality.

Anais ploughed her fingers through his hair, enjoying the contrast of the rich colour against her milky skin. It was damp from his fever. A fever that seemed to have finally broken. He'd had her worried. She wasn't sure how many hours had passed since he had lost consciousness, but it felt like more than a day's worth. She had been startled when she had gone to fetch a fresh pail of cold water to bathe him and had heard him yelling her name.

She had been afraid when she had seen him crawling towards the ledge and had reacted on instinct to stop him, fearing he would fall over the edge again and she wouldn't be able to save him this time.

"Anais?" he murmured and she pulled her eyes away from his short wild hair and dropped them to his.

They were soft and calm again, bright with flecks of gold fire that seemed to shimmer and swirl.

They sought an answer to his unspoken question from hers and she sighed as she feathered her fingers down his cheek.

"I'm crushing your wound." She decided to say it straight and not dance around the truth. She had wanted things to continue, but not when it had been in danger of hurting him.

He loosened his hold further and she slid off his right side. His eyes rolled back in his head and he groaned, and she realised with dismay that she had forgotten something else in the heat of passion too.

He was naked.

Anais glanced down and fire flashed through her. His cock jutted proudly from a nest of deep blue curls, thick and long, and Heavens she wanted to run her hand down it and hear him moan again.

She dragged her eyes away instead and avoided Loke's fierce gaze. He breathed hard, his chest pressing against hers, tempting her gaze down to it. She couldn't let it lure her eyes there to roam over his muscles as they strained, because those same eyes would want to drift down the hard ridges of his stomach and from there it was barely a leap to his cock.

"Come back," he murmured and tried to pull her back on top of him, but gave up when she resisted. "You felt good pressed against me."

Hell, he had felt good pressed beneath her too but she had been putting weight on his wound. She drew in a deep breath, steadied herself, and then focused on the bandage around his waist. She needed to check the wound and make sure she hadn't reopened it.

Anais reluctantly pulled herself away from him and kneeled beside him. He huffed and propped himself up onto his elbows, his gaze on his left hip. She focused there too, refusing to let the way his entire torso had tensed, revealing every muscle, sway her into looking at his body. He didn't flinch as she untied the strip of black material and unwound it, revealing the wound.

The ragged line where she had cauterised the wound was still pink and raw, but there was no blood.

Loke prodded it. Hard.

"What did you do?" His deep voice echoed around the cave, a touch of irritation in it.

"I cauterised it." When he frowned at her, she realised he didn't understand and put it in terms he would. "I heated your knife on the fire and used it to seal the wound shut."

Loke looked less than pleased and she folded her arms across her chest.

"Would you rather have bled to death?" she snapped and his frown eased.

He shook his head. "No. Dragons heal quickly, Little Amazon. There is a chance I would not have bled out."

"A chance? You'd rather bank on a chance over being certain?" She frowned now. He made no sense at all. He prodded the scar again and she grabbed his hand. "Stop that. You'll open it again."

"No, I will not. It is healed... and now I am left with this scar."

Thanks to her.

He didn't say it, but it was there in his tone and his eyes. She glared at him and pushed his hand away from his left hip before he could prod the scar again.

She pointed to his chest and the scars on it, long slashes from the claw marks that had littered him. "You would have scarred anyway."

"But it would have been less noticeable."

Anais resisted the urge to roll her eyes and box him around the ears.

She sighed and stroked her fingers over the wide scar that darted over his left hip, her gaze locked on it as she tried to think of something to say that would make him shut up about what she had done and appreciate it instead of complaining about it.

His gaze left her face and she glanced at him, finding his eyes following her fingers as she caressed his skin, one finger on either side of the three-inch line of the scar. The fascination was back in them again, making them almost glow and the golden flecks burn.

"Some girls like scars." She let the words tumble from her lips and his eyes slowly lifted from her fingers to her face, the fire in them growing hotter as they met hers and held them, rendering her powerless and under his command.

"A girl like you?" he husked and her fingers stilled against his hip.

She nodded.

His expression turned pained and he groaned as he frowned at her.

He rocked his hips upwards, tearing a gasp from her throat as his hard length pressed against her forearm. His nostrils flared and his eyes darkened further, flooding with need and rekindling the embers of her desire.

"Touch me," he groaned and rolled his hips again, thrusting against her arm, rubbing the head back and forth across her skin. "I need it. It has been too long and you drive me to the edge of despair... I need you, Little Amazon. Gods, I need you."

And *gods*, she needed him too and wanted to give him what he desired, but part of her was stuck on what he had said.

It had been too long.

"How long?"

He cast her another pained look and rubbed himself against her arm, and she thought he wouldn't answer her question. She opened her mouth to say it again and he spoke over her.

"Centuries… one… two… a long time. I am not sure. Will you touch me now?" He groaned and bit his lower lip as he rocked his hips again. "Please, Anais. I fear I might burst or die if you do not."

A little melodramatic.

But he hadn't been with a woman in a long time. Longer than she had been alive. For some reason, she found that pleasing. Appealing. She liked the fact that it had been centuries since he had last taken a lover, because it wasn't as if he hadn't had the opportunity. The red female dragon acted as if she would leap on Loke given the chance and other females had admired him too.

He didn't want them.

But he *needed* her.

Anais twisted her blonde hair into a thick strand and knotted it at the back of her head. If she was going to give him his first touch from a woman in centuries, she was going to make sure he roared the cave down and never wanted another woman again.

She was going to blow his mind.

She hooked her leg over his and sat back, pinning them beneath her. He stared down the length of his incredible body at her, his eyes narrowed and hot with hunger and his teeth still buried in his lower lip.

Anais held his gaze and feathered two fingers down the length of his rigid cock.

Loke tipped his head back and growled, his sexy throat working on a hard swallow and his lips parting as his eyes slipped shut. If he liked that, he was going to love what she had in mind.

She danced her fingers up and down his length, giving him time to grow used to her touch. It jerked beneath her, pulsing with need that made her want to press her thighs together and wriggle. It was all she could do to resist crawling up his body, settling herself over his shaft and rocking against him. She battled that need and stroked him, up and down, from root to tip and back again. When she dipped to the base, she let her fingers drift over his balls and he shuddered and moaned, the wanton sound filling the thick silence.

"Anais," he murmured, his expression half-mad already, and she smiled as she leaned over him and decided to drive him all the way to full-crazy.

She lowered her mouth and stroked her tongue over the length of his cock, flicking the head when she reached it. He jerked hard against her and moaned as he shook all over. She didn't give him a chance to grow accustomed to things this time. She swirled her tongue around the sensitive blunt head of his length and ran it over the slit, ripping a feral grunt from his lips. He rocked, a desperate edge to his actions, and she pressed her hands to his hips and pinned them.

Another groan escaped him.

Anais set about earning another one as she stroked her tongue over his flesh and then wrapped her lips around him. He thrust upwards, driving his cock into her mouth, and growled. His hand clamped down hard on her head and he tried to push her away but she refused to let him. She curled one hand around his length and began sucking him, taking him deep into her mouth before withdrawing and swirling her tongue over every sensitive spot he had.

He bucked and groaned, and she opened her eyes and looked up the length of him. Delicious. Every inch of him was tensed, taut and pronounced, on display for her to devour. The man was a god. Wicked perfection. A warrior who she swore was going to war on her heart and wouldn't stop until she surrendered.

Maybe she would turn the tables on him and not stop until he surrendered to her.

She smiled wickedly and sucked him again. Each moan he loosed stirred her desire, sending her passion and need soaring to new heights. She swayed her hips, feeling the moisture as it pooled between her thighs, her need as it burned through her, and she found herself thinking about taking him inside her or finding release in some way.

He had said that he wanted her, but Hell, she wanted him too. Needed him just as he needed her.

"Anais," he whispered, hoarse and strained, and then muttered something in his beautiful tongue.

He pushed against her again, harder this time, and she couldn't resist him. He was too strong. He easily lifted her mouth away from him and she relented when she looked up at him and saw him breathing hard and fighting for control. Hunger burned in his striking eyes, calling her to him, beckoning her in a way she didn't want to resist.

She needed him.

"Gods," he muttered and dropped his hand to her shoulder. He tugged at the strap of her bra and eyed the garment. "Take this off... before I tear it off you."

She appreciated the warning and the chance to save her bra from being torn into pieces, and tamped down the urge to tell him to take it off her so she could see his expression sour and hear him confess that he didn't know how. She didn't think he would like her teasing him, not when he was so far gone, on fire with need and mad with desire.

Anais sat back on his knees, undid her bra and slipped it off her breasts.

Loke's gaze instantly zeroed in on them and he swiftly sat up. His left arm snaked around her back and he grabbed her bottom and hauled her up onto her knees. His lips descended on her right breast and she gasped and clutched his shoulders as he pulled her nipple into his mouth. The exquisite feel of his teeth rolling the sensitive bead between them tore a moan from her lips and had her tossing her head back and trembling against him.

He groaned against her breast and pulled her closer, sucking harder on her nipple, sending hot sparks shooting outwards from it and blazing across her overheating skin.

"Loke," she husked and he groaned again and wrapped his other arm around her, pinning her to him.

It wasn't enough. She needed more.

Anais couldn't stop herself from flexing her hips. The need to feel his hands on her was too fierce, controlling her and sending her out of her mind. She needed some relief.

She tore at the button on her trousers and shoved the fly down, and reached around her back to grab Loke's right hand. She seized it, pressed it flat against her stomach and then guided it downwards into her underwear.

Loke stilled, breathing hard against her breast, his hand trembling as she nudged it between her thighs. A groan left him and she echoed it as she began to move his hand against her, rubbing his fingers over her sensitive bud. He growled and she gasped as he took control, his hand no longer shaking as he caressed her.

Anais grabbed his shoulders again, steadying herself as pleasure rocked her, promising sweet relief. She was so close already. On the precipice just as he was.

Another growl left his lips as he tried to dip his hand lower and her trousers hindered him. She shoved at them at the same time as he did, trying to get them down her hips. They refused to budge while she had her legs spread to accommodate his between them.

Loke found a solution to that.

He pulled them so hard she ended up on her back with her bottom in the air. It didn't stop him. He saw his chance and he took it, yanking her black trousers down her legs together with her underwear. The ground was cold and rough beneath her back, but she didn't care, not when Loke edged her knees apart and wedged his shoulders between them.

The first brush of his tongue over her flesh was bliss.

The second tore a moan from her throat that startled her. She couldn't remember ever sounding so wild and abandoned, untamed and lost in the pleasure of a man's touch.

He groaned and lapped at her, teasing her sensitive nub with the tip of his tongue before laving it with the flat, sending her soaring higher towards Heaven.

She reached down with one hand and grabbed his hair, twining the blue lengths between her fingers, and threw the other one above her head. Her hips rocked of their own accord, rubbing her against his wicked tongue as he mastered her body. He moaned and she balanced on the edge, flexing and reaching for her climax. It refused to come. She still needed more, that extra push.

The feel of him inside her.

She wanted to know what he would feel like as he eased into her, joining them and completing her.

Damn, she needed that.

"Loke," she whispered and then bit her tongue, her cheeks heating as her courage faltered.

He lifted his head and she cursed him for stopping. When he showed no sign of going back to his work of driving her mad, she risked looking down at him. His dark blue gaze locked with hers, sending a blast of heat through her. She had never had a man look at her as he did, as if he wanted to eat her whole. Devour her.

"Touch me."

His eyes darkened further as she issued that command, not with anger but with passion and need, hunger she had awoken in him with a simple but brave request. She had also never dared to tell a man what she wanted before, but as Loke lowered his head and stroked his tongue over her nub, harder than before, and eased two fingers into her sheath, she decided that it was worth the risk of embarrassing herself.

Anais threw her head back, arching off the ground as she rode each thrust of his fingers and each swirl of his tongue. Heat blasted through her, ebbing and flowing, bouncing around inside her until she was on fire. She clutched her own hair with one hand and his with the other, moaning and writhing, seeking a release that seemed so elusive, forever coming within reach before slipping beyond her grasp.

"Loke," she husked and he slid his other arm beneath her, raising her backside off the ground, and stroked her harder with his tongue as he thrust deeper with his fingers.

The heat pooling within her reached boiling point.

Loke swept his tongue over her nub and she shattered, her entire body jolting upwards as fire and lightning shot through her, a million sparks that cascaded down her legs and over her torso. She quivered around his fingers, moaning with each thrust as he brought her down from her climax, adding to her pleasure.

He pulled his fingers from her and licked her, lapping at her entrance and tearing another hazy moan from her lips.

He growled and she gasped as he was suddenly above her, his hands pressed against the black ground on either side of her head, bracing his body away from hers. His eyes glowed blue fire and she trembled under his intense gaze.

She knew what he needed, because she needed it too.

Anais pressed her right hand to his chest and slowly drifted it downwards, feeling his heart hammering against it and how tight his muscles were, coiled strength beneath her palm. She twisted her hand when she reached his hip and swept across, towards his length. It flexed and pulsed when she cupped it, and he moaned, his eyes turning hooded as his breath left him in a rush.

"Little Amazon needs," he murmured sexily and she nodded as he looked at her.

"Loke needs too," she whispered and stroked him, eliciting another groan from him as he frowned, his nostrils flaring and eyes closing.

"Gods." He lowered his head and his arms visibly trembled.

Anais stroked him one more time and then pushed down the length of him, encouraging him to move backwards. He did so without hesitation and she didn't hesitate either. She wanted this—*him*—and she was going to have it.

He lowered his hips and she brought him to her, guiding the tip down to her sheath.

He froze and pulled away, his expression fierce and icy, and his lips flattening into a thin line.

Cold swept through her as he sat back and she sat up and covered herself with her arms, unsure what she had done wrong.

Frustration etched deep lines on his handsome face. "Someone comes."

Relief filled her for a split-second before what he had said sank in.

Someone was coming.

And she was naked.

Anais leaped to her feet and Loke groaned, drawing her gaze back to him. His pained expression spoke to her, telling her that he wasn't happy that they had been interrupted. She was plenty pissed about it too and she was going to make sure whoever was coming knew it.

She tugged her trousers on and quickly donned her bra, making sure she was covered before their intruder landed.

She presumed it was a dragon anyway. She hadn't really thought to ask.

Loke gripped the black rough wall of the cave and pulled himself onto his feet, and she paused and frowned at him. Someone had been pretending to be in better shape than they really were. She would have words with him about that later. The last thing she wanted was Loke hurting himself.

"I am fine." He gave her a look that warned her to hold her tongue and his blue leather trousers materialised on his legs.

If fine was another way of him saying wobbly and paling, she might have agreed with him.

"You need to rest." She took hold of his arm and he shot her another look, this one dark with passion and hunger, fanning the desire that still burned within her.

He opened his mouth to answer her and quickly turned away, giving her his back and coming to face the mouth of the cave. He caught her hip and shoved her behind him, and she peered around him, wanting to see who had come to visit and fearing it would be Zephyr or the irritating red female dragon.

It was neither of them.

An incredible violet dragon landed on the ledge.

Anais stared at it, stunned by its colouring. She hadn't realised that dragons could come in twin colours. The violet scales gave way to white down the front of its throat and its chest. It flapped enormous wings that were two-tone too, with purple scales over the muscles and bones, but white membranes, and settled them against its back.

She remained behind Loke as the dragon transformed.

Into a beautiful woman with shoulder-length violet-to-white hair and the most amazing eyes Anais had ever seen. Her irises were deep purple around the outside, but white around her pupils.

A very naked beautiful woman.

One who Loke clearly knew as he released Anais and walked towards her, speaking to the woman in their native tongue.

Anais folded her arms across her chest and remained where she was, refusing to move, even when Loke looked back at her. He frowned and canted his head, a flicker of confusion in his eyes as she glared at him. How many beautiful female dragons did he know?

Had he slept with this one?

They seemed close as Loke gestured towards the fire, smiling at the woman, and she finally made an effort to dress. Unlike the redheaded bitch in the village, this one covered herself in both violet leather trousers and a white top.

It didn't change how Anais felt about her.

She wanted the woman gone.

Damn, didn't that make her sound and feel like a jealous little bitch?

Loke wasn't hers. They barely knew each other, no matter how differently she felt on that front. She hadn't known him for months or years, and definitely not for centuries, but she felt as if she had.

She felt as if she had always known him.

But she hadn't.

She looked back at the beautiful woman and Loke as they approached. How long had the woman known him? Had they been lovers?

Anais dragged her gaze away from them and tried to quieten that vicious voice, stopping it from raising questions that only hurt her. She went to the fire and sat on the furs near it, staring at it and paying no attention to Loke or the female.

Or how her heart caught fire in her chest and felt as if it was burning to ashes.

She felt Loke's gaze on her but couldn't bring herself to look at him as her thoughts weighed her down. Just minutes ago, she had been filled with light and something akin to happiness, and now she had plunged into darkness and it was cold, chilling her to the marrow.

She wrapped her arms around herself, drew her knees up to her chest, and kept her eyes on the fire as the reason for her jealousy dawned on her.

She was falling in love with a dragon.

CHAPTER 11

Loke wasn't sure what was wrong with Anais or why her mood had changed so abruptly, but he wanted to know. He kept glancing at her, but she refused to look at him, her eyes constantly fixed on the fire in the middle of his cave, a distant and unfocused quality to them. Was she unwell? Her cheeks were flushed, but he had thought it was from their lovemaking. Perhaps he was wrong and she had caught a fever.

The thought of his little mortal ailing made ice form in his veins and he barely held himself back as desire to go to her where she sat on the pile of furs and demand to know whether she was sick rushed through him. Only his other desire to keep his attraction to her from Taryn kept him in place near the female dragon.

He willed Anais to at least look at him and let him know she was well without words but her eyes didn't leave the flames.

Taryn glanced down at Anais too, an inquisitive edge to her violet-to-white gaze that had him drawing his focus away from Anais in order to protect her from the dragon's curiosity. It had been a while since Taryn had visited him, and she was much changed from the last time they had seen each other. There were dark arcs beneath Taryn's eyes and she was far thinner, a greyness to her skin that worried him.

"What happened?" he said in the dragon tongue and she drew her eyes away from Anais and fixed him with the same curious look.

"She is pretty."

"She is mortal," he countered and Taryn's eyes grew concerned. "I took her from a battle in the Third Realm."

"A spoil of war? That isn't like you, Loke."

He shook his head. "I saw her future and I wanted to change it."

He wasn't sure he had changed it though. He still kept seeing her die.

Loke pushed his own problems out of his mind and focused on his old friend. "What happened, Taryn? I have not seen you in years and now you show up looking as you do."

She diverted her gaze off to her left and the fire there and rubbed her arms, a faint but uneasy smile on her lips. "Slavers caught me… I was repeatedly sold on the black market."

Fury raced through his veins, making him burn with a need to track down the vile monsters who had captured and sold her into slavery and butcher them all.

He closed the gap between them and took hold of her shoulders, and she slowly lifted her eyes to meet his. Pain shone in them, terror that he struggled to comprehend. Slavers rarely caught dragons. When they did, they were sold for a high price as an exotic slave. He had heard horror stories about the things dragons in captivity were forced to do by their masters, but they had only been stories. No dragon had ever escaped the slavers or their master. Those who were taken never returned.

But Taryn had.

Somehow, she had survived everything and had returned. Scarred and broken. A piece of herself dead and gone. He could see it in her eyes as she looked at him.

Her life had been difficult enough before she had been taken by slavers.

He smoothed his palm across her pale cheek and wished she had better fortune, a better life than the one she had been born into and forced to endure.

She shied away from his touch, slipping beyond his reach as she stepped back, gaining some distance from him. He sighed and then frowned as he felt Anais's gaze boring into his back and smelled the dark taint of anger in her scent.

He looked over his shoulder at her, wanting to see why she was upset with him, but she pinned her gaze back on the fire and refused to look at him.

"The female is jealous," Taryn whispered in the dragon tongue. "She is more than a ward to you, is she not, Loke?"

He forced his eyes away from Anais and looked at Taryn. Her hard expression demanded an answer from him. He had wanted to avoid such questions, because he wasn't sure how she would react to the news he had developed feelings for a mortal and one under his protection. He didn't want her thinking less of him, placing him with the other males who took spoils of war. He needed her to understand that it had never been his intention to fall for the little Amazon.

But fall for her he had, and he had fallen hard.

He nodded but left it at that as he tried to pull her attention back to herself and away from his private life. "Are you running from slavers?"

Taryn's expression shifted, turning troubled again. "No."

But she was on the run from someone. There was fear in the depths of her eyes and lacing her scent. She was afraid of whoever was after her. If it wasn't slavers, who was it? Who had Taryn running scared?

He wanted to know.

"Who then, Taryn?"

She heaved a sigh and looked down at her bare feet. "He is no one... of no consequence to you."

But he was someone. This unknown male had rattled Taryn, so much so that she clearly didn't even feel safe here in the realm of dragons. She feared the male would find her.

Loke growled and couldn't suppress his need to know what awaited Taryn. It was born from a need to protect her, one that had run deep in him for thousands of years. He had always tried to shield her, because she had always felt like a sister to him, even when she already had a brother.

He closed the distance between them with a single stride, caught her chin before she could protest and raised her eyes up to meet his. He stared hard into them and tapped into his magic, using it to force a vision. Sharp pain pierced his skull and his eyes ached, but he pushed through it all, weathering it until his magic triggered his natural ability of foresight.

Darkness swirled, filling the cave and blotting everything out, and then abated, revealing a green land. He lifted his eyes and saw Taryn laying on the grass, bloodied and beaten, her violet-to-white hair spilling around her and stained crimson in places. Three males stood in the distance, dressed in black skin-tight armour.

Elves.

He snarled at them but they didn't respond. They remained with their purple eyes narrowed on Taryn.

A male stepped past Loke, coming to loom over her broken form. His pointed ears flared back through overlong blue-black hair and his violet eyes fixed on Taryn, merciless and cold as he stared down at her. His fingers flexed around the shaft of a black spear and he raised it.

Loke launched himself at the male on instinct, even when he knew he couldn't affect the outcome of the vision. He ghosted through the male and the darkness closed in again, evaporating a heartbeat later to reveal the black mountains of the dragon realm and the deep grey sky.

Taryn flew through it, her wings beating heavily, rhythmically. She swooped and spread those wings, a blaze of violet across the tops of the trees before she gave another hard beat and launched upwards to somersault in the air. A carefree and joy-filled cry left her, speaking to him of her happiness.

The inky black closed in on him once more and when it parted, he was standing in the middle of the cave and staring down into Taryn's eyes.

"What did you see?" Those words were quiet and edged with fear and trepidation.

He lowered his hand from her face. "Your future is undecided. One path is dark... the other light. Something you are destined to do will cause one or the other to happen. You must be careful and choose your steps wisely, Taryn."

She nodded. "I will keep running. I must speak with my brother. Where is he?"

Loke shook his head and she faltered, the certainty that had been in her eyes fading as she looked up at him, replaced with concern.

"Do not." The last thing he wanted to do was hurt her, but he refused to send her marching into her grave. If he had to hurt her to keep her from dying, he would do it. Her brother meant the world to her, but she was blinded by her love for him, and Loke feared it would get her killed one day. "Stay away from him, Taryn. Your brother has grown more dangerous. His lust for power has tainted him. Please? I fear that if you go to him, the first glimpse of your future I saw will be the one that comes to pass. You will die."

Her cheeks paled and her dark violet eyebrows furrowed as she went to shake her head, but only managed to move it mere millimetres. "I must see him. He is my brother."

Loke closed his eyes and sighed. The bond between sibling dragons was always strong, but Taryn's bond with Tenak was stronger than usual because he was her twin. It was rare among dragons. Loke hadn't heard of twins being born since Taryn and her brother, and that had happened thousands of years ago.

"Loke?" Taryn whispered and he sensed her need for him to look at her and reassure her.

He forced a smile and opened his eyes, fixing them straight on hers. He wanted to lie and say something that would lighten her heart and destroy her fears, but the words wouldn't line up on his tongue. Others replaced them, and he couldn't hold them back.

"Be careful." He brushed his fingers across her cheek and shook his head as he looked down into her eyes, his heart aching at the thought of her being swallowed by the madness and violence that surrounded her brother. "Tenak is worse... the tales coming from where he resides say that he is insane. He kills any who draw too close to him. What if he does not recognise you, Taryn? What if he turns his vile craving for violence towards you?"

Taryn lowered her head, drew in a deep breath, and then lifted her chin and pinned him with eyes that were calm and soft, filled with hope and light. No trace of fear.

"I still must see him." She smiled softly and he realised that there was no changing her mind. She was set on going to her brother and risking her life. "He needs me, Loke."

He wished he could believe that. Her brother needed no one. He lusted after power and would stop at nothing to achieve his grand vision of being lord of all dragons and the ruler of Hell.

Her brother had gone to war with many of the realms, leading legions of dragons to their deaths. Fools. They had thought they would achieve power and wealth if they followed him. They had been seduced by his words and promises. Those who had survived had returned to tell their clans that Tenak had used them as shields, sending them to their graves so he could weaken the forces of his enemy before setting foot on the battlefield to claim victory.

Loke could see the resolve in her eyes though and he knew she would keep pressing him until he told her where her brother resided or she would go to the clan village to ask one of the dragons there.

Those dragons were liable to attack her, pinning her brother's crimes on her and seeking to avenge their fallen kin. He had no choice but to tell her, if only to spare her from the wrath of the other dragons.

He sighed and reluctantly nodded. "Go then. He has moved to the borderlands with the Devil's domain, at the furthest reaches of our realm. He has taken the Valley of the Dark Edge as his own kingdom."

"I am come for the blade too."

He had known that the moment she had landed.

She had given him the elven blade before disappearing, entrusting him with it.

"It may not make your brother recognise you. He may kill you for it." Loke looked into her eyes, making sure she knew what she was getting herself into, because once she set foot in the valley, there would be no turning back for her.

Either Tenak would kill her, or he would recognise her as his sister.

Even then, there was a chance that Tenak might choose to kill her. Loke doubted that her brother's love for her reached the depths that her love for him did. When Tenak saw the blade she had stolen from him, he would want it back. His dragon need to reclaim his property, his prized possession, would rule him.

She nodded. "I accept whatever fate awaits me."

He wanted to mention that he had seen elves in his vision and now she asked for a blade of their making, a weapon capable of piercing dragon armour and killing them.

He had seen her bloodied and broken.

He prayed to the dragon gods that taking this blade wasn't what would set her on the path to her death. If elves found her with it, they would kill her just as he had seen. The blade was sacred to them.

"I hope you know what you are doing." He turned away from her and made haste to his treasure room, taking the right-hand tunnel at the back of the cave and following it down into a lower chamber.

The black blade lay on a stone altar where he had placed it many years ago. Markings carved into the obsidian stone shielded the weapon, making it impossible to detect. When he removed it, those linked to it would feel its presence in the world again. They would know it hadn't been lost.

They would search for it.

The princes of the elves.

Tenak.

Both parties would want it returned to them, and would stop at nothing to attain it.

The blade was power.

The strongest of the elven metals and dragon blood forged into a single weapon that gave the one who wielded it control over ancient magic and all the powers of the elves and the miraculous ability of the metal. The power to cut through any armour or weapon combined with the ability to condense that power into an arc of pure light using magic.

That arc could slice through a horde of enemies in a single sweep of the blade.

Part of Loke wanted to leave it shielded and tell Taryn she couldn't have it, but he had vowed to trust her with it when she asked for it back, and he had to do just that. If anyone had the strength to face her brother and live, it was Taryn.

He placed his hand on the hilt and it vibrated with power beneath his touch, warm against his skin.

A flash of the elves standing over Taryn's body shot across his eyes and he frowned at the blade.

Elves.

They were already after Taryn. They were the reason she was running scared.

He grabbed the blade and hurried back up to the cave with it. When he entered, she lifted her gaze away from Anais and her smile died.

"It is elves who chase you, Taryn, and do not lie to me." He held the black sword up. "Or I will destroy this."

Her eyes shot wide and she lurched forwards a step, her hands coming up in front of her. "Do not. Please, Loke? I know what I am doing."

"Who are the elves after you?" He lowered the weapon back to his side and wondered if he actually could destroy it. Taryn seemed to think it possible. If he had known that, he might have burned it to ashes shortly after she had given it to him.

"He is no one. I can handle him."

Just one male.

The one he had witnessed standing over her?

"This male wields a spear." He made it a statement and the way her cheeks paled and her gaze darted to take in anything but him confirmed his suspicions. "Be careful, Taryn. It is he I see at your death."

She closed her eyes, drew in a deep breath, and then resolutely raised her head and looked at him. "He is dangerous, but I will not let him outwit me. He has not outwitted me yet."

Loke growled at that. "How long has he been after you?"

"Centuries." She didn't hesitate and he could see she was finally telling him the truth.

Loke frowned as it dawned on him. "Since the blade was stolen."

She nodded and held her hand out for it. "He has not killed me yet and he will not kill me. I know it. Whatever you saw, it was wrong."

Wrong? A vision was never wrong. He had seen her die. He had seen the male standing over her, merciless and cold. It was possible that the male hadn't killed her though, but that didn't change the outcome. She still died.

"I saw you dead. I saw that male present." Loke looked down at the black blade he gripped. "Is this worth killing yourself over? Is your brother worth it?"

"I believe so. A life in slavery has more appeal, was better, than a life spent in constant fear. I must end this."

He sighed and held the blade out to her. "Very well."

She placed her hand over his on the hilt. "I will be careful, Loke. Please do not worry."

Impossible. He felt he was sending her to her death by handing her this blade and telling her where to find her brother. He could only hope that she managed to pull off whatever she was planning. The thought of the elven blade in the hands of her brother disturbed him. It was the one thing guaranteed to give Tenak enough power to lay waste to every realm in Hell and set himself up as the ruler of them all.

Taryn took the blade and backed away from him. He couldn't bring himself to look at her as she left the cave, fearing it would be the last time he saw her. Only when the steady beats of her wings drifted into the distance did he look at the cave mouth.

"What just happened?" Anais's soft voice breaking the silence drew his gaze down to her where she sat near the fire.

Another female whose death he felt doomed to witness.

"Taryn has gone to face her brother. Either she will die or she will set herself free. Pray to the gods that she knows what she is doing, for if she fails, all Hell will be at her brother's mercy." He scrubbed a hand over his face.

"You seemed pretty close to this Taryn woman." The sharp edge to her tone drew a frown from him and Taryn's voice rang around his head.

She was jealous.

Loke's heart soared as he realised that Taryn had been right and Anais was jealous of his closeness to her.

"Taryn is only my friend." His words didn't ease the darkness in her eyes or the fierceness of her expression.

"What about the others at the village? The bitch who took me?"

Loke's mood darkened now and he folded his arms across his bare chest, pressing his short claws into his biceps as he thought about what Rayna had done. "I will deal with her, Little Amazon. She will pay for what she did."

"She did it because she wants you."

He couldn't deny that, but he could set her mind at ease. "I do not want her. I grew tired of that traditional sort of behaviour many centuries ago. I am not looking for dalliances."

Saying that stirred a deep need within him, a possessiveness that demanded he finish what he had started with Anais. It was born of more than an attraction to her. Born of more than his growing feelings for her.

It ran in his blood and burned in his soul.

It was an unshakable need, fierce in its strength, consuming in its hunger for her.

It owned him, controlled him, and commanded he obey it.

Instinct.

Ancient and powerful.

Impossible to resist.

His earlier fears came back full force. They settled in his heart and refused to shift from it, no matter how hard he tried to push them out.

One of the prince of elves and a king of demons had been given a mortal mate.

Had fate done the same to him?

He wanted to know whether she was more than merely a female he desired and had feelings for.

He needed to know the answer to the question beating within his heart.

Was Anais his fated mate?

CHAPTER 12

Loke took slow measured steps towards Anais where she sat on the furs near the fire. Her eyes slowly lifted away from the flames, rising up the height of him, coming to meet his. The darkness in them began to fade, burned away by the heat of desire as her pupils widened, swallowing the rich sapphire of her irises.

The air around them thickened as he closed in on her and her lips parted, luring his gaze down to them.

They had been warm against his, her taste sweet on his tongue. He wanted to taste them again.

He wanted to taste her again.

He halted in front of her and she swallowed as he held his hand out to her. She hesitated only for a fragment of time before placing hers into it and allowing him to pull her onto her feet.

His cock stirred in the tight confines of his leather trousers, his desire rising again as he stared down into her eyes. Was she his mate? There was a way of finding out, but it was dangerous. If he made love with her, he would know if she had been made for him, but he would discover it by awakening his deepest instincts as a male dragon.

He would rouse a fierce need to mate with her to complete the bond.

Loke looked down at her delicate hand. It was callused from her battles, a sign of her strength, but it was also weak. It felt fragile in his. Breakable.

She was mortal.

A mortal was no match for an immortal, and definitely not for a dragon.

A mating between a dragon and another immortal was dangerous enough. A mating between a dragon and a mortal was unthinkable. He would hurt her.

He could kill her.

But he needed to know whether the beautiful creature standing in front of him was his mate.

He couldn't survive another moment without knowing, and definitely couldn't face the next thousand years or more wondering whether she had been his one true fated female and he might have been able to have forever with her.

He needed to risk awakening his dragon instincts to mate in order to find out.

He pulled his arm back, luring her towards him, and her head tilted up as she approached. His gaze lifted to meet hers and the heat in her eyes stole his breath away and shattered every last fear and reservation he had.

She wanted this. Him. She welcomed it.

His little Amazon still needed him, and he would satisfy her.

Loke dipped his head and captured her lips, swallowing her gasp as her free hand leaped to clutch his shoulder and the one he held crushed his. She leaned into him, rising on her toes, seeking more that he gave to her willingly. A need filled him, a dark commanding urge to give her everything she desired. He released her hand, slid both arms around her waist and hauled her up the length of his body, so her mouth was level with his.

She moaned again, the soft sound drawing a groan from him as heat chased through him and his hard length kicked against his trousers. He lowered one hand to her backside and clutched it as he kissed her, stealing her breath and leaving no part of her untouched. She mewled and wrapped her legs around his waist, and he concealed his pain from her as the wound above his left hip burned. He didn't want her to worry, because she would stop him from making love with her. He was strong enough now.

He kneeled and slowly lowered her onto the furs, covering her body with his. She flexed beneath him, rubbing herself up and down his cock, and he grunted as he joined her, thrusting against her and cursing his clothing and hers. It dampened everything, stealing the pleasure from it and leaving only a frustrating glimpse of what they might have experienced if they had been naked.

Loke wanted her naked again.

He sat back between her legs and attacked her trousers, dealing with the complicated fastenings. She lowered her hands from his shoulders and helped him, tackling her trousers with ease before shoving them down her thighs.

He groaned and tore his gaze away from the triangle of pale curls at the juncture of her thighs.

When she reached her knees, he took over from her, pulling the black trousers down her legs and off over her bare feet. He tossed them to one side and focused on his own trousers, using a sliver of magic to make them disappear.

Loke shuffled backwards on the furs, wedged himself between her knees and delved his tongue between her soft petals. She cried out, the sound filling the cave, stirring his need for her. He growled and stroked her with his tongue, tasting her. Gods, he needed more of her. That need only increased when she dug her fingers into his hair and held on to him, gripping him tightly as he pleasured her.

"Loke," she husked, breathless and beautiful. His little Amazon.

He knew what she needed.

He eased two fingers into her and she tensed around him, muscles flexing and drawing him in deeper. She moaned and writhed against him as he began to stroke her as he laved his tongue over her sweet bud. Her actions grew more frantic with each plunge of his fingers into her hot moist sheath and he could feel the wildness rising within her as she careened towards the point where she would become a slave to her need for release. He drove her to it and then eased off, giving her a moment to come down, before he sent her soaring again.

His cock pulsed against the furs, as hard as steel and aching for her touch and for some relief.

She arched against his mouth and moaned, the strained sound of her pleasure too much for him to handle.

He pulled away from her and rose over her, bracing himself on his hands above her. Her eyes slowly opened and locked with his, dark with desire and need. He growled and swooped on her lips, claiming them in a kiss that seared them both.

She responded by wrapping her arms around his neck and pulling him down against her.

The soft feel of her warm body giving beneath his and the wet heat of her against his length tore a groan from his throat. He couldn't stop himself from rocking, rubbing his erection against her, his face screwing up as a ripple of pleasure flowed through him.

Still not enough.

She kissed him harder and he took the hint, crushing her lips with his as he drove against her and swallowing her cry of bliss. Another growl curled up his throat and rumbled through his chest, and need overwhelmed him. He shoved back, gripped his cock and rubbed the tip of it down between her folds, towards her sheath. She moaned and arched again, raising her hips towards his, an invitation he wouldn't turn down and couldn't resist.

He groaned as he edged inside her and his arm trembled beneath his weight, threatening to give out.

Her moan joined his as he eased into her inch by inch, holding himself back and forcing himself to take it slowly. She was hot and slick with need, but tight around his length. He didn't want to hurt her. He gently moved deeper and then eased back, working his way into her. She moaned with each move he made, driving him into thrusting into her, and he struggled to hold himself back.

Anais took that struggle out of his hands as she wrapped her legs around him, pressed her feet into his bare backside and drove him into her. She cried out and he grunted as she flexed around him, giving him a brief flicker of exquisite pain. She dragged him back down to her and her lips sought his, her kiss searing him as she slowly relaxed beneath him, loosening her hold on him and freeing him to move.

Loke clutched her shoulder with one hand, resting on his elbow, and her hip with the other, raising it off the furs. He held her hard as he thrust into her, long slow strokes that had him reaching every part of her.

He drank her moans as she shuddered in his arms, her kiss turning frantic even when he tried to keep it slow and tender. Her need stoked his, fanning it into the same wild inferno and stripping control from him. He clung to a fraction of it as he began to pump her harder, clinging to the piece of his sanity that constantly reminded him to be gentle with her.

His little mortal.

He groaned and kissed her harder as he plunged into her.

A deeper connection bloomed between them, a stronger thread that tied them. It strengthened with each thrust and kiss, with every meeting of their hips, becoming a powerful force that slowly seized control of him and filled him with heat and light.

She broke the kiss and pressed her forehead to his, her fingertips digging into his shoulders as she moaned with each panted breath that left her lips. He clung to her as he drove into her, a flicker of awareness stirring in his soul, growing stronger with each passing heartbeat.

She stole that awareness from him as she flipped him onto his back and rose off him.

He snarled and clutched her hips as she rode his cock. She was beautiful as she threw her head back, her tangled knot of blonde hair fraying and causing spun gold to cascade down her shoulders and over her breasts.

Loke groaned and could only lay beneath her and drink her in as she bounced on him, pleasure written across her face. It echoed within him, an intoxicating kind of bliss that had him melting into the furs even as his body cranked tighter, his balls drawing up and his cock thickening as release coiled at its base. She moaned and held his hands as he began to counter her thrusts, driving up into her as she came down and withdrawing as she rose off him.

"Loke," she whispered, her face screwing up and her actions turning rougher.

He could sense her need. It blasted through him too.

He drove deeper into her, losing himself for a moment and unleashing a fraction of his strength on her. She groaned louder and he grunted as she tightened around him, stealing more of his control from him.

He gripped her hips harder and seized control of her movements as he thrust into her. She tangled her hands in her messy blonde hair, her face etched in lines of frustration and pleasure, impending bliss. He brought her down harder, driving deeper into her, and she threw her head back and cried out. Her body shuddered around his, heat scalding his length as her release took her. He grunted and pumped harder, seeking his own release as her sheath milked him, drawing him towards it.

It came swiftly, staggering him and sending a hot rush through every inch of his body as his cock throbbed inside her, spilling his seed. He grunted softly with each pulse, still thrusting shallowly as he fought for air and to stop his head from spinning.

Anais slowly drifted down to rest on his chest, her moist breath fanning across his pectorals and her body trembling against his.

He wrapped his arms around her and stared at the roof of the cave as the awareness that had been growing within him finally sharpened into focus and his deepest instincts roared to life.

Demanding he claim his mate.

CHAPTER 13

Anais rested in Loke's arms, her gaze on the fire as the flames flickered, sending warm light dancing across the black ground around it. When he shifted and sighed, she pulled her focus from the flames, twisted so her front pressed against his left side while carefully avoiding his wound, and looked at him. He lay with one arm bent beneath his head, cushioning it, and his eyes closed. He looked content. Happy. Handsome.

Hours had passed since they had surrendered to their desire and they hadn't moved from this spot. They had passed every minute in each other's arms and in silence, sharing the moment.

Loke's eyes opened and lowered to her, their striking aquamarine depths warmed by the light of the fire off to his right. He raised a single dark blue eyebrow at her and she had the feeling he was trying to figure out why she was staring at him.

Why wouldn't she be staring at him?

He was gorgeous, and the way he was laying, with his arm beneath his head, showed off his muscles and rekindled the heat within her, making her think about climbing on top of him and seeing if he was interested in an encore.

It had been a long time since she had experienced anything as intense and blissful as making love with Loke. When he had unleashed his strength on her, she had found Heaven. He had sent her shooting into the stratosphere, or possibly beyond it. Heat pooled in her belly and she had to close her eyes to shut him out as she fought the urge to lower her mouth and kiss a trail across his chest to awaken his hunger for her.

There was something she had to ask him first, and it was something that was liable to ruin the moment. She didn't want that to happen and she didn't want to upset him, but she had to know or it was going to hover at the back of her mind and mar her time with him.

"Are the dragons who took the other hunters like you?" Her voice sounded too loud in the silence, even when she felt sure she had whispered that question.

He frowned, raised his other hand away from the small of her back and brushed her hair behind her ear for her. "Like me?"

She nodded and when his frown didn't shift, the quizzical look in his eyes remaining, she decided she needed to say it straight. "Are those dragons going to be nice to my friends like you are to me… or are they going to be like Zephyr?"

He looked away from her, towards the fire, and his expression gained a troubled edge. Her heart sank into her stomach and she couldn't stop her mind from filling with images of her fellow huntresses being mistreated.

"I do not know if they had a reason for taking their females... but if they did... their reason would not be as mine was. It would not be noble."

She frowned as the slender ribbon of hope she had been clinging to slowly dissipated. "That blond one back at the village said they were spoils of war, Loke. What does that mean? Zephyr made it clear he had been abusing whoever he took."

She felt sick just mentioning that and her mind raced through every female hunter she had known in her team, wondering which he had taken.

"Not all will be like him. Others will charm the female... but if that fails, they may employ magic to convince them."

"Like drugging them?" She stared wide-eyed at him.

When he nodded, she barely tamped down the urge to spring to her feet and demand he take her to every dragon home he knew of so she could help her kin.

Zephyr had fought him and had almost won. The green-haired bastard had wanted her as a second spoil of war, a replacement for one he had broken. She had no doubts that the other dragons would fight to defend whichever huntress they had stolen from the battle. The thought of Loke having to fight again turned her stomach and she looked down the length of his body to the thick scar over his left hip.

He was in no condition to help her save her fellow huntresses, not right now. As much as she wanted to head out and rescue them, she needed to gain enough information to form a plan first and give him a chance to regain his strength.

"Could you fly me around to the homes of the dragons you know? We could scout them and see if they have any of my friends. If they do, we could help them."

He nodded. "I will do that for you. I will be able to scent whether they have company."

She smiled and thanked him with a kiss, pressing her lips to his cheek. The light dusting of dark blue hair on his jaw scratched at them, taking her back to kissing him on the mouth while making love with him, and it was difficult to tamp down the desire that rose within her and focus on their conversation. When she pulled back, he was smiling too.

"When you're better though. Not right now." She stroked his bare chest and avoided his glare as he narrowed his eyes on her.

"I am fine." He kept saying that, but it didn't mean she had to believe it.

She had noticed him flinching when she had wrapped her legs around him.

She would give him another day in which she would use the time to strategize with him and learn more about the other dragons who had fought as part of his clan in the battle. Once she was sure he was strong enough, she would take him up on his offer to help her. First, they would scout the locations and see if the dragons who lived there had one of her friends, and then they would plan their mission to save them.

They would have to move quickly once they decided to take back her friends and do it all in one perfect run. If word spread about what they were doing, there was a chance the other dragons might go into hiding or might prepare themselves to fight Loke. She didn't want him to fight again.

She didn't think she ever wanted to see him fight again.

It had terrified her.

"Anais?" he whispered and she pulled herself out of her thoughts and smiled at him, trying to show him that she was fine.

"I want to help them." She didn't hide how much she wanted that as she looked at him, right into his eyes. They were more than just her friends. They were part of her family.

He nodded. "And you will... but I will not place you in danger."

"Because of the visions?" She studied him for a reaction, wanting to see whether there was another reason he might not want to place her in danger, one that might hint at whether what they had shared was more to him than just mutual attraction at play.

He had said he wasn't interested in dalliances.

Did that mean what was happening between them was more than just a fleeting moment in his eyes?

His handsome face darkened and he gave a clipped nod, and her foolish heart took it as an answer to her unspoken question.

"Tell me about them." She refused to give up when he shot her a warning look that said he didn't want to talk about them. She did. "You've had more than one now, Loke. Do you see the same thing?"

He shook his head and wrapped his free arm back around her. "Let us not speak of them. My visions are mine to know and deal with."

She tossed him her best glare and shirked his grip, knocking his arm away from her as he ran his fingers up and down her side. He wasn't going to get around her by stroking her and distracting her.

"They're about me. I have a right to know." She pressed her hand against his chest and went to get up, but his arm clamped around her waist and he pinned her to his side.

"I am only trying to protect you, Little Amazon." His gaze implored her to listen to him and let it go, but she couldn't, no matter how badly she was spoiling the moment.

"I can protect myself." She tried to wriggle free of his arms but he held her tighter, crushing her against him, and she gave up and settled for glaring at him instead.

"Can you not let me protect you?" he whispered and she faltered as he gave her a boyish look that made her want to sigh.

She didn't mean to trample on his male pride, and she wasn't saying that he couldn't protect her too, but she was a big girl and she was used to taking care of herself.

It had been a long time since someone had wanted to take care of her.

It felt strange.

She sighed. "Fine. You can protect me too... but you have to let me in. I need to know what you see."

"I see your death. Is that not enough?" He looked away from her and the pain in his eyes clawed at her, making her feel awful for pushing him. "I will tell you soon. If the visions come again... I will tell you. I swear it."

She nodded when he looked back at her. She could go along with that, because part of her hoped that he never had another vision, and therefore she wouldn't have to worry if she ever found herself in a similar place or situation to what he had seen.

"Let us focus on finding your friends." He smiled at her, flashing straight white teeth, his attempt at charming her not failing to hit its mark.

He had realised that her friends were important to her and she could see that he was going to use it to place himself in her good book and score some points with her. She didn't mind. She needed help and he was the best there was. He knew the local dragons, could fly around the forbidding terrain and cut travel time down exponentially, and he was strong enough to convince whichever dragons had her friends to hand them over.

Sable would probably love him and she was sure her leader would appreciate his help when she came to save them.

"Sable," Anais muttered as she realised that her leader would be coming for her and the others.

"The other huntress?" Loke said and she nodded. "What of her?"

"She's the leader of the Archangel team that came to Hell to fight in the battle. I know her. She won't leave us behind. She will come for us all." Even though part of Anais hoped that Sable never found her, because that part of her was happy here with Loke.

Loke's expression turned grave. "You desire to be rescued?"

Anais wasn't sure how to answer that question. There was a part of her that wanted to stay here with him, but the rest wanted to return to her world and her job.

"No," he barked and his face blackened into a scowl. "It cannot happen. I will not let it happen. I must stay with you to protect you. I must save you."

She smiled and shook her head. "You're making no sense. You can't save me from yourself."

He looked blankly at her and then frowned again. "I was speaking of saving you from the foe in my vision."

Foe? There was someone he kept seeing then? Someone who was going to kill her. An icy shiver blasted through her and she wished he would tell her about the things that he had seen. His gaze flitted between hers, a flicker of

fear in it that she knew came from the thought that she was going to press him
to tell her about the visions. She wanted to know what he had seen that had left
him so shaken, but she didn't have the heart to ask him, not when she knew it
would hurt him.

She would wait for him to tell her as he had asked.

His handsome face softened and his blue eyes warmed, turning tender as he
brushed his fingers through her hair and held her gaze. "You are safe with me,
Little Amazon. I swear it. I will keep you safe... with me."

She knew that, but she also knew that she didn't belong in this world. She
wasn't sure she could stay as he clearly wanted, and part of her also wanted.
The thought of leaving him didn't sit well with her. It turned her stomach and
sent her thoughts churning, filling her with dread and making her want to wrap
her arms around him and hold on to him.

She didn't want this time with him to end, even when she felt deep in her
heart that it would.

No matter what they did to stop it.

They would end up parted.

Ice formed in her veins and she did the only thing she could to make it go
away.

She pulled herself up Loke and kissed him.

He was quick to respond, wrapping both arms around her as he craned his
neck and returned the kiss, his lips dancing softly across hers and filling her
with heat that melted the ice.

Anais didn't resist him when he rolled her onto her back, his right leg
wedging between her thighs and pressing against her mound. She slipped her
arms around his neck and ploughed her fingers through his blue hair, clutching
him to her as he kissed her breath away. She moaned and he followed her,
groaning as he slid one hand down her side, tracing the curve of her waist
before stroking her hip and then her left thigh.

She raised it and he nudged it with his hand, pushing it open. A soft gasp
escaped her as he trailed his fingers down the inside of her thigh, tickling and
teasing her. His lips left hers to blaze a path down her cheek and she tilted her
head back as he devoured her throat, his mouth working magic on her as a
thousand hot shivers tumbled through her.

His right hand slipped between her thighs and she gasped louder, arching
up to meet his touch as his fingers eased between her folds, seeking her nub. A
fiercer bolt of desire shot through her as he found it and rolled it between his
finger and thumb, torturing her with a touch of pain before giving her pleasure.
He lowered his hand and stroked the entrance of her sheath, drawing moisture
from her and cranking her desire higher.

She closed her eyes and gripped his head as he kissed her throat, pressing
his tongue in hard to the line of her artery, and drew his fingers back up,
swirling them around her aching nub. She tensed her muscles, desperate for

another hot blast of pleasure. It came swiftly, sending her rocketing higher as he stroked and teased her.

"Loke." She couldn't hold back as she rocked against his fingers, flexing her body beneath his.

He grunted against her neck and then he was kissing her again, fiercer this time, his mouth dominating hers as he ground against her hip, rubbing his hot hard length between them.

She moaned and unleashed her passion, trying to match him as he took her mouth. His hand dipped lower and tore a gasp from her as he plunged two fingers into her sheath and began to pump her. She gave up trying to match him and surrendered to him instead, giving him control over her and letting him master her body, sure that he would give her another earth-shattering climax.

She moaned as her passion hijacked her body, making her roll her hips to meet every wicked thrust of his fingers. She breathed harder, straining for the one push that would send her tumbling into bliss.

Loke denied her.

He withdrew his fingers at the critical moment and snatched his lips away from hers.

She growled in frustration and tried to pull him back to her, but he easily resisted, her strength no match for his. She flicked her eyes open and moaned, heat sweeping through her as she saw him kneeling in front of her, a glorious vision of pure unadulterated masculinity.

Thick ropes of muscle coiled tightly beneath pale skin. His hard cock rose from its nest of curls, dark with need that made her body yearn in response to the sight, aching for him to fill her and to give him pleasure.

Anais shifted before he could make a move, coming to kneel on all fours in front of him, her hand seizing his cock. He grunted and then moaned as she stroked him, the guttural sound filling the cave. She wanted to hear him making that noise when he was in her mouth and she was tasting him.

She lowered her head and wrapped her lips around the blunt head of his cock.

He grunted again and his hands seized her shoulders, his nails pressing in hard as she swirled her tongue around the crown, seeking his sensitive spots. He moaned whenever she found one and went to war on it, not relenting until his hands trembled against her and he was as hard as steel in her mouth.

"Anais," he husked, his passion-drenched deep voice commanding her to give him some relief from the torture.

She took him deeper into her mouth and began sucking him, pressing her tongue hard into the underside of his cock on each withdraw and swirling the tip around the crown. She raised her right hand and played with his sac as she sucked him, ripping a feral grunt from him. He gripped her shoulders harder and began to rock into her mouth, shallow thrusts accompanied by soft grunts of pleasure. She moaned, the sound of his pleasure giving her a shot of it too, drugging her and making her hungrier for him.

When he was on the verge, she pulled away, giving him a taste of his own medicine. She looked up the height of him and met bright blue eyes that swirled with gold flecks of fire. His handsome face turned deadly serious, a dark edge to it that thrilled her.

She had pushed too far and she had a feeling he was going to make her pay for it.

He clamped his hand down on the back of her neck and pulled her up to him, searing her with a kiss that sent an inferno sweeping through her. His other hand delved between her thighs and she moaned and shuddered as he thrust two fingers into her, spearing her and making her quiver with a need for more. His answering groan was deep and guttural, more beast than man.

It thrilled her.

It made her want to climb up him and impale herself on his long hard cock.

Loke had a different idea.

He grabbed her behind her thighs and pulled them upwards, sending her flat on her back with her bottom in the air. She lay at a diagonal, her eyes on his, goading him into doing it. She needed him inside her again, filling and completing her.

He snarled, flashing twin rows of sharp white teeth, and grasped his cock.

He gripped her hip with one hand and fed his cock into her with the other. He didn't take things slowly this time. The moment the head was inside, he drove home, filling her with one deep stroke. She cried out as her body stretched around him and he struck the deepest point inside her.

He paused only long enough to catch the desire in her eyes, the passion and need for him that commanded him not to stop, and began thrusting. His hands clamped down on her hips and his eyes locked with hers, dark and hungry, making her burn for him. She moaned in time with him, the sound tearing from her lips whenever their hips met and he filled her.

The cave filled with the sounds of their lovemaking, their wild noises and each hard meeting of their bodies drowning out the crackle of the fire.

Anais threw her hands above her head and clutched the furs, twisting them in her fists as Loke took her, hard and fast, every delicious inch of him tensed. The sight of him only added fuel to the fire as she stared up at him and he stared back at her.

He was incredible.

A perfect blend of danger, sensuality and lethal beauty.

One hundred percent male, and that masculinity spoke to her feminine side, filling her with appreciation and need.

She moaned and tried to hold his gaze, but it was impossible as her desire reached a crescendo. She screwed her face up, lost in her passion and her spiralling need. He grunted and thrust harder, leaving no part of her untouched with each powerful stroke of his cock.

The universe detonated in a shower of stars across the darkness of her closed eyes and she cried out as fire swept through her and her entire body quaked from the force of it, her limbs trembling as it pulsed through her, each wave growing stronger rather than weaker. She breathed harder, her heart pumping faster as Loke kept thrusting, driving her towards a second climax. It came in a blinding rush as his cock jerked and began to pulse inside her, shooting hot jets into her core. She cried out with him, her hoarse shout matching his as they shook and found Heaven together.

Awareness of the world slowly came back, the thick sound of her rapid breaths and Loke's panting filling her ears at first. The feel of his hands clutching her hips, his grip so tight her bones ached came next, followed by how big he still felt inside her, filling her completely.

She slowly opened her eyes and looked up at him.

His eyes blazed blue fire at her, his expression still deadly serious, and she had half a mind to ask what that look was for, but he took her back out of her head before she could get the words out.

He eased back, making her think he was going to withdraw completely and release her.

He didn't.

He slowly rocked into her, filling her again, the fire in his eyes growing hotter. Each slow thrust stirred passion in her veins again, reawakening her desire for him and driving the last two climaxes to the back of her mind as her body came alive to seek a third with him.

Anais had the feeling that she had seriously underestimated the power and stamina of a dragon shifter and she was about to find out just how high Loke could take her.

He leaned over her, not breaking his rhythm, and his lips crushed hers in a kiss that seared her right down to her soul and left her in no doubt of what lay ahead of her.

Heaven.

She had found Heaven in Hell.

And she never wanted to leave.

CHAPTER 14

Loke beat his broad leathery wings, the slow methodical rhythm and the feel of the breeze against his face soothing him and giving him something to focus on other than the fears crowding his mind. At the forefront was the terrifying thought of dropping the precious cargo he held tucked in his huge front paws, close to the broad blue plates of armour that protected his chest. That precious cargo was stroking her palms back and forth over his talons, the steady consistent tempo of her caress only adding to the calm front that battled the storm of his emotions.

He could feel her disappointment and he wanted to reassure her that their scouting mission tomorrow would go better and they would locate some of her friends. The journey today had turned up nothing, but they had only checked ten caves from a distance, using his superior senses to see whether the dragons residing in them had a mortal with them. There were many more in the area and he felt sure that they would discover which dragons had taken a huntress soon enough, and then they could set in motion her plan to save them.

He angled his head to one side and dropped his blue gaze to her, the vertical slits of his pupils narrowing as he watched her as he continued to fly over the valleys and mountains, carrying her home.

Home.

Over the past two days, his cave had begun to feel different, but it was only now that he realised what that difference was.

Anais had made it feel like a home.

A home for him and for her.

He snorted at that feeling, knowing deep in his heart that her home was many miles away. Ice filled that same heart as the most constant of his fears pushed forwards to fill his mind and flood his veins—the fear that she would leave him.

The other huntress was coming for her.

Anais's words had played on his mind for the past two days, throughout all the time they had spent planning the route they would take in order to scout for her fellow huntresses and discussing the dragons of his clan and their locations, and all the time they had spent in each other's arms, lost in bliss. They plagued him and he couldn't shake them. She had told him with such confidence that Sable would be coming and there had been a look in her blue eyes, an edge to her emotions that warned him she wanted her friend to come and she wanted to return to her world.

Never.

She cared for him. He felt sure of that. She had revealed a hint of her feelings for him when he had suggested they fly to Zephyr's cave first to see whether he really did have one of her friends.

Anais had rebelled against that idea, quickly gripping his arms and forcing a promise out of him, a vow that he would avoid Zephyr's cave until they knew of the locations of all the other huntresses. She hadn't pressed him to promise that because she feared the other dragons would discover what they were doing and would hide the females they had taken.

She had pressed him for that promise because she feared he would fight Zephyr again.

She wanted to keep him safe.

He could understand her concern and it warmed him right down to his aching soul.

She cared for him.

As deeply as he cared for her?

And what if she did?

Loke carefully adjusted his paws, holding her close to him, so she was sandwiched between his paws and his chest, locked to him and safe. Perhaps he could convince her to stay. He would do whatever it took to make her see that she belonged with him, even when he feared what would happen if she agreed.

The need to mate with her was already growing stronger, increasing in ferocity whenever they made love, and it was getting more difficult to hold back that urge. It was primal and powerful, stronger than his will and his desire not to hurt her. It controlled him and left him feeling weak, vulnerable in a way he didn't like. He was used to being the master of his body and his mind, but the instinct to claim his fated female kept pushing and breaking through, seizing command of him.

He fought it as hard as he could, battling to suppress it and somehow mastering it, but each time it swept over him, it was a longer fight and a harder battle, and he feared that next time he would lose the war and his ability to hold back his instincts.

He would claim her, whether she was willing or not.

He would kill her.

Loke closed his eyes and beat his wings harder, a growl rumbling up his throat that tore a startled gasp from Anais. He silently apologised to her, and vowed once again that he would never allow his instincts to control him like that. He would find a way to master them so she would be safe with him.

Her steady stroking started again, this time against his chest, offering him comfort that he drank down, greedily stealing every drop of it because he needed it. He needed to know she was safe and she felt something for him. He needed her, close to him like this, touching him with love in her caress.

Forever.

He held her closer to him, fearing that something would take her from him and there was nothing he could do to stop it from happening.

Whether it was the one called Sable or the grim shadow of death he kept seeing in his vision.

He was going to lose her.

His heart stung at the thought and his grip on her tightened. It was only when she pushed her palms against his chest that he realised he was holding her too tightly and was hurting her. He loosened his grip as he flew over the peaks of the mountains surrounding his valley and looked down at her.

Her expression softened as her sapphire blue eyes met his and her eyebrows furrowed as she tucked the wild strands of her golden hair behind her ears, holding it back from her face. She was so small and fragile. His little Amazon. So easily breakable. So vulnerable. A need to clutch her to him filled him and it was only her sweet action that stopped him from pressing her back against him to protect her and shield her from the world.

She placed her right hand on his chest, over his heart, and held his gaze, hers filled with affection and tenderness, as if she had felt his pain and his conflict, and all of his fears, and wanted to soothe him.

Perhaps she had.

He knew of bonds, but not of bonds between a mortal and a dragon. It was possible that the connection he had started the first time they had made love gave her insight into his emotions, tying them with an invisible string.

That invisible string linked his heart to hers, and it was short. Even venturing as far from her as his larder or the bathing pools made him ache with a need to return to her, that thread pulling tight and tugging him back to her.

He felt sure that if she returned to the mortal world that the string would break or yank free of his heart, rupturing the fragile organ, and he would bleed out and die.

Gods, he needed her.

That need was fierce, like a fever. He couldn't get enough of her and no matter what they did together, how many times he made love with her, he was left unsatisfied in a way. His body was always sated, but his soul wasn't.

It craved a bond with her.

One that would tie them together forever with an unbreakable string.

He scouted his cave from a distance, afraid that the one called Sable would have found it and would be waiting for them.

Waiting to take his precious mate from him.

When no signs of life flickered on his senses, the relief he expected to feel didn't come. The threat of her friend coming for her hung over him.

Haunted him.

He carefully landed on the broad deep ledge of his cave and furled his wings against his back before reluctantly setting Anais down. She smoothed her black combats and the strip of dark cloth she had tied around her chest to cover the garment she had called a bra.

Would she leave him when her friend came?

He had promised to return her to her people, but now he wanted to break that promise and refuse to let her go. The thought of her leaving chilled his blood and hollowed out his chest, making him feel dead inside. He couldn't bear it. It stirred a deep need to clutch her to him and kiss her, to somehow drown in her so he could shake the dreadful feeling and replace it with something good and beautiful.

It refused to go though, only growing stronger the longer he stared down at her.

He was going to lose her.

No matter what he did, she would want to return to Archangel and her world, and he couldn't follow her into that realm, even though he would fiercely desire to do such a thing. A darkness grew inside him, a desperate need to make her see that she belonged to him now and belonged here with him, and somehow find a way to make her stay.

He had to make her stay.

He couldn't lose her.

He focused on his body and shifted, and her blue eyes followed his as he shrank down to her level, his wings folding into his back and his horns withdrawing into his skull.

He stood before her on the ledge of his cave, naked both physically and emotionally. He had never felt so vulnerable as he did as he stood there, waiting for her to react, hoping she would do something to ease the pain in his heart and make him believe that she wanted to remain here with him in his world, where he needed her.

She took a slow step towards him, her face softening again as her eyes searched his, and he felt certain she could feel his emotions. She knew he was suffering and she wanted to ease his pain, even when she didn't understand where it stemmed from.

Her irises gradually darkened with each step, the hunger that filled them awakening his own fierce need of her and setting his heart pounding. When she reached him, she stopped so close their fronts were pressed together, tiptoed and looped her arms around his neck. Her fingers ploughed into his hair and she drew a swift breath before obliterating his fears and driving them out of his mind.

Her kiss wasn't tender. It wasn't sweet as he had expected it.

It was intense as her lips claimed his, passionate as she delved her tongue into his mouth, and fierce as she pulled him down to her, bending him to her will. It relayed every drop of her need, telling him that she craved him as ferociously as he craved her.

It stoked the fire in his veins until it burned as an inferno, a wildfire that was impossible to tame and bring back under control. He growled as his need of her roared to the surface, breaking free of its tethers and demanding he satisfy it this time.

Both his body and his soul.

He growled into her mouth as he claimed her hips and then ran his hands down, over her bottom, and lifted her off the ground. He didn't break the kiss as he walked with her, carrying her into his cave. His mouth fused with hers, devouring her, unable to get enough of her. He rocked his hips, grinding his hard aching length against her, and she responded by wrapping her legs around his waist and rocking against him.

Her breathless little gasp tore another growl from him and he diverted course, unable to make it as far as the furs and the fire.

He needed her now.

He needed her taste on his tongue and the sound of her crying his name in his ears.

Loke set her down close to the wall near the entrance of his cave and swiftly tackled the fastenings of her trousers. She wriggled as he shoved them and her underwear down her legs and yanked them off her, her eagerness only driving him on, increasing his need. He needed to satisfy his female.

He kneeled on the ground before her and looked up at her, meeting her hungry blue gaze, seeing her desire and need burning in it. His female needed.

He narrowed his eyes on her and growled low in his throat as she responded by leaning back against the black wall, lifting her left leg, and placing it over his shoulder. The scent of her arousal swept over him and he couldn't hold himself back. He grabbed her hips, pulled her to him and delved his tongue between her petals. A jolt rocked him as her sweet taste flooded his mouth and his cock pulsed, as hard as steel and aching for more.

He clung to the tattered threads of control, barely holding his instincts at bay as he licked her, flicking her pert nub and eliciting a soft gasp of pleasure from her. Pleasure that flowed over him, through him, heightening his desire and his need. He groaned and laved her, sweeping his tongue over her, relentlessly pursuing another sweet sound of bliss from her lips. She moaned and rocked against his face, her right hand coming down to clutch at his blue hair.

She tangled the threads between her fingers and tugged as she angled her hips, rolling them and rubbing herself against his tongue. He hungrily devoured each gasp she gave, each breathless moan and each frantic jerk of her hips, but it wasn't enough. He wanted more from her.

Needed more.

He ran two fingers down her, from her nub to her sheath, and groaned as he eased them into her. She was hot and wet, already needy of him, and he wanted to replace his fingers with his cock and give her what she desired. He held back, forcing himself to remain where he was, kneeling before her and worshipping her. His female.

His little Amazon.

His mate.

His primal instincts rushed back to the fore and he snarled again as he pumped her with his fingers, ripping a moan from her throat and feeling her tense around him. His mate. She belonged to him. He would make her see that. He would make her confess it. He wouldn't stop teasing her until she was weeping for him, begging him to fill her and take her, telling him that he was the only male she needed.

The only male she wanted.

A feral growl rumbled through him as he felt her dancing on the precipice of release and halted his assault. She mewled and writhed, the sound born of pure frustration, but he refused to move his fingers inside her and grasped her hip with his free hand, pinning her in place so she couldn't shift her body on his. He slowly laved her bud, teasing her back down but keeping her balanced on the edge, filled with need and hungry for him to push her over into the warm abyss of bliss.

Anais tugged at his hair, moaning softly and sweetly, each breathless gasp filling him with a need to start pumping her with his fingers again. Not yet. He held back, lapping at her with his tongue, refusing to submit to her and obey her silent commands.

"Loke," she whispered, a desperate edge to her voice.

He groaned and his cock kicked, jerking with a need to hear her say his name like that when he was inside her.

He began thrusting his fingers into her again, a slow steady invasion that had her gasping with each plunge and each flick of his tongue over her sensitive flesh. She reached the precipice faster this time and he backed off again, weathering her frustrated growl and her vicious yank on his hair. He smiled against her, withdrew his fingers and tongued her there, tasting her need. She moaned and shuddered, her body quaking against his.

"Loke." It was more frantic this time and he could feel her desperation.

It pulled at him, his primal instincts telling him that his female needed him and demanding he satisfy her now.

Demanding he make her belong to him now.

He growled as that need blazed through him, a hunger he couldn't deny. He needed to possess her.

Anais gasped as he shot to his feet, knocking her back towards the black wall of the cave. She bumped against it and he eyed it, and then her, and then snarled as his need to possess her and make her know that she belonged to him now overwhelmed him.

He caught her waist, spun her to face the wall and grabbed her hip. He drew it back with one hand and pushed between her shoulder blades with his other one, forcing her to bend over. She moaned and planted her hands against the wall, and he swallowed hard as he looked down at her pert backside.

Gods.

He couldn't contain the deep growl that rumbled through him as he grabbed his cock, fisted it hard and then guided the head to her entrance. He nudged inside, her moist heat scalding him and tearing at his fragile control. He needed to possess her. She belonged to him. She needed to know it. She needed to be his.

He entered her in one swift hard plunge, ripping a startled cry from her that turned into a moan as he pressed deep, as far as she could take him, filling her completely. Her fingers tensed against the wall as he withdrew, her short nails digging into the rough black rock. Her golden hair spilled down her back and he wrapped his right hand around it, gripped it tightly, and pressed forwards with his hips, rocking back into her. She cried out, the sound of her pleasure drugging him and filling him with a need to do it again in order to have another fix of that addictive sound.

Loke grasped her hip with his left hand and her hair with his right and began thrusting deep and hard, frantic plunges that had her rocking forwards with each meeting of their bodies. She moaned and arched into him, and he groaned as she welcomed his dominance and surrendered to him. The knowledge that she enjoyed being at his mercy only increased the ferocity of his need to master her and show her that she was his now.

He grunted and quickened his pace, filling the cave with the sound of their lovemaking. He devoured each gasp and moan she offered up to him, his hunger for her feeding off them and demanding he elicit more. He pressed deeper, each swift stroke of his cock sending a hot thrill chasing through him and ripping another moan from her. He groaned and then growled as he lost himself in the feel of being inside her.

She responded so sweetly to each thrust of his cock, shuddering and moaning, whispering his name, and then she did something that threatened to tip him over the edge.

"Loke, please. More. God, I need more." She pressed back against him, forcing his cock into her.

He growled through sharpening teeth and tightened his grip on her hip and her hair, a deep need flooding him, a hunger he couldn't master.

It mastered him.

It owned him.

He snarled and thrust deeper and faster, possessing her and claiming her body. Her gasps of pleasure only drove him deeper into his instincts, allowing them to possess and claim him.

His gaze zeroed in on her neck and he bared his sharp teeth, hungry with a need to sink them into her soft warm flesh and mark her as his mate.

He would do just that.

He released her hip and reached for her arm, intending to pull her up to him so he could reach her neck and complete their bond.

She cried out in that moment, the sudden flexing of her body around his cock shattering the hold his instincts had on him and he grunted in shock as her climax ripped one from him. He screwed his eyes shut and breathed hard as waves of heat tore through him, shivers following in their wake, and he pulsed inside her, seeing stars in the darkness of his closed eyes as he struggled to cope with the sudden onslaught of bliss.

Anais sagged against the wall, her own breathing ragged and fast, her ecstasy washing over him as his slowly waned, allowing his scattered senses to fall back into place.

He opened his eyes and stared at his hand where it still reached for her with the intent of bringing her up to him so he could bite her.

So he could claim her against her will.

Loke closed his eyes and lowered his hand and his head, shame engulfing him as he thought about what he had been about to do. He stepped back, slipping free of her, and schooled his features when she straightened and turned to look at him. Her smile was stunning, brightening her blue eyes and enchanting him.

When that smile wobbled and her eyes gained a curious edge that warned she could see through him and knew something was wrong, he managed a smile of his own and opened his arms to her. She stepped into them and nestled close to his chest, her cheek pressing against it.

"Your heart is racing," she whispered, a smile in her voice.

"You have that effect on me." He lowered his head and pressed a kiss to her golden hair.

He closed his eyes again and breathed her in, afraid of the other effect she had on him. He wouldn't claim her against her will but he wouldn't let her go either.

He would find a way to make her see that they belonged together.

He would find a way to explain that she was his fated female and that he couldn't live without her now.

He would find a way to tell her that he was in love with her and that heart she spoke of was hers forever if she wanted it.

CHAPTER 15

Loke stared across the rippling dark water to the far end of the cavern, not seeing the black stalagmites that rose around the bathing pool. He had turned his focus inwards the second he had eased into the hot water and had lost track of time after that.

The past few days had been a strange yet pleasant experience, blissful in a way but terrifying in others.

They had been together the whole time, growing closer to each other every day. It felt nice. He had never lived with anyone before, not in all his six thousand years. He had easily fallen into it though, settling into a routine of bathing with her, feeding her and learning about her, and then taking her scouting for her friends. They were yet to find any of them and he suspected the dragons who had taken them were the older generation that lived in the mountains beyond the village. He would take her there tomorrow.

Today, he needed to do something else.

He sighed and tipped his head back, staring at the black ceiling of the cave.

He was enjoying her company and how well they were getting along. It reassured him, chasing away his fears about her leaving him and filling him with the belief that he could have the forever he wanted with her.

She had shown interest in his life, culture and his species too. They had passed every evening sitting in each other's arms near the fire and exchanging tales. She told him of the battles she had fought and the various creatures who had come close to taking her life, which, if her accounts were anything to go by, happened too often. He had told her about the wars he had fought in and the way Hell had changed over the millennia.

Change happened more slowly in Hell, but it still happened. The elves had started it by bringing light into their new realm and technology from the mortal realm, harnessing the winds of Hell to grind seeds and their light to grow food. The demons had followed their lead, and he had seen technology in the Third Realm that had astounded him.

Anais called them wind farms.

Huge turbines that generated what she had termed electricity.

He had pushed her to her limit asking her about electricity. It seemed he needed a better source of information if he wanted his deepest questions about it answered. She had faltered and had admitted that she was no scientist and she couldn't explain how it worked or where it came from.

He wanted the information though and then he would somehow procure himself one of these turbines. The winds were strong in the valleys and could easily generate enough electricity to power items in his cave.

He could make it more comfortable.

For her.

Loke grimaced at his thoughts. He was treating her as a nesting female, desiring to give her all the comforts she craved. He wanted her to view him as a good potential mate. One who could provide for her and take care of her.

Gods, if she would have him, she would want for nothing.

But acquiring everything he wanted to give to her to convince her that his cave was more than basic and she could happily live there required him to work with the demons or those in the free realm who could use the portals to reach the mortal world.

He couldn't venture there himself.

The demons of the Seventh Realm were the most amiable of the kingdoms. They had procured things from the mortal realm for the dragons in the past. Perhaps he could seek out a few different demons of that realm and form a working relationship with them.

Although all he had to offer was gold.

Anais had been astounded when he had finally shown her his hoard. Her eyes had lit up, reflecting the bright gold that had surrounded her in the torch lit room. The diamonds had drawn her the strongest and she had zeroed in on a beautiful necklace made of white gold and teardrop diamonds. She had lovingly stroked it as she had told him that the stone was her birth one. He'd had no idea what that meant until she had explained it, telling him that in the mortal world, diamond was considered the stone for those born in April, but that she had never owned a diamond.

He had responded to that by placing the necklace on her, gifting her with it. She hadn't taken it off since then. Not even to bathe.

It got in his way whenever he wanted to kiss her neck.

Loke closed his eyes and tipped his head back, trying to shut out the sudden surge of thoughts of kissing her neck and more wicked things.

It was getting more difficult.

More dangerous.

Every time they made love, the urge to claim her as his mate grew stronger. He wasn't sure how much longer he could resist the deep need that rose within him whenever they were being intimate. The last time it had been so strong that he had almost lost control. He had barely managed to hold back.

He feared what might happen next time.

He sighed out his breath and sank lower into the water, so it lapped over his shoulders and against his chin. He needed to speak with Anais about it, because he was constantly losing himself in his thoughts and he had been avoiding touching her since yesterday evening. The concerned looks she gave to him, an edge of confusion and hurt in her blue eyes, haunted him. He didn't want to be distant from her or for her to feel she had done something wrong.

He needed to tell her that she was his fated female.

She had feelings for him that went beyond simple attraction and desire. He was confident of that. He would speak to her about it today, when she woke, because he was sure that together they could work something out.

He leaned the back of his head on the smooth side of the pool and tried to relax, preparing himself to talk with her about something that was liable to confuse, upset and place pressure on her. She was strong. He felt certain that she would find a way to handle what he had to tell her.

His little Amazon.

A sharp spear pierced his mind at the same time as unfamiliar scents reached him.

People were in his cave.

He snarled and shot out of the water, using his magic to cover his legs with his leather trousers as he sprinted towards the cave entrance. His senses located two intruders.

Close to Anais.

He roared and ran harder, eating up the distance between him and his female. The second he burst into the cave, he took in everything with one swift assessing glance. A huge demon male blocked his path to Anais, charging at him, his dusky horns curling from behind his pointed ears as he flashed fangs at Loke.

The Third King.

Anais turned fearful blue eyes on Loke and he snarled as he set his sights on her, determined to reach her and pull her away from the black-haired female standing in front of her.

The one called Sable.

They had come to take his little Amazon from him.

Never.

His dragon instincts burst to the fore, screaming that the two before him meant to take his most precious possession from him—his fated female.

A red veil descended and his focus sharpened, narrowing on his enemies, and his claws extended.

He roared and diverted course, launching himself at the broader demon male. They clashed hard, the demon king stumbling back a step before he found solid footing and drove forwards. The male grappled with him, his strength matching Loke's, and almost managed to pin him.

Loke twisted out of his grip, using his natural agility to escape the demon's hold, and came around behind him.

The cave was too small for him to shift in it near the tunnels, but if he could reach Anais, he could grab her and transform as he sprinted towards the mouth of the cave, changing in time to take flight with her before the end of the ledge.

The demon growled, turned on the spot and grabbed Loke's arm before he could start towards Anais and the huntress. He dragged Loke back and wrapped his other arm across the front of Loke's throat, cutting off his air supply.

It wouldn't stop him.

Loke sank sharp teeth into the male's arm and blood flooded his mouth at the same time as the male cursed him in the demon tongue. He bit harder, cutting flesh and severing tendons, and the male released him, shoving him in the back for good measure. Loke slammed face first into the black wall of the cave and grunted as his head struck it hard. Pain spider-webbed across his skull and his eyes stung as he struggled to regain his senses.

The demon king didn't give him the chance.

He grabbed Loke's wrist and Loke twisted to face him, throwing a hard right hook at the same time. It connected with the demon's jaw, snapping his head to one side and sending him back a step. The demon flashed his fangs on a snarl and his red eyes glowed like the fires of Hell as his dusky horns curled from behind his pointed ears, twisting around themselves to flare forwards like twin daggers beside his temples.

He stepped into Loke and his fist slammed into Loke's stomach, striking on the left side and hitting the healing scar there.

Agony tore through him, hot and fierce, a rush of blinding pain. He doubled over and breathed hard, fighting for air as his head swam and the cave turned around him. Voices rang in his ears, a mashed up cacophony of sounds that he couldn't pull apart and understand. Perhaps he hadn't been as healed as he had said to Anais or as he had thought.

It didn't matter.

His gaze slid to Anais where she stood beyond the huntress, her blue eyes wide and filled with fear.

He needed to keep fighting for her sake.

He needed to reach her and take her far away from here.

He sucked down a hard breath and began to straighten, determined to overcome the pain and protect Anais. He would take her fear away and make her feel safe again. He would never let anything happen to her.

He would keep his promise to protect her.

The Third King slammed his fist into the side of Loke's head.

Cold black ground struck his right side.

Oblivion swallowed him.

CHAPTER 16

Anais woke alone. It unsettled her. She stared at the fire for a moment, taking in the fact that Loke had risen before her and hadn't bothered to wake her with a kiss as he had the last few days they had been together.

Cold tried to fill her and she rejected it, not allowing the whispered poisonous voice at the back of her mind to get the better of her.

He had been acting strangely for the past day, but that didn't mean she had anything to worry about. She really didn't.

It was amazing that telling herself that on repeat every five minutes hadn't done a thing to change her outlook.

Something was wrong, and she wished he would speak with her about it. She knew it was about her. Had he seen her death again?

She shoved that question and fear away. He had promised to tell her if he saw her death again and she believed that he would. He kept his promises.

So what was wrong then?

Part of her wanted to believe it was just another vision that had shaken him, because she felt comfortable with that explanation and it at least provided a reason for his behaviour. Not knowing the reason for it was driving her crazy. She needed to just man up and ask him what was wrong.

She would. When he came back from wherever he had gone, she was going to ask him why he was being distant.

She made herself get up and dress, straighten the furs, and begin her morning routine. She was about to head towards the larder when a noise at the entrance of the cave sent a sudden bolt of fear through her and she whirled to face it, afraid that a dragon had come to snatch her while Loke was away.

Her eyes widened as she took in the impossible sight of Thorne setting Sable down onto her feet.

They had come for her.

Sable drew a short blade from the sheath at the waist of her black leather trousers and advanced swiftly, her light brown eyes quickly scanning the cave. Thorne trudged along behind her, his dark red gaze fixed on Anais, a curious but dangerous edge to it.

Anais folded her arms across her chest, covering her black bra. When Sable's eyes finally landed on her, taking her in from head to toe, they darkened too, coming to match Thorne's. Anais knew it didn't look good, but she could explain everything.

"We're getting you out of here." Sable grabbed her arm before she could say a word, the strength of her grip shocking Anais together with how her hand trembled. "Is the bastard still here?"

Anais stared blankly at her, her mind racing as she realised that Sable was going to fight Loke. She couldn't let that happen. She didn't want to leave him, but she would if it meant she could lure Sable and Thorne away from him. She would find a way back to him somehow. She just needed to ensure he was safe first.

"The dragon is here," Thorne said in English, his deep voice gruff and filled with menace as he folded his arms across his broad bare chest. "I sense him."

Sable looked her over again, the darkness in her eyes increasing. Anais searched for her voice and how to explain what her leader was seeing. She was in her bra but it wasn't as Sable thought. The whole thing was a huge misunderstanding and she had to make her see that before things got out of hand and Loke was dragged into a fight.

Well, it was sort of a misunderstanding since Loke had abducted her, but he hadn't done it to claim her as a prize of war like the others.

"Sable," Anais started.

"There's only one exit?" Sable spoke over her and flicked her a glance.

Anais didn't get a chance to answer that question.

A deafening roar filled the cave and Loke was suddenly charging towards her from the tunnels. She shook her head, silently asking him not to do what she could see coming, but he didn't see it. He took one look at her, and then at Sable where she had jumped in front of her to shield her and Thorne where the immense demon had placed himself between Loke and them, and attacked.

Anais didn't want to watch as Loke fought Thorne, grappling with the broader male at first before managing to gain some space and land a blow. Thorne didn't relent and her heart flipped in her chest when he slammed his fist hard into Loke's stomach and the dragon doubled over.

"Wait… please." Anais started forwards and Sable grabbed her.

"What are you doing?" Sable pulled her back. "Let Thorne handle the bastard."

She shook her head and managed to break free of Sable's grip. "Don't kill him."

Sable looked at her as if she had lost her mind and then cracked a smile. "I'm not going to kill him. He's coming with us."

He was?

Anais's heart sank as the true meaning of those words dawned on her and she stared at Loke. *Run.* She willed him to look at her and see that command in her eyes or somehow hear her. He looked at her and she opened her mouth to shout at him to flee and then flinched away as Thorne dealt a hard blow to his head, sending him crashing onto the black ground.

"Now that our guest is in a fit state to travel, we should get going. We need to get him to an interview room before he wakes up and then we can get the information we need from him so we can find the others," Sable said and

Anais clung to those words, stealing a piece of hope from them and using it to settle her fears.

She wanted to save her friends too and Loke did have information on the other dragons that Archangel could use, and Sable had said he would be their guest. She trusted her leader. They had been on missions before where Sable had captured someone for information, and Archangel had treated them as a guest, returning them once they had what they wanted. Anais looked at Loke and told herself that it would be the same deal this time. Loke would be taken to an interview room, Sable would question him and Anais would be there with him the whole time. She wouldn't let him out of her sight, not even when they had returned him to his cave and Sable was gone. She would make sure he was safe and unharmed.

"We already saved a few, but their captors fled. None of them tried to fight." Sable glanced at her but she kept her eyes on Loke where he lay unconscious on the black ground.

Loke had fought because he had wanted to protect her. He had viewed Sable and Thorne as a threat, people who would steal her away from him and possibly place her in danger, and he had wanted to stop them.

He had been keeping his promise.

A cold feeling went through her, rousing a need to rebel against Sable's idea and stop Thorne from taking Loke to the mortal world. She needed to do something to protect him, but she couldn't convince her feet to move or her voice to work.

Blood pooled at the corner of Loke's lips and then tracked down his cheek. Her heart ached at the sight of him, burning with a need to go to him, but the part of her that still wanted to go home kept her feet rooted to the spot and her voice silent.

It told her to trust in Sable. She had no reason to fear for Loke. They only wanted information from him. Archangel would use that information to help her friends. It didn't matter that Loke had sworn to help her with that mission and that she might be able to convince Thorne and Sable to leave him alone and allow him to help them now rather than at Archangel's headquarters if she could only find her voice.

The presence of Sable, a woman who had been a good friend to her for too many years to count, and the thought of going back to a familiar and safe place, to her home, overwhelmed her and she couldn't stop herself from going along with their plans.

Loke would be alright. She would make sure of it. She had faith in Sable and in Archangel. He would give them the information they needed and together they would help the other huntresses. She had to do this. She was a hunter for Archangel. They were her family. She had to help them if she could.

Thorne dragged Loke roughly onto his feet and slung him over his shoulder. More blood spilled from his lips and her stomach clenched, the quieter voice in her heart telling her that she was making a mistake and fooling herself.

"Be careful," she whispered before she could stop herself and the demon looked across at her, one single russet-brown eyebrow raised.

"The dragon is no threat to me."

It wasn't what she had meant. She didn't want him to hurt Loke any more than he already had.

Sable eyed her, a piercing edge to her honey-coloured gaze, and Anais felt as if she was trying to see right through her and attempting to divine her feelings for Loke. She looked away and her eyes settled on Loke. The voice in her heart said to speak up and explain the situation now before it was too late.

The one that wanted to go home and was holding on to her faith in Archangel overwhelmed it.

She would make sure that Loke was safe. They would speak with him as Sable had said and then they would return him. He would be safe. She swore it. Archangel had no reason to hurt him if she told them why he had taken her and that he hadn't hurt her. She would clear his name with her superiors, he would help Archangel and they would leave him alone.

As she followed Sable's lead and took hold of Thorne's hand, and they fell into a pool of darkness that opened beneath them, a terrible feeling went through her.

She was going to regret this.

Loke was never going to forgive her.

She was going to lose the man she had fallen in love with.

CHAPTER 17

Loke slowly became aware that he was no longer in his cave. The brightness of the room surrounding him was blinding even through his closed eyelids. He squinted to shut the white light out and covered his eyes with his forearm as he waited for his senses to gradually come back. The darkness was a relief, immediate and sweet, but it didn't soothe his heart.

It ached in his chest, burning fiercely for some reason unknown to him. He struggled to remember what had happened. He recalled bathing and pondering how to approach Anais about her being his fated one.

He remembered sensing that she was in danger.

He groaned. He remembered the demon brute using his weakness against him and knocking him out.

Anais.

He needed to see that she was safe. His every instinct roared at him to protect her.

He peeled his arm away from his closed eyes and grimaced as the brightness assaulted them again. Long minutes passed, strained seconds in which he forced himself to wait for his eyes to become more accustomed to the high light level before he dared to open them. The last thing he needed was to blind himself when he was in an unfamiliar location.

What place in Hell was this?

He had never seen so much light, not even in the elf kingdom. He had dared to fly close to their borders once to see their paradise. The light that had bathed the green land had been bright, but not blinding. Not like this.

He drew in a deep breath of air that tasted strange and risked opening his eyes.

White surrounded him. Piercing and painful.

He grunted and squinted again, narrowing his eyes to the point that he could just about see out of them. The pain lessened and he muttered a ripe curse when he swung his gaze around his surroundings.

Three white walls and one open side. A cube barely twenty feet across. He rolled off the bench against the back wall where he lay and staggered onto his feet. His knees gave out and he almost hit the floor, stopping himself by shooting his hand out to his right and grasping the smooth wall there. He used it as a support as he stumbled forwards, towards the open side of the cell. There was a corridor and another cell across it from his. Empty.

He needed to investigate.

Loke reached the open side and walked straight into an invisible obstruction, cracking his head on it. He grimaced and growled, and rubbed his forehead. What strange power was this?

He carefully reached out, his heart hammering against his chest as his hand neared the point where a barrier had stopped him. He gasped as his palm touched it. It felt solid and cold beneath his fingers, but gave him no pain.

He stepped closer to it and angled his head, looking along the length of it. It shone, reflecting the light filling the room, and distorted the corridor. He dropped his gaze to his bare feet and raised an eyebrow. There was a gully in the floor where the barrier was, around five inches wide. In the ceiling, there was another gully, this one dark but light enough that he could make out metal attached to the barrier.

"What is this magic?" he muttered to himself in the dragon tongue.

"It's called glass, Dumbass." Came a male voice from Loke's right.

It was muffled by the barriers between them but he could make out the words, and the fact the male had spoken Loke's language. Well, everything apart from the final word. Loke wasn't sure what a dumbass was, but he presumed it was rude and meant to be derogatory.

"Are you dragon?" He couldn't scent the male through the walls and the object the male had called glass.

Loke had heard of glass, but he had never seen it.

Apparently, it was difficult to see.

He rapped his knuckles against it and it sounded as solid as it had felt when he had walked into it.

"Nope." The male voice was louder now. Had he moved closer? "Not a dragon… but it helps in my line of business if you know your languages."

He wanted to know more about the male, sure that he would be able to help him understand where he was and what was happening.

"Where am I?" Loke leaned his back against the wall, using it for support as his head turned again and his legs trembled beneath him.

Something was wrong.

He should have been growing stronger and recovering from the blows the demon had dealt, but he felt as if he was growing weaker.

"A complex filled with bastards. From the twittering I've heard during the past day, they're quite excited about you."

Excited about him? A complex?

"Where is Anais?" Because he needed to see her and know she was alright.

He tried to peer along the corridor to his right and see into the other cells, but the glass made it impossible. The only cell he could see was the empty one opposite him. Was she in one of the other cells, waiting for him to help her?

"She a dragon too?"

Loke shook his head and then remembered the male couldn't see him. "She is mortal."

The male didn't answer him and an unsettling feeling went through Loke, a sensation that she had done something terrible to him.

She had betrayed him.

She had allowed Sable and the king of demons to capture him and she had placed him into this cell. Why? He sank down the wall, landing on his backside with his leather-clad knees against his bare chest, all hope and warmth fading from him and leaving him cold inside. He stared at the wall opposite, struggling to comprehend what she had done.

She had feelings for him. Didn't she?

Had it all been a lie?

She was a hunter of immortals.

Had she been playing him the whole time?

She had used her feminine wiles to grow close to him and he had told her about his kin. He had given her information that she could use against them. What had he done?

A more resilient fragment of his heart told him to believe that this hadn't all been a game to her and it had been real for both of them. It told him that she was in one of the other cells, waiting for him to save her and take her home to his cave.

It was difficult to cling to that belief when anger began to burn within him, devouring the chilling cold with white-hot fire that demanded he find her and hear the truth from her. He would escape this cell, track her down and make her confess what she had done and why.

Loke pressed his right hand to the glass again. It was strong, but fragile. If he shifted, the pressure of his larger form trying to fit into the small space would fracture or shatter it, allowing him to escape. Being so confined during a shift would hurt him too, but it was his only option.

He called on his other form.

Nothing happened.

Loke rose onto his feet and tried again, and met with the same result. Failure. He couldn't shift. Was it some form of magic inside the cell that was stopping him?

He focused on it, detecting no magic in the air or in the walls and glass. There was no barrier preventing him from shifting. He turned his focus inwards, seeking the source of the restriction, fearing it was something they had done to him.

His eyes slowly widened.

The restriction came from within, but it was nothing Anais had done.

Only one place could bind his powers in this way.

One realm.

The forbidden land.

She had taken him to the mortal realm.

He shook his head and staggered backwards, breathing hard as the white walls closed in on him and he fought for air. He couldn't be here. No dragon could survive in the mortal realm since they had been banished long before he had been born. Dread filled him, sucking the air from his lungs and leaving him shaking as he realised the weakness he was experiencing was because the laws of the banishment were already in effect.

It had stripped the power to shift from him and now it was stripping his strength.

He threw his head back and roared, the ferocity of it rattling the glass.

He had to escape.

He ran at the barrier and slammed his right shoulder into it, intent on still breaking it by force. Pain splintered across his shoulder and down his arm. It didn't stop him. He drove into it again, battering it and himself at the same time. Agony ripped through him and he snarled as he hit it a third time. He stumbled back a step and pressed his hand to where he had struck. Blood smeared across the glass but beneath it was perfect. Not even a scratch.

He unleashed another roar of fury and clawed at the glass, trying to dig his way through. His nails ached, threatening to rip away from their soft beds as he desperately fought the vile glass holding him in his cell.

"Loke!" Her soft voice didn't soothe him as it travelled down the corridor.

Neither did the sight of her as she stopped in front of his cell, dressed in a fresh black t-shirt and trousers, her blonde hair tied in a long ponytail.

He bared his fangs at her and hammered his fists against the glass, growling the whole time. He would get to her, and when he did, she would pay for what she had done to him.

The pain in his heart burned fiercely, tearing him apart. She had told him of her sister and how she protected her niece and her brother-in-law from Archangel. It hurt that she fought so hard to protect her family, but had handed him over to the fiends she worked for. He had thought he meant something to her.

He battled the part of him that screamed that she had betrayed him and had played him, and everything had been a lie. He didn't want to believe it, because it hurt too much, more than anything he had been through before.

He had never experienced such pain.

It felt as if he was dying.

"Stop!" She pressed her hands to the glass, her blue eyes imploring him, and for a heartbeat he swore she was hurting and he could feel it.

She quickly looked off to her right and snatched her hands away from the glass as she backed off. The emotions drained from her face and her eyes, leaving them blank.

Cold.

He snarled at the two males dressed in white who appeared in view and stopped near her. Too close to her. His mate. She feared these males. Every instinct he possessed told him that.

He would eliminate them for her.

No.

He dragged his hands from the bloodied glass and shook his head as he backed off, his eyes locked on her. She had betrayed him. She was with her people now. Her fear was another lie. A fabrication designed to make him lower his guard for some nefarious reason. He couldn't allow himself to be duped by her again. He needed to remain distant from her and clearheaded, and focus on his escape.

"Loke… you know where you are?" She stepped forwards and he backed off another one. The hurt returned to her eyes, briefly flickering amidst the blue before she schooled her expression again.

"I am where I cannot be. Your world." He shifted his gaze to the two males. Scientists. Both wore a look that told him of their intentions. There was too much fascination in it. Too much pleasure and desire. They wanted to *study* him. He lowered his gaze and fought a crippling wave of nausea as it crashed over him. When it receded, he felt weaker. He could feel his life draining from him. He whispered to his bare feet, "I cannot be here."

"We just need information so we can help our friends."

"I gave you information," he snarled, pinning her with a black look, and she averted her gaze. "I gave you all I could… I took you from that battle to save you… to stop the death that awaited you… and in doing so I have condemned myself."

Her eyes shot up to meet his and she frowned. "What do you mean?"

The fear returned to her expression and she didn't attempt to hide it from her comrades this time. She approached the glass and pressed her hands to it.

"Loke… what do you mean?" Her eyes pleaded him to answer.

So he did, because he wanted to see her hurt. He needed to see it so he could begin to believe again that what they had shared had been real. He ached to know that she felt something for him and seeing him caged upset her.

"This place is killing me. It will be my death. I cannot be in this realm."

"No." Her hands flattened against the glass as she leaned into it, as if bracing herself against a terrible blow. A blow her eyes confirmed as tears lined them. She swallowed hard and her voice was strained as she spoke. "They just want to see."

"See what?" He tossed a glare at the two males. If it was his insides they wanted to see, they would pay for the pleasure of attempting it with their lives.

"Your dragon. They will release you if you let them see you in your dragon form." She believed that. He could see it in her eyes.

She was fooling herself.

The males in the white coats had a different look in their eyes, a glint that warned they wanted to do more than just see.

"Show them, Loke." She pressed closer to the glass. "They'll release you if you show them."

Her feelings ran through him, her fear a driving force that demanded he do as she asked to relieve her and steal her pain away. Dread slithered through his veins and icy claws sank deep into his heart as he realised that he had lived for six thousand years dreaming of the mortal realm and his life was going to end because he had been brought to it. He wasn't even going to get to see it. All he would know of it was a cell and the torture chamber of two scientists.

He had always imagined the mortal realm to be a sort of paradise.

He had been wrong.

It was Hell.

A Hell far worse than the one he lived in and called home.

The two males looked as if they were losing patience and Anais seemed to sense it because the tears in her eyes trembled on the brink of falling from her lashes.

"I cannot." Those two words leaving his lips seemed to deal another terrible blow to her and she paled, her eyes growing enormous as she shook her head and sent tears tumbling down her cheeks.

"You can," she said and her expression shifted, turning resolute, even when he could feel the hope draining from her. "Change or they will make you. Please, Loke. Just change and then they will let you go."

It touched him that she clearly didn't want them to hurt him and rekindled his faith in her, adding fuel to it so it grew stronger and could finally stand against the part of his heart that insisted she had betrayed him.

He walked on unsteady legs to the glass.

To her.

He pressed his hands to the barrier where hers were on the other side, wishing he could touch her and could feel the soft warmth of her skin against his again. He ached with a need to dash away her tears for her and reassure her somehow, but he wouldn't lie to her.

Loke looked down into her eyes. "I would shift if I could... but I cannot."

She shook her head.

He smiled faintly.

"No dragon can shift in this realm."

CHAPTER 18

"No dragon can shift in this realm."

Anais believed Loke when he said that, but she had the feeling the two men with her didn't and it wasn't going to stop them from attempting to force him to shift. Her stomach churned and her mind raced, her feelings colliding within her as she tried to think of what to do.

She stared at Loke, weathering the curious gazes of the scientists, feeling as if she was the one they were studying now.

The past day had been a blur. From the moment Thorne had teleported them into the Archangel cafeteria in the London headquarters, she had been separated from Loke and pulled from one office to the next, never given a moment to catch her breath. Everyone she had asked had refused to tell her where Loke was.

Only an hour ago, she had been brought into a meeting of the heads of each department and told by them that she would be their bridge—the one who would speak to Loke first and explain the situation to him and gain his compliance.

Anais had the feeling she was being used and tested.

They wanted to see where her allegiance laid.

That stung. They had no reason to doubt her dedication to their cause. She had given them almost a decade of service, risking her life time and again for them, and this was how they repaid her?

She had told them everything that had happened since Loke had taken her from the battlefield and had explained his reasons to them. Of course, she had omitted that they had been together in an intimate way. Archangel didn't need to know about her personal life. It had nothing to do with them. Her feelings for Loke wouldn't change her dedication to protecting the humans and good non-humans from those who meant them harm.

Anais had gone along with what they wanted because she had needed to see Loke again. She had expected to find him in one of the secure rooms they used for questioning non-humans. She hadn't expected the heads of departments to tell her that she would find him in the cellblock.

She stared into the stark white cell at him, her heart on fire, burning with the agony of seeing him caged and knowing it was her fault. If she had spoken up when Sable had come for her, if she had found her courage in that moment when Thorne had fought Loke, all this could have been avoided.

Loke wouldn't have been looking at her as if she had driven a knife into his back and straight through his heart.

Her act of indifference had shattered the moment she had heard him say that he couldn't shift and that he was dying. Hearing that had made her die a little inside too. She needed to find a way to get him out of the cell and out of the hands of Archangel. Now. Before it was too late.

He stared at her, aquamarine eyes incredibly bright under the white lights, his bare chest rising and falling at a steady pace. His hands pressed to the glass on the other side of hers and she wanted to reach through it to him and take hold of them. She wanted to clutch them and explain everything, and ask for his forgiveness. She had made a terrible mistake. She had trusted Sable and Archangel, and she shouldn't have.

She had spent almost a decade protecting her brother-in-law and niece from Archangel, and now she had let them get their hands on Loke.

On the man that she loved.

The one who meant the world to her.

Her stomach turned again, rebelling at the reality of what she had done.

She had sentenced Loke to death because she had clung to her blind faith in Archangel.

Now the people she had trusted were going to subject him to what amounted to torture. She had never condoned what Archangel did to some species by capturing them for study or the methods they employed during those studies. It was the side of Archangel that she didn't like and she had passed almost a decade pretending that darker side didn't exist so she could focus on doing her job of protecting the humans and good non-humans. She had refused to believe Archangel's propaganda that they fed to their hunters, telling them that the studies were necessary. To fight against their enemies effectively, they needed to know that enemy, and that meant knowing every species inside and out.

But Loke wasn't their enemy.

He hadn't harmed her or anyone outside of Hell. He hadn't gone after a good non-human and terrorised them or attempted to kill them.

He had been living a peaceful life until he had saved her from death.

He was right. He had condemned himself by taking her from the battlefield that day and for the first time since it had happened, she wished with all of her heart that he had left her there.

He should have let her die.

"We'll prep a room for the study and draw up a plan. See if you can convince him to drop the act and admit he can shift." The lead scientist, a brunet male with steel-grey eyes, stared at her and she managed to pull her gaze away from Loke and nod, when all she really wanted to do was throw up.

The two men left her alone with Loke and she could feel him watching her, his steady gaze boring into her. She couldn't bring herself to look at him, because she feared seeing his expression and the anger and hurt she knew would be in his eyes. No. She was stronger than this and he deserved the chance to make his feelings clear to her. He deserved the right to punish her for what she had done.

She sucked down a fortifying breath and pulled her courage up from the pit of despair in her heart, holding on to it this time.

Anais turned to face him and met his cold gaze. It froze her right down to her soul but seared her at the same time, leaving her in no doubt of his feelings. She deserved all of his fury and hatred. She would take every last drop of it, but she wouldn't let it push her away. She would find a way to make things right between them and set him free.

She knew he wouldn't thank her for it or forgive her, but it wouldn't stop her from doing it. She would cast aside her life with Archangel in order to set things right with Loke. He was more important to her than an organisation that had lied to her.

"Why?" Loke's deep voice reached through the five-inch-thick glass to her and his eyes bore into her, piercing her and holding her immobile.

That single word held so much power.

It rendered her speechless. Stole the air from her lungs. Shattered her heart.

There was so much pain in it. Anger. She had dealt a mortal blow to him and to herself at the same time. She had known that from the moment her superiors had announced their plans for him. Hell, she had known it from the second she had let Sable and Thorne take him from his cave without standing up and fighting them to protect Loke. She had known it, but she had never felt it as keenly as she did now as he glared at her, the ice in his eyes confirming her worst fears.

He despised her.

He believed that she had betrayed him.

Played him.

She wanted to tell him that she had thought it wouldn't be like this. She had been convinced that Sable would keep her word and that he wouldn't be treated as if he was a threat. She had believed he would be a guest. She had gone along with it all because she had wanted to help her friends, not because she had wanted to hurt him.

She wanted to unburden her heart and tell him all of that, but the darkness in his eyes warned he wouldn't believe her. He felt she had betrayed him and she couldn't blame him for it.

All she could do was make amends by finding a way to set him free before being in her world killed him.

"I'm sorry." She resisted the temptation to lower her head and forced herself to hold his gaze, to let him see that she meant those words, even if he refused to believe her.

His handsome face lost all emotion, his eyes turning flat and hard.

He took his hands away from the glass and backed off a step, distancing himself from her.

"I am sorry too." Those four words cut her as no blade ever had, slicing deep into her heart.

The bitterness in them, the hurt and hatred, spoke of the meaning behind them. He wasn't sorry about what she had done to him.

He was sorry he had ever met her.

Tears burned her eyes and she lost her nerve as her heart shattered all over again. She couldn't take it. She couldn't remain where she was. She had to leave before she made a bigger fool of herself.

Anais turned on her heel and ran along the corridor, aching inside as the distance between her and Loke grew, feeling as if something inside her was about to stretch tight and break and she was going to die. He could hate her all he wanted. It wouldn't change what she was about to do.

Time was precious and she would need every last second of it if she was going to pull off something as dangerous as setting Loke free.

CHAPTER 19

Loke cursed himself under his breath as Anais fled, leaving him alone and staring at the space where she had been. What he had done had been necessary. He had needed to drive her away from him.

He hadn't expected it to hurt as much as it had though.

The pain that had flared in her eyes and on his senses, running through him as if it had been his own incredible hurt, had torn down his strength and resolve, and he had been on the verge of taking back his words and comforting her when she had run away from him.

He staggered to the right wall of his cell, pressed his back to it and slid down it again. He stretched his legs out in front of him and looked along the corridor in the direction she had run, aching with a need to make her come back to him. He needed to take her pain away. It was still strong within him and he couldn't shake it. It mingled with his own hurt and tore at him, stripping away the guards around his heart until it felt exposed and vulnerable, a weak thing that would never be strong again.

Because he had driven away the one divine being who had filled him with strength and power the likes of which he had never felt before.

His little Amazon.

His fated female.

Just being around her, being close to her, had made him stronger, until he had felt invincible. Just a smile from her had made the earth tremble beneath his feet and had set his heart pounding. A look was all it had taken to shake his world to its foundations and leave him burning with a need for more of her.

A kiss from her had ruined him.

Gods, he needed her.

He raked his fingers through his blue hair, tugging it back as he fought that need.

It was better this way. He had seen her pain and her guilt, and her fear. He couldn't take those things away from her, but he could stop them from growing stronger and destroying her.

If his words had struck a deep enough mark, as he had intended, she would stay away from him while the scientists studied him. He didn't want her to witness what they did to him. He didn't want her to have to endure seeing him go through everything they had planned for him and blaming herself for it.

The male in the next cell began chanting about revenge, a mission and escaping. The first and last of those sounded appealing, but escaping took precedence over revenge. He wasn't even sure who he wanted revenge on. Archangel for containing and studying him? King Thorne of the demons for defeating him? Anais for handing him over?

The darker, angry part of himself whispered to make her suffer for what she had done to him.

The rest of him said he had hurt her enough when she was already hurting over what she had done. There was no need to punish her for it. He had driven her away and now he would wait for an opportunity to escape. Hopefully it would come before he lost too much of his strength or the laws of the banishment killed him.

The male continued to mutter as he started to pace, a clipped edge to it as he moved closer to Loke and then drifted further away.

Loke closed his eyes and settled more heavily against the white wall, resting and conserving his strength as he waited for someone to come to take him to the scientists.

There was a knock on the wall behind him.

"That the woman you were looking for?"

Loke sighed. "Yes."

"They sent a woman to trick you, too?" Those words stuck a knife in his heart and he tried to ignore the sick feeling that swept through him, chilling him and stirring the darker part of himself that blamed Anais for what had happened.

Had she betrayed him as a hunter from the same clan had clearly betrayed the male in the other cell?

He couldn't bear the thought that she might have, that what had happened between them might not have been real after all. He shunned that feeling, clinging to his belief in her and her feelings. She felt something for him. She hadn't betrayed him. She hadn't used him. Her pain had been real. His grip on that belief began to slip again and he clung more fiercely to it, refusing to listen to the darker part of his nature.

It was difficult when he was weak and hurting, and afraid. He might be a warrior, but he was strong enough to admit when he was scared. He feared what lay ahead for him, what torture the scientists would inflict upon him in their quest for knowledge of his species.

Anais had done this to him.

The male twisted the knife in his heart. "Did she sleep with you and then betray you?"

Loke screwed his eyes shut and scrubbed a hand down his face. He growled, "Yes."

The male spat out a foul curse. "They did the same thing to me… and then they attacked my pride. They killed my sister and mother."

Loke's eyes shot open and his heart raced as the male's words sank in. His clan were in danger.

The hunters knew where they were.

Anais or the other huntresses would lead Archangel to them and they would all be killed, as this male's family had been.

He snarled and shoved onto his feet, and began pounding on the glass again, unable to stop himself as his rage burned beyond his control, turning his heart to ash in his chest as his mind filled with images of these wretches harming his kin, all because he had dared to save one of them.

Because he had fallen in love with one of them.

Lies.

The male in the next cell had been tricked in the same manner. Loke had wanted to believe that Anais hadn't betrayed him, but that belief died again as he ran over what the male had said. A female hunter had seduced and betrayed him.

"What is your name?" Loke pressed his hand to the white wall between his cell and the male's and breathed hard, struggling to calm himself.

He was wasting his energy and his strength. He needed to conserve them. Weakened as he was, he was still superior in strength to the mortals in the complex. None of them would be a match for him.

"Harbin." Came the reply.

"My name is Loke. You heard my conversation with the huntress. I cannot be here. I must escape these fiends… and therefore I need your help. I need your knowledge of this facility."

Harbin began chanting about his mission again and Loke couldn't help but wonder whether he had lost his mind during his containment. Had they studied him too? Was this madness what awaited Loke if he allowed them to conduct their study?

He needed to escape.

He refused to allow his life to end here.

He roared and hammered his fists against the glass. It shook beneath his furious blows but still refused to break.

"Bad move," Harbin called through the wall. "They don't like it when we're rowdy."

Loke stopped.

Too late.

Thick white smoke poured into the room from above the barrier and swirled around him. He tried not to breathe it in but he ran out of air and was forced to take a breath. The moment he did, his head turned and his vision wobbled.

The last thing he heard before passing out was the deep vicious growl of Harbin's voice.

"Two scientists. Bonds are weak. Shatter them. Scalpels are weapons. Four guards. Two observers. Eight throats to cut. Kill the fuckers and come get me. I know a portal back to Hell."

CHAPTER 20

Anais tried to focus on what Sable was telling her as she explained how she had gathered intelligence on the dragons with Olivia and Thorne's help. She couldn't take her eyes off the silver cuff that Sable wore around her right wrist. The black-haired woman kept playing with it, her fingers constantly twisting it around. A nervous trait?

What did Sable have to feel nervous about?

Was it because they were both standing in the black-walled observation room waiting for the guards to bring Loke into the other brighter white room beyond the one-way glass?

Her stomach churned and she had to breathe slowly to stop herself from running out of the low-lit room to intercept the guards who would be bringing Loke to the scientists. She settled her hand on the short sword sheathed at her waist. She would put her plan into action soon enough. All she could do right now was bide her time and somehow find a glimmer of patience.

She focused back on what Sable had said when the huntress looked at her, golden eyes expectant, as if she was waiting for an answer to a question. Anais hadn't heard one, so she did the only thing she could. She changed the course of the conversation in the hope of finding answers to some questions of her own.

"Isn't it better to study them in their natural environment?" She swallowed the sudden surge of nerves as Sable stared at her.

Sable remained silent for so long that Anais was close to losing her nerve and halting the conversation altogether by the time she did speak.

"Olivia feels the same way." Sable returned her golden gaze to the window.

Anais eyed the two men in the next room as they prepared all the tools on the metal trolley next to the gurney.

Sable shook her head and twisted the silver cuff again. "Olivia doesn't want to see a dragon on the chopping board. She's changed."

"Have you changed too?" Anais weathered the cool gaze of her leader and refused to let it silence her. "Does falling for one of them change you?"

Sable's expression shifted, her golden eyes gaining a knowing but shocked edge, and Anais averted her gaze. She didn't want Sable to see her feelings for the dragon they were about to place into the other room. Her stomach turned again and a need built within her, an urgency that she couldn't ignore.

Her time to strike was coming, but she had no escape plan.

She wouldn't make it out with Loke without help.

Nerves joined her colliding emotions, fear of what she was about to do. Archangel had been her home, her family, for close to a decade, and she was about to turn her back on them. She flexed her fingers at her sides, trying to loosen up her tight muscles and shake the sudden surge of adrenaline.

"It does, and it doesn't." Sable's soft voice filled the quiet room, laced with understanding and a touch of unsteadiness that sounded like nerves. "I have to lie more these days."

Anais looked across at her, seeing the emotions that had been in Sable's voice shining in her eyes as she stared into the room beyond the glass, a distant but sharp edge to her expression, as if what was about to happen didn't sit well with her either.

As if she didn't want Loke to end up hurt because of what they had done.

Anais had felt the strength in Sable, power that went beyond anything a human was capable of. Sable had mated with a powerful demon, and it must have affected her. If Anais could convince her that what was about to happen was wrong and they had to stop it, she might have a shot at saving Loke.

But in order to convince Sable to help her, she would have to play on Sable's feelings for her mate by confessing her feelings for Loke.

"This goes no further than this room, Anais." Sable turned deadly serious eyes on her and Anais nodded. "After the war ended, I filed a report through those returning here, but I didn't come back. When I returned with you, I was detained and questioned, and I lied through my teeth. I said that I had been looking for you and the other huntresses the whole time."

"But you hadn't. You were gathering information on the dragons so you could search for us... but you had been staying at the castle with Thorne." Anais's eyes slowly widened as Sable's reason for weaving a huge lie dawned on her. "Archangel doesn't know that you bound yourself to him."

Sable shook her head, causing her sleek black hair to sway across the shoulders of her black t-shirt. "They wouldn't understand."

"What are you going to do?" Anais wanted to ask more questions but movement in the next room caught her attention and her heart lurched as two heavily muscled guards dragged Loke into the room and dumped him unceremoniously on the inspection table.

She covered her mouth with her hand and stared at him, unable to breathe as guilt ripped at her and her heart demanded she do something now to help him.

"I've seen the way he looks at you... and the way you look at him." Sable's voice was distant in her ears as she forced herself to watch the guards strapping Loke down. He tried to resist them, weakly pushing them away and growling at them through sharp teeth.

They had drugged him, but it wasn't the only reason he didn't have the strength to fight them. He was pale and gaunt, as if all of the life was leaching from him, draining right before her eyes. It was all her fault.

"Did I do the wrong thing? Did I step in when I should have stepped back?"

Anais did look at Sable now. The guilt in her amber eyes turned to pain as Anais stared into them, searching for something to say. She should have spoken up when Sable had found them. She should have told her, because she knew that Sable of all people would have understood.

Would understand.

She turned her cheek to Sable and fixed her gaze on Loke where he lay strapped to the table, the two scientists hovering around him. She forced herself to stand where she was and see what was happening to him because of her and everything she had once stood for and held dear.

"I'm in love with him." The words slipped easily from her lips and some of the weight pressing down on her heart lifted, easing it and restoring a sliver of her strength, enough to boost her resolve and her courage. "I should have spoken up when you came... and now I feel it's too late but I have to do something. If he stays in this world much longer... he'll die... because of me. It will be all my fault and I hate myself for it."

Her hand went to the hilt of the blade strapped to her waist.

Sable's hand clamped down on it. "It is never too late."

She looked at her superior.

Sable closed her eyes and rubbed a black and silver band around her left wrist.

"What are you doing?" Anais frowned at her fingers as she kept rubbing the band. It wasn't a nervous trait this time. Sable was up to something, and whatever it was, there was power behind it.

It charged the air in the room, making the hairs on the back of her neck stand on end.

"Calling in a favour... well... I'm requesting help in exchange for a favour as right now I'm a little low on favours to call in," Sable whispered as she frowned, her eyes still closed. Anais opened her mouth to ask whether she was calling for Thorne just as Sable added, "The elves will help us."

Her hope soared.

Elves could teleport, were agile and swift, and had armour that Archangel's human-made weapons couldn't penetrate. If anyone was strong enough to help her save Loke, it was that species.

The static charge in the air grew stronger and a spark flickered out of the corner of her eye.

Anais turned her back to the window at the same time as Sable did, coming to face the white-blue arc of light as it flashed again in the middle of the room, brighter this time.

Blinding her.

She flinched away and waited for the light to fade before opening her eyes.

An immense and beautiful man with a thick head of onyx-black hair and incredible silver eyes stood in the room opposite them, his presence sucking the air from it.

But he wasn't an elf.

Loke had been right.
Angels existed.

CHAPTER 21

He flinched as a piercing shrieking noise filled the pleasant stunned silence, grating on his nerves and fraying the weak threads holding his temper in check. On opening his eyes, he realised it was the female he had come to detain who had dared to raise the alarm. She stood further away from him now, the blonde female held behind her and her other hand still on the red button on the black wall. The hard sharp edge to her golden eyes challenged him to make a move against her.

Movement in the adjoining room gained his attention for barely a second, long enough to see they were removing the semi-nude shifter male from it and the mortal males who had accompanied him were fleeing in fear.

Pathetic creatures.

He calmly returned his gaze to the reason he had been sent to this wretched realm.

Two more females rushed into the room and flanked her, their silver swords drawn and aimed at him. As if such paltry weapons could pierce his flesh.

"What do you want?" the one called Sable spat at him, her icy glare declaring her intent to fight him.

Brave. Courageous. He gave her that. But also foolish. She knew she was no match for him, and yet she sought to intimidate him. Many had attempted to cover their fears with such a poor façade when faced with him and all had eventually cracked and crumbled, falling to their knees to cower before him.

He furled his white wings against his back. Their longest feathers grazed his bare shins and feet and he decided that he should have gone with wearing his armour rather than a simple white and gold tunic. It would have made a stronger impression on the puny mortal females huddled before him and might have sped things along. It certainly would have stopped the bastard offspring of an angel from being so mouthy.

"I came as soon as I learned of your existence. I am come for you." He pointed to the silver cuff around her wrist and she looked down at it, the colour slowly draining from her face, adding a satisfyingly fearful pallor to it.

Now he was getting somewhere. Perhaps she would be more compliant now.

"What's he talking about?" the blonde female whispered with a curious edge to her frown as she looked at Sable.

"It's not important. I'll tell you later." Sable turned from her comrade to face him again. "Listen, Buddy, I'm not going anywhere and definitely not with you. I don't even know who you are."

Perhaps she wouldn't be more compliant after all.

They had warned him that she was a difficult thing, but he hadn't listened to them. Mostly because they had said she had a difficulty rating the same as his and he tired of their taunts about his temper. He had stated that he would easily take her into custody and he meant to do that. Swiftly. He had no desire to linger in this realm, around such lowly beings.

"You got a name? Other than Tall, Dark and Pompous?"

Pompous?

He glared at her and unleashed a fraction of his power. She straightened her spine in response, resisting the pressing weight of his power as it buffeted her. Her three comrades didn't fare so well. They all staggered back a few steps towards the door and beads of sweat broke out on the brow of the weakest.

"Give me your sword, Anais." Sable held her hand out to the blonde female, who did as she instructed, drawing her weapon and placing it into her palm. Her fingers closed around it and she held it out in front of her, pointing it at him. "I'm giving you to the count of three. Tell me your name or bugger off. Fail to do one of those things and I'll kick your arse. Choice is yours."

Amusing, but boring. He had heard better threats, from more dangerous foes. She was part angel, but no match for him in a fight. Still, he had strict orders to bring her back with him, unharmed, and that meant he had to lower himself to select the first ridiculous choice she had given him.

In a manner of speaking anyway.

"I have no name. No angels do. All I can give to you is that I am of the Echelon."

He held his right arm out to her, revealing the cross marked on the inside of his wrist.

A cross she also bore on her skin in the exact same spot.

The irritation that had been building in her eyes gave way to a flicker of curiosity and something akin to hope, but she didn't move from her spot near the other females. He needed her away from them. While their weapons couldn't kill him, they might land blows while he was attempting to detain Sable and he would lose his temper.

He didn't think the council would forgive him if he killed three mortals.

They hadn't mentioned any restrictions when it came to mortals, but the council rarely took a favourable view on killing them.

"I met an angel with a name. Aurora. Heard of her?" Sable said and he barely held back his irritated sigh.

"The one you speak of is no longer an angel… and you will come with me."

She pinned him with a glare when he considered just crossing the distance between them and grabbing her, putting an end to this farce. It seemed she was better attuned to the feelings of others than the council had suspected. She could read him. A rare gift.

The huntress who had sweated when he had unleashed a fraction of his power edged backwards towards the door. He shifted his focus to her and used another gift of his to change her mind about sneaking away and going for reinforcements. She stilled and stared blankly at him. A weak mind was always a glorious thing. So easy to influence. He wished the other two were weak too, but he had tested their minds and found them strong. As strong as Sable was.

Influencing them would hurt them.

"What's it like having no name?" Sable waved the sword at him, the curiosity back in her eyes. "How does that work? How do other angels get your attention?"

Her constant questions perplexed him. He couldn't remember ever appearing before anyone who had been so irritatingly unaffected and able to string words into sentences in his presence rather than just staring in a dumbfounded manner at him.

"They address me as Fourth Commander of the Echelon if they desire my attention." He wasn't sure why she needed to know or why she had such a problem with angels having no name.

He had a rank, and that was all he required.

"That seems like a pretty crappy way of getting someone's attention… and you're only the fourth commander?" She frowned and shook her head, a teasing edge to her tone and expression that he found annoying. None of the people he had graced with his presence had ever dared to tease him before either. She smiled and he knew she had read him again, had felt his irritation and dislike of her conversation, and she was going to use that knowledge against him. "That must grate a little. Who's the first? Oh, wait! He doesn't have a name so I guess he's just First Commander of the Echelon."

He frowned at her now, his pride a little chafed by her taunting and his patience wearing thin.

"How many are there?" She swung the sword up to rest on her shoulder.

So casual.

Would she be so casual if he exerted a little power and popped one of her comrades' heads with nothing more than a thought?

"How many what?" He played along with her, lost in the pleasing thought of terrifying her by killing her little friends in front of her.

"Commanders."

"Six." He could see where this was heading and he folded his arms across his chest, warning her not to go there.

She did. With a huge grin. "Six, and you're only number four. Ouch. How long did it take you to reach number four?"

"Silence," he barked and even the alarms stopped shrieking. "I am not here to speak of my rank. You will come with me. Echelon are rare now and all must serve Heaven."

Sable shook her head. "If you haven't got the memo, maybe I should tell you… I'm a queen of demons."

That surprised him, moderately, but didn't sway him. "You will come with me. The demons are of little consequence. They may find another queen."

Her expression turned horrified and she had the sword pointing at him again before he could blink, the darkness in her eyes warning him that he wasn't the only one close to losing his temper now. "That's my husband you're talking about so callously. My people! I'm not going to Heaven. I'm going back to Hell."

His temper snapped and the room darkened, the light sucking out of it as he stepped towards her, glaring down at her as he spread his wings. They spanned the room and drew fearful glances from the three mortal females. Sable stood firm in front of him, her blade never wavering, not even when his power began to slip beyond his grasp. He held his hand out in front of him, filled with a dark need to call his blade to him and teach her a lesson in humility and respect.

The steely determination in her steady gaze challenged him to try.

A sensation shot down his spine and fire arced through his blood, a warning from those on high that he was close to overstepping the line.

Again.

He drew a deep calming breath, reined in his temper enough to regain control of his powers, and tried again. "I am not known for my patience. I would not test it. You will come with me. By force, if necessary."

The blonde female called Anais and a second female jumped in front of Sable, blocking his path to her.

His gaze caught on the second female, a slender brunette with fierce green eyes. Strange warmth flooded him at the sight of her but it was swiftly followed by fury so dark and deep that it threatened to shatter his carefully controlled calm and send him into a killing rage.

She bore wounds on her fair skin.

She had been beaten.

"What did this to you?" The words seemed to leave his lips of their own volition, coming from an unfamiliar part of him, one that felt alien and shook him with the strength of its will and the depth of its feelings.

She shook her head and backed away from him, her green eyes gradually widening and filling with fear.

Her lips wouldn't answer him, so he sought it from her eyes.

He stared deep into them and saw it all for himself. He witnessed her suffering at the hands of a dragon.

His blade was in his hand before he knew what he was doing. Blue flames flickered along the length of it, darkest near the hilt. Almost black. A need filled him, a terrible hunger that he couldn't hold back or deny.

"A dragon resides in this place. I will slay him for you." He swept the blade down at his side and focused his senses to find the dragon who had been in the other room when he had arrived.

143

Sable shoved the two huntresses behind her. "Don't you bloody dare! That dragon had nothing to do with what happened to Emelia."

Emelia?

His gaze drifted back to the slender female. She had bowed her head, her dark hair falling down to obscure her face and steal the pleasure of seeing it from him, and had wrapped her arms around herself, holding herself so tightly he felt she feared she might fall apart.

"Where does the dragon who did this to you reside?" He spoke to her but it was Sable who answered.

"In Hell."

His mood darkened again on hearing that, but he recalled that all dragons had been banished from the mortal realm millennia ago by a powerful witch. He flexed his fingers around the hilt of his blade, his mind working to find a solution to his problem so he could hunt and slay the dragon, but none presented itself.

Irritated by a seemingly irremovable object in his path, he muttered, "I cannot enter Hell."

And regretted it when Sable's eyes lit up.

"What a shame," she said with a victorious smile.

She believed she would be safe from him there, but he wasn't going to give her a chance to escape him.

He lunged for her.

A huge demon male appeared in his path, his eyes blazing red and dusky horns curling from above his pointed ears, twisting around themselves to flare forwards like daggers on either side of his temples. The male bared sharp fangs and grew even larger, coming to tower over him as his leathery dark wings brushed the walls and ceiling as he hunched over in the room.

He readied his sword.

The demon didn't give him a chance to use it.

The enormous male spoke in the demon tongue, each word piercing his ears like white-hot needles and slithering through him like oily darkness, warning him away from the female.

She had not lied.

She was a queen of demons.

But she was Echelon too.

"This is not over," he spat the words at the demon and teleported just as the male swung at him.

He reappeared on the balcony of his home in the vast white of Heaven and looked down on them, seeing through the layers of the building to the room where he had been just a second before.

It wasn't Sable or the demon who was the focus of his gaze though.

It was Emelia.

He watched her as she shrank away from the group, still holding herself, entranced by her beauty and angered by her suffering.

144

He would find a way to slay her dragon for her.
He would bring the wrath of Heaven down upon all of Hell.

CHAPTER 22

Awareness slowly grew within Loke as the effects of the gas began to wear off. Two men were dragging him through the corridors, but his surroundings were no longer white. They flashed red in time with the piercing wail that drove through his mind like a sharp spear, repeatedly stabbing him until he growled groggily and prayed to the gods it would shut up.

The man holding him under his right arm looked down at him and then up at his comrade. "Better hurry before he comes around."

Where were they taking him?

He hazily remembered being in a different room with the two scientists.

A clearer memory rose and rage blasted through him, born of a need to protect his mate.

He had sensed her close to him when he had been in that room, and had instinctively known that she was beyond the mirror that had reflected his stark gaunt image back at him. He had sensed another presence too. Shortly after they had shoved him down onto the strange table and strapped him in place, he had felt a powerful being in the other room with Anais.

A heartbeat after that, the lights had begun flashing and the irritating noise had started.

He had been unshackled and pulled from the room.

But Anais had remained back there, in that other room where the presence had appeared.

She was in danger.

He needed to get to her.

He tried to fight the hold of the two mortal males, but the weakness infesting him and the debilitating effects of the gas they had given him made it impossible to break free. Shame swept through him, chafing at the pride he had as a warrior and a dragon. He had been reduced to a creature weaker than a human.

The men dumped him back in his cell and he lay on the white floor, breathing hard and shaking all over as he fought a dizzy spell that threatened to have what little contents were in his stomach rising up his throat. He closed his eyes and clung to the floor as it rocked and whirled.

It wasn't the gas that was affecting him now.

It was being in this realm.

He had to escape, but the one chance he had been given had been stolen away from him by whatever creature had appeared in the room with Anais and the other huntress.

Hope drained from him, fear and the reality of his situation combining to siphon it from him and leave him cold and exhausted, on the brink of surrendering and allowing death to claim him.

"What's happening?" Harbin's voice rang loudly through the wall as the male banged on it.

It roused Loke from his stupor and gave him something else to focus on as he pulled himself back together.

He couldn't give up.

No matter how much he desired it.

A warrior never surrendered, not even to death. He would fight it until he could fight no more.

He managed to push himself up into a kneeling position on the white floor and pressed his right hand to the wall that separated him and Harbin.

"I do not know." Just as he said that, the screeching noise fell silent. He looked up at the ceiling and thanked the gods for their mercy. "I sensed a strong presence near me and then the infernal lights began flashing and that noise began."

"It's called an alarm. They raise it when something bad happens."

Loke pulled himself closer to the wall and rested against it. "Then something bad has happened."

He stared at the corridor, filled with an impotent need to reach Anais and ensure that she was safe. Had whatever invaded the complex come for her? The fear returned, running through his veins and making his blood burn even as it chilled. This time, it wasn't fear for his own life. It was fear for hers. He had seen her death so many times now.

But never in a place like this.

He clung to that, using it as a balm to soothe his heart and give him hope.

She was strong, and so was the one called Sable. Together they could manage to escape whatever had entered the room with them.

Minutes ticked by slowly, each second like an hour as he struggled to remain awake, his eyes constantly locked on the corridor beyond the glass. He willed Anais to appear in it and show him that she was safe. He needed to see her.

The alarms began again, the red flashing lights hurting his eyes. He wanted to close them and to cover his ears, but he forced himself to keep his gaze on the corridor. Anais had to come to him. He needed her.

A shriek rose above the wail of the alarm, followed by a heavy thud. There was a series of harsh grunts and then the metallic ring of weapons clashing. Someone was fighting.

Loke pulled himself closer to the glass, needing to see what was happening in the corridor. Was someone attacking the complex?

He growled at the thought, the need to break free of his cell and protect Anais sweeping through him, stronger than ever.

"Can you see anything?" Harbin called through the wall.

"Nothing." And it was frustrating him, wearing at his patience and his temper.

He pressed his hand to the glass and tried to focus beyond it and use his senses to detect what species were wreaking havoc in the corridor just out of sight. His head turned again, spinning violently, and he had to close his eyes against the sudden whirling that made the world around him nothing but streaks of white and red.

All he could detect was that there was two of them, and they were not the presence he had sensed in the room with Anais.

These two were strong, but far weaker than the one he had felt.

A tall male with blue-black hair and obsidian armour that hugged his lithe figure stopped directly in front of Loke's cell and glared at the ceiling. The alarms ceased and the lights stopped flashing. It was the male's doing.

An elf.

A powerful one too.

The male turned violet eyes on Loke, a curious but disappointed flicker in them, and then moved on. Who was the male searching for?

The answer became apparent when he stopped to the right of Loke.

"Hartt!" Harbin's voice rang through the wall and the elf looked thoroughly annoyed.

"What the Devil made you toss yourself into this predicament?" The male called Hartt moved towards the glass of Harbin's cell.

Loke became slowly aware that someone was staring at him and he shifted his gaze to the male standing in the corridor in front of him.

Another elf.

But this one had darkness in his eyes.

They were jet black.

The male curled his lip at Loke, flashing a hint of fang, and produced a cloth from the air. He wiped his long black blade on it, his gaze on Loke the whole time, leaving him feeling that the male wanted to kill him as he had slain the guards. Loke had seen many males with that same darkness in their eyes during his lifetime, that same hunger for bloodshed, violence and death. This male didn't care who his foe was or whether they were his foe at all. He craved death and he fed that hunger, making it grow more voracious.

The elves had a name for those who succumbed to the darkness.

They called them tainted.

The male standing before him looked more than merely tainted to Loke.

He looked dangerous, crazed, and consumed by the darkness. It ruled him.

"Fuery, get your backside in gear and deal with those guards." Hartt pointed towards the end of the corridor they had entered through.

The one called Fuery smiled, a glimmer of joy in his black eyes as he turned to face his new opponents and beckoned them with a crook of his armoured clawed finger. His pointed ears flared back against his overlong blue-black hair that was drawn back to reveal them, the top half of his hair tied into a small ponytail with a silver clasp and the rest allowed to brush his neck. He bared his fangs at his enemies and disappeared in a flash.

Hartt watched him go, his expression emotionless but holding a touch of wariness, as if he regretted what they were doing.

Butchering creatures far weaker than they were.

"Stand back." Hartt twisted a small black device that Loke couldn't quite see and it looked as if he pressed it to the glass front of Harbin's cell. The elf male turned violet eyes on Loke. "I suggest you move back too."

Loke mustered his strength and shuffled back to a safer distance. The moment he was nearing the back of his cell, Hartt sprinted down the corridor towards where Fuery was fighting.

A bright violet flash blinded Loke and a violent explosion deafened him, making his ears ring as it rocked his cell.

The glass barrier fractured, deep splinters racing across the surface of it. The glass that had contained Harbin completely exploded, raining down in the corridor, and the male growled and muttered several ripe curses.

Hartt appeared back in view and glanced at Loke. "I suggest you escape this place."

A suggestion that Loke was going to take, just as soon as he had rested enough to regain the necessary strength to shatter the glass wall and actually make it out of the complex alive.

"Desist!" A deep commanding voice caused Hartt to turn wide violet eyes on the end of the corridor where Fuery had been fighting.

Fuery who was suddenly beside Hartt, a similarly stunned expression on his face. It lasted only a second before he looked ready to take on this new foe. Loke wasn't sure that was a wise decision. Whoever this new male was, he was far more powerful than the two elves combined.

Hartt knew it. Loke could see it in his eyes. He wanted to follow that command and halt the attack.

"Take the dragon." Harbin's voice sounded in the corridor and Hartt looked at him.

"I cannot teleport three. I am sorry." Hartt lowered his gaze to his feet, a regretful edge to his expression, and then drew in a deep breath and burst into action.

Loke had a brief glimpse of a silver-haired male with equally silver eyes as Hartt grabbed Harbin with one hand and caught hold of Fuery with the other.

The elf teleported both of them in a flash of silver-violet light.

The male who had issued the command appeared in view, a black look on his noble face, his violet eyes narrowed in displeasure. His pointed ears flared against the sides of his head through his neat blue-black hair as he bared his fangs. Another elf.

Loke knew this one.

Prince Loren.

The elf prince huffed, looked back along the corridor and raised his hand in a sort of signal. Who was he beckoning?

More elves?

Loke growled at the male and lumbered onto his feet, preparing to fight him. They had been at war in the Third Realm and if the male had come to finish what had been started there, Loke would teach him that an elf was no match for a dragon. He swayed and pressed his hand to the wall, determined to overcome the weakness battering him and threatening to send him plunging into the waiting arms of darkness.

And death.

He roared and hurled himself at the glass, smashing his fists against it in an effort to break it. He would take down the elf and flee. He would find the portal that Harbin had spoken of.

He would be free.

Anais suddenly sprinted into view, her thick boots crunching on the glass sprayed across the corridor. His fists instantly stilled against the glass as he took in the sight of her and weathered the rush of emotions that blasted through him.

She was unharmed.

She smiled at him, her blue eyes bright with it and with hope.

"It's time to go," she said.

The last of his strength and his fight drained from him on seeing that she was safe and hearing that she had come for him. He tried to hold on for her, clinging to consciousness, but the effect of being in the mortal realm had reached its crescendo and he was too close to the endless black abyss of death.

He pressed his hand to the fractured glass, wishing he could touch her and know the warmth and softness of her skin.

She placed her hand to the glass on the other side and her smile widened, the affection in it flooding him with heat.

His beautiful mate.

It was the last thought he had before the darkness consumed him again, plunging him into a nightmarish vision.

The inky black parted to reveal an unfamiliar interior of a building with several thick columns supporting a high ceiling. The walls were painted in tones of darkness and colourful orbs of light barely chased back the gloom.

Anais stood before him, near a high and broad black bench, but she wasn't alone.

The shadowy male loomed over her.

His eyes glowed brightly, fixed on Loke where he stood bearing witness to it all, unable to do anything but watch as Anais turned towards the male and her fear flooded the room.

Loke reached for her.

The male raised vicious talons to strike her down.

CHAPTER 23

The prince of elves had teleported into the room shortly after the angel had left it. Anais had met him before in Hell, and Sable had called on him using the band around her wrist, but his sudden appearance had still startled her and she had launched herself forwards to attack him and protect Sable, barely stopping herself from striking him.

That had drawn a very unimpressed look from the handsome man until Sable had explained everything that had happened.

Her explanation had made Thorne grow larger and growl something in the demon tongue, his eyes burning crimson and his leathery wings shifting restlessly against his back. Loren had spoken to the larger male in the same language. When Sable had pressed them to speak in English, neither male had looked inclined to agree and both had kept their conversation to themselves.

Anais suspected it had something to do with the angel who had appeared and tried to take Sable with him.

Because apparently she was part angel.

That had definitely shocked Anais and she knew it had shocked Emelia too. Sable's status as half-angel wasn't the only reason Emelia had to feel shocked though. The male angel had made it clear he was interested in her. Anais had been around long enough to know how men operated and it seemed angels were just like all the rest of them. He wanted to slay the dragon for Emelia, and there was only one reason he would want to do such a thing and it wasn't because he was amazingly magnanimous.

He desired Emelia.

Anais could understand why that had made Emelia withdraw into herself. Since returning, she had discovered that Emelia had been held by Zephyr.

She was the huntress he had broken.

Sable had used the communication system in the room to call in what had happened and a very kind looking woman in a suit had come to take Emelia away. Anais could only hope that Archangel only had Emelia's health in mind and that they weren't about to use her to get their hands on an angel, not as Anais felt they had used her to get their hands on a dragon.

Loke.

"I have to go." Anais started for the door but Sable caught her wrist, holding her back.

"*We* have to go. You think I'm going to owe an elf prince for nothing, think again. I brought him here to help us and he's going to help us. Aren't you, Loren?" Sable looked from Anais to the black-haired elegant male.

He sighed and preened his hair back, revealing the pointed tips of his ears. "I came to help and I intend to fulfil that duty, but I cannot see how it will be easy to remove the dragon from his cell unnoticed. Archangel will know that you had some part in his escape. Both of you."

Anais shrugged. "Archangel can go fuck themselves. I'm getting Loke out of here, before it's too late."

Loren nodded. "He is not doing well?"

"Understatement of your long life," Anais said and tried not to think about what state she would find Loke in when they made it down to the cellblock. "I'm worried he isn't going to make it."

"He's going to make it." Sable clapped a hand down on her shoulder. "Let's go."

Loren stared up at the ceiling and Anais was about to ask what he was doing when the room went dark. A hand caught her wrist, cold against her skin, the grip too strong to be Sable, and then ice blasted across her and she shivered and tried to pull away.

"Do not." Loren's deep voice sounded in the pitch-darkness and she realised he was teleporting her.

She immediately grabbed his arm, locking onto it as fear swept through her, adding to the iciness in her veins. She didn't want to end up in some random place in Hell and she had learned that would happen if she let go of an elf mid-teleport.

Her feet struck something solid and Loren held her steady as her knees gave out, keeping her upright.

It was still dark. Were they still teleporting?

"You had to kill *all* the lights?" Sable's voice held a reprimanding note and Anais heard Thorne grunt in agreement. "We might have ended up in a wall or something!"

Loren made a small clicking noise of irritation. "Thorne knows the layout of the building well enough to avoid such a thing."

Anais wanted to agree with Sable but she held her tongue. She wasn't sure how Loren expected them to walk around when they couldn't see where they were going. Unlike him and Thorne, she and Sable didn't have incredible night vision.

Red lights chased the darkness back, flashing across her eyes, and the alarm sounded again.

"Another intruder?" Sable said as the lights darted over her face, allowing Anais to pinpoint her in the darkness. The touch of fear that had been in her voice and was in her eyes too told Anais that she was afraid that the angel had returned already.

If he had, he was going to have a fight on his hands. Anais wouldn't let the bastard take Sable from Thorne.

Loren's handsome face darkened. "Elves."

"Elves? Is it Bleu?" Sable looked hopeful now, but wary, and after everything she had witnessed in the Third Realm, Anais could understand why being around the elf who had wanted her for his own unsettled her.

Loren shook his head. "I am not familiar with these elves."

"Where are they?" Anais said and Loren shifted his violet gaze to her. It looked a strange colour in the murky red flashing light.

"Beneath us. I would estimate they are in the cellblock and would suggest we move swiftly, because I can smell blood."

Anais began running at the same time as Sable, thundering along the corridor and then down the steps towards the cellblock. Sable had her blade at the ready and Anais drew hers, clutching it tightly as she tried to steel herself for what might lay ahead of her. Her heart beat hard against her chest, growing faster as they approached the cellblock.

The overhead lights were still on in the lowest level.

Anais almost slowed as the red lights stopped flashing and the alarm ceased.

She did slow when a huge explosion rocked the corridor, sending her stumbling backwards and drawing her focus to what lay ahead of her.

Carnage.

Sable stopped and stared at it, her lips parted and golden eyes wide. Anais covered her mouth and swallowed hard. Whoever had invaded Archangel this time, they had swept through the guards with ease. Most of the fallen hadn't even had a chance to draw their weapons. They were still sheathed against their bloodied bodies. Crimson drenched the floor and splattered across the white walls, rolling down it in places.

Loren appeared in front of them and pushed them both backwards, and Thorne's hands clamped down on them, grabbing Anais's right shoulder and Sable's left.

"Keep back," Loren said and looked over his shoulder towards the dead hunters and the grim red corridor.

Anais looked beyond him and saw the reason he had stopped them.

Two males stood in the corridor ahead of them. The one closest to them had black eyes and blood all over his obsidian armour, his sword still stuck in the belly of a dead hunter. The one at the back stood in a pile of glass, swirls of smoke curling around him, his focus on whoever he was breaking out of Archangel's cells.

The cell that was right next to Loke's one.

Her heart started at a rapid pace again.

"Desist," Loren shouted and both elves looked at him.

The darkest one backed towards his companion, his shock on seeing Loren quickly subsiding, replaced by a hunger to attack him. The one with violet eyes didn't give him the chance. He grabbed him and a silver-haired male, and teleported in a blinding flash of light.

Loren growled and raced forwards, nimbly leaping over the fallen hunters. He stopped in front of Loke's cell and her heart leaped as she heard Loke roar and the blows of his fists against the glass. She moved as swiftly as she could, not looking down as she picked her way through the dead. Right now, she had to focus on the living.

She reached Loke's cell and he stopped striking the glass and stared at her. He was too pale, his skin milk-white in the stark light. The darkness around his eyes and the obvious difficulty he had standing warned her that he was losing his fight against whatever prevented him from being in the mortal world.

"It's time to go," she said and he pressed his hand to the glass.

She placed hers over it on the other side of the barrier and gasped as he passed out, collapsing in a heap on the ground.

Loren shoved her back with one hand as his black armour covered his other fist. He snarled and launched a punch at the cracked glass. It shattered under the force of his blow and he grunted as he staggered back and shook his hand, pain contorting his face and darkening his violet eyes.

"Thank you." She raced forwards again and he shook his head.

"Thank me later, when he is actually safe. I do not think we have much time." Loren stepped over the remains of the glass barrier and she followed him into the cell, her gaze on Loke where he lay out cold on the white floor.

She kneeled beside him and reached out to touch him.

He jerked awake and snarled at her, flashing twin rows of sharp white teeth. His eyes blazed bright aquamarine as he lashed out at her. She darted back to avoid the blow and tried to reach him again, not blaming him for defending himself. He didn't seem aware of where he was or what he was doing.

"Instinct is a dangerous thing sometimes." Loren dropped to his knees on the other side of Loke and tried to grab hold of him.

Loke growled and attacked him, landing futile blows on Loren's black armour, his claws raking over the small scales but leaving no marks behind.

Anais sat with her heart in her mouth as Loke fought the elf, agreeing with Loren that instincts were dangerous things, because her every instinct said to intervene and stop Loren from hurting Loke and driving him mad with a need to defend and protect himself.

Instinct told her to protect him and soothe him.

She reached out to do just that.

Loke launched his left hand at her and she gasped as fiery lines cut across her right upper arm in the wake of his claws.

He immediately stilled.

Sniffed.

Growled low in his throat.

Turned murderous blue eyes on Loren.

He blamed the elf prince for her bleeding. He was going to attack him again and this time he looked as if he was serious about it.

Anais lunged at Loke, grabbed both of his wrists and pinned them to his bare chest, using all of her weight to press them down. It wasn't enough. He shoved and she almost flew across the cell, but Loren caught her with one hand and pressed his other one over hers where she still gripped Loke's wrists.

He effortlessly pressed down and pinned Loke's hands to his chest.

Anais wished she was as strong as a five thousand year old elf prince.

"We will move him away from here." Loren took Loke's arms from her and held them pinned in place.

"To Hell?" Anais looked from Loke to Loren when the elf didn't answer. The grave look on his face unsettled her. "What's wrong?"

"We cannot teleport him straight to Hell. He is not strong enough to survive travelling such a vast distance."

Her blood chilled. "We have to take him home."

Loren reached out to touch her and she leaned back, evading him. She paused and realised with dismay that he could take his hands away from Loke because he had passed out again. Her heart seized in her chest and she couldn't stop herself from lowering her hand and brushing the tangled strands of blue hair from Loke's damp forehead. He had to be alright. He couldn't die. She didn't think she could live with herself if she lost him.

It was all her fault.

But what she had done wasn't the only reason her heart felt close to breaking.

She couldn't lose the man she loved with all of that heart.

Understanding dawned in the elf prince's purple eyes, a look that cut her and made her want to glance away. "It is too dangerous. He must regain some strength or we shall put his life in danger—"

"His life is in danger here," Anais interjected. "Being in this realm is the thing that is killing him."

"If you would allow me to finish." Loren's calm tone didn't hide the fierce glimmer of irritation that shone in his eyes and she nodded, holding her tongue and giving him a chance to speak. "We will take him somewhere safe in this world, very close to here, and there I will use what knowledge I have of his kind to assist you in helping him."

"Helping him how?" Anais stared at the elf, finding it hard to believe that it was possible to help Loke without taking him back to Hell where he belonged.

Loren settled his hand on her shoulder. "Dragons draw energy from nature and they can draw it from everything created by nature, especially if that thing is born of this realm... I propose to help you give some of your energy... your life... to him."

Anais lowered her gaze to Loke, her eyebrows pinned high on her forehead as she absorbed what Loren had said. Was it possible? Could she sacrifice part of herself for his sake and give him the strength to survive the teleport to Hell?

"You will agree to it?"

She nodded without even needing to think about it. "If I can help him, I will, no matter how much of my life I have to give to him."

"Anais," Sable started and she silenced her by shaking her head.

"I'm set on this. He needs me and I have to make things right. It's my fault he's in this situation… but more than that… I'm doing it because I love him." She lifted her gaze to meet Sable's.

Sable's golden eyes softened and she nodded.

Loren rose to his feet in one fluid movement and had Loke slung over his shoulder with the effortless grace she was coming to associate with elves. He was powerful and shared a deep connection with nature, and if anyone could help her save Loke, it was him. She was going to owe him big time if he pulled this off and the way he smiled at her said that he knew it.

That smile eased her heart too, because it spoke of his confidence. He was certain that what he had proposed was possible and that it would save Loke.

"Where can we take him that will be safe?" Anais looked between Sable and Thorne, and finally at Loren.

He had suggested moving Loke to a safe location nearby, so she presumed he had one in mind.

"Where else would you take a shifter?" Loren's smile widened.

It was Sable who answered that question.

"Underworld."

CHAPTER 24

It turned out that Underworld was a nightclub run by a very gruff jaguar shifter called Kyter. He had opened the black steel door with a disgruntled look on his handsome face and had pinned each of them with a glare, his golden eyes dark with it and warning that the disturbance wasn't a welcomed one.

Kyter yawned as he scrubbed a hand through his sandy hair, the action raising the baggy dark grey tee he wore and flashing a hint of toned stomach muscles between the hem of it and his loose grey sweats.

Anais couldn't blame him for being annoyed. It was three in the morning after all, and he had probably only just gotten to sleep after closing the club for the night.

Kyter motioned for them to come in and Loren led the way, carrying Loke into the dimly lit expansive room.

Anais wrinkled her nose at the smell of booze, too much perfume, and undertones of sweat. She caught Kyter watching her and smiled politely, hoping he hadn't noticed her reaction.

"You think it reeks? Try being a shifter with a sensitive nose," he grunted and shut the door.

It slammed and the sound echoed around the empty nightclub. It was strange being in a nightclub after hours. Most of the lights were off, but the coloured ones above the bar still rotated, their whirr the only sound in the silent room. It felt as if a vital piece of Underworld was missing and all that was left in its place was a ghost of a nightclub.

Loren carefully laid Loke down on the long black bar to her right and she moved to catch up with him, taking long strides into the heart of the club. She halted near Loke and stared down at him, her heart throbbing in her chest as she took in how pale he was now and the beads of sweat that dotted his brow.

"You do know dragons can't be in this realm?" Kyter said at her elbow and peered over her at Loke. "It's kinda detrimental to their health."

"We know. I just need to get him strong enough and then we're taking him back to Hell." Anais looked over her shoulder at the sandy-haired jaguar.

His eyes took on the same knowing look as Loren had had back at Archangel. "He your mate?"

A shiver ran through her and she stared blankly at Kyter as those words crashed over her. Was he? She wasn't sure and she had no way of telling. Was it even possible? She looked at Sable where the black-haired huntress stood beside her imposing demon mate. Thorne had his arm slung around her shoulders, holding her tucked close to his side, and had rested his chin on top of her head, his concerned red gaze on Loke.

It was possible.

Sable had fallen in love with Thorne and was his mate.

Anais looked at Loren as he checked Loke over. Olivia had fallen in love with Loren and was his mate.

She settled her gaze on Loke. There was every chance that she was his mate. Did he know? She wanted him to wake so she could ask him, but reminded herself that she had more important matters that required her attention. She could ask him later, when she had saved his life.

Loren gestured for her to move closer. "The process will be quite simple, but it might hurt and it will require all of your focus."

She nodded and came up beside him. He took hold of her hands and placed one on Loke's bare chest over his heart and the other on his forehead. It was hot beneath her palm and his heart thudded slowly against her other one. She closed her eyes and drew in a deep breath to steady herself and drive away some of her fear. Loke would be fine again soon, and then she had some serious apologising to do.

Loren placed his hand on the back of her neck and she tensed, her shoulders jumping up. "I apologise. I require a connection to both of you and it requires bare skin."

She nodded and tried to relax, but it was difficult with Loren's hand against her neck. She kept wanting to tense or wriggle free of his grip. It felt as if he was going to snap her neck or throttle her, and the voice at the back of her mind kept chanting how easy it would be for him to do either of those things. He was extremely powerful. One swift jerk of his hand and it would be lights out for her. Permanently.

She opened her eyes and settled them on Loke's face, using the sight of him to drive awareness of Loren's hand on her neck from her mind.

Loren placed his other hand on Loke's chest next to hers. "Focus on him and the thought of transferring some of your energy into him."

It sounded ridiculous, but she did as he instructed. The first few minutes ticked by slowly, her head filling with too many thoughts, cluttering it and making it impossible for her to focus as Loren needed. He spoke quietly to her, guiding and soothing her, encouraging her when she needed it and praising her whenever he felt the connection between the three of them begin to open.

She fell into a sort of trance after that, a blankness where only Loke and Loren existed, and she could almost feel her strength flowing from her and into Loke. He cooled beneath her palms and his heartbeat began to level out. It was working.

Her trance shattered as loud voices filled the silent room.

She whipped her head around and caught sight of the elves who had been at the complex.

The ones who had killed her fellow hunters.

Loren's hand tensed against her neck. "Ignore them. Thorne and Sable will deal with them."

She nodded and went back to focusing on Loke as Thorne and Sable moved off to intercept the two elves and the silver-haired male they had brought with them.

Another, larger silver-haired male wearing only pale grey sweats came out from the back of the club, shattering her focus again. Her gaze tracked him as he made a beeline for the man who looked similar to him, his pale eyes filled with incredulity.

Kyter moved between Thorne and Sable, and the trio who had entered his club unannounced, blocking their path. "I have a no fighting policy in this club, as you're well aware. At least until I know what the fuck they want."

Sable looked as if she wanted to ignore Kyter and keep heading towards the three men. The big silver-haired male reached them and the slighter man who looked like him blew out his breath and sucked down another.

"Brother." That word leaving his lips had Kyter looking over his shoulder at the man.

"You know them, Cavanaugh?" he said to the bigger man.

The one called Cavanaugh nodded. "I like to think I knew one of them anyway... it's been a while since we've seen each other. I might be wrong."

The other man looked away and the two elves with him shifted further apart, forming what looked like a very offensive line to Anais. They were prepared to fight, despite Kyter's announcement that he didn't condone violence in his club.

"Focus," Loren whispered behind her and she dragged her gaze back to Loke and fixed it on him.

The sensation of her life flowing from her started again and she struggled to tune out everyone as they all began talking at once. Her side argued with the elves about what they had done, and Cavanaugh argued with them about something else entirely.

Anais took another deep breath, released it slowly, and focused on her hands where they pressed against Loke's chest and forehead.

"That is good. Like that." Loren's deep voice was close to her ear and she nodded, beginning to slip back into the strange trance state.

The door in the wall ahead of her opened again, throwing light into the dim room.

"Hartt?" The soft female voice caused silence to fall in the room but the tension in the air ratcheted up a thousand degrees.

Anais glanced up at the beautiful, tall and elegant black-haired woman where she stood near the end of the bar, dressed in only a long black satin negligee.

There was a sudden and strange sounding roar off to her left and all Hell broke loose as Kyter launched himself at one of the elves—the one who had looked as if he had wanted to stop fighting the hunters when Loren had commanded them to halt their attack.

159

The male defended himself, blocking Kyter's fierce blows and gaining some distance between them by teleporting away from the jaguar shifter. He reappeared right in front of the woman.

It didn't help matters.

Kyter's roar shattered the silence again and he was suddenly right behind the elf, his eyes glowing dangerously in the low light. The elf dodged the blow he had aimed at the back of his head and twirled to face him, a smile on his lips.

"How the hell do you know my mate?" Kyter snarled and lashed out with his claws before the male could answer.

Anais couldn't help noticing he seemed to have forgotten his no-fighting policy.

Hartt's smile became a wicked grin as he evaded Kyter, nimbly strafing to his left and coming around behind the shifter.

"We were engaged once." Those four words only served to infuriate Kyter and Anais had the feeling that Hartt was doing it on purpose.

He was intentionally provoking Kyter.

"Kyter," the woman said in a firm tone and he paid her no heed.

Anais tried to focus on Loke and shut out the lover's quarrel but it was impossible. Her calm dissipated as the noise level rose, anger and frustration growing where it had been, and she closed her eyes and sought the strength to ignore what was happening.

She had just started to feel the connection between her and Loke opening again, when a new voice rose above the din.

"You must stop disappearing like this, my prince."

Loren's hand tensed against her neck and she squeaked at the sudden pressure. "I am sorry."

She wasn't sure whether he was apologising to her or to the man now standing right in front of her, near Loke's head. Another elf. She recognised this one. Bleu was as tall as Loren and wore the same black skin-tight armour, but his hair was dishevelled and wild, and he had a teasing edge to his gaze as he chastised Loren.

The woman in the negligee turned wide purple eyes on him. "Bleu?"

He looked over his shoulder in her direction, and then at the fight happening between Kyter and Hartt. Everyone had moved back to allow them space, forming a rough circle around them and dodging either left or right whenever the two of them brought their fight a little too close for comfort.

Anais gritted her teeth and wondered if she was ever going to get some peace and quiet so she could help Loke.

"What did you do this time to get in deep shit with assassins, Io?" Bleu said and the woman looked mortified.

"I am not in trouble. Hartt is not here because of me." She grimaced as Kyter landed a hard blow on Hartt's jaw, sending him stumbling sideways.

The elf male snarled at Kyter through bloodied fangs.

She huffed. "Oh, that is enough."

She disappeared in a flash of green-purple light and reappeared between Kyter and Hartt. She shoved Hartt in the chest and he flew across the room, slammed into the far black wall with a grunt, and dropped like a sack of bricks to the floor.

Kyter stood behind her, breathing hard, his t-shirt bearing long gashes in it.

Bleu stared at the elf male, his gaze narrowed and troubled, as if he was trying to place him but couldn't quite recall why he knew him.

Hartt picked himself up off the floor and wiped the back of his hand across his mouth, smearing blood over his cheek. "If I had known you would turn out so damned beautiful, I might have married you after all."

Bleu's eyes widened and recognition shone in them.

Kyter roared and hunkered down, preparing to launch himself at Hartt.

Bleu beat him to it.

He teleported in front of Hartt as he walked back towards the female elf and slammed his fist into the assassin's face, sending him flying across the room again. Hartt growled and teleported, reappearing in Bleu's face.

Bleu didn't even flinch.

He grabbed Hartt by the throat and shoved him away.

"Focus," Loren said from behind her. "Bleu will handle this mess. Will you not, Bleu?"

"Yes, my prince." Bleu nodded stiffly and drew a black blade out of the air.

Anais blew out her breath and locked her gaze on Loke again. She fell into the trance more quickly this time, slipping deep into it and feeling the connection between the three of them blossom again. It was stronger now and she fought a dizzy spell as her energy leached out of her.

Hartt hit the black bar, making it shudder and jolting Loke.

Anais's temper broke its tethers.

"Will you all go in the other damned room or something. I'm trying to fucking concentrate!" She turned a glare on every immortal present, uncaring that every single one of them was infinitely more powerful than she was.

They all stared at her in stunned silence.

Even Hartt had an edge of guilt to his violet eyes.

"Take the fight elsewhere, Bleu," Loren snapped.

Bleu didn't seem to listen.

He pinned Hartt with a black glare. "Stay away from my sister, you assassin scum. I hear even a rumour that you merely looked at her in the wrong way and I will kill you. Tainted bastards like you deserve to be put down."

"Tainted?" The female elf stared at Hartt, shock dancing across her pretty face.

"It's nothing." Hartt pushed himself off the bar and set his gaze on the other elf he had appeared with and the silver-haired man. "Get a move on, Harbin, or we're leaving you behind."

Hartt teleported and reappeared next to the other elf in his group.

Bleu looked there and his eyes widened again. "Commander Fuery? I thought you were dead."

The darker elf's expression shifted dangerously, turning even blacker than it had been before.

Bleu took a step towards him, the shock on his face remaining as he stared across the open space at the other elf. The one he had called Fuery didn't seem to recognise him. He looked as if he was considering attacking Bleu, and possibly everyone else present.

"How did you survive Vail's attack?" Bleu whispered and Loren's hand dropped away from Anais's neck.

She looked back at him and found him staring at Fuery, his wide eyes matching his stunned expression.

Fuery didn't answer. He continued to stare at Bleu through cold black eyes.

"What happened to you?" Bleu took another step towards the other elf.

This time, Fuery backed away one and cast a panicked look at Hartt, his dark eyes gaining a wild edge as he started to shake his head. Hartt closed the gap between them and placed his hand on Fuery's shoulder. The touch seemed to comfort him and Fuery drew in a shuddering deep breath.

"The elf is tainted," Loren said and Bleu looked over his shoulder at him. "The male you knew no longer exists, Bleu."

The elf male looked as if he didn't want to believe that. Had they been close to each other once, back before the attack Bleu had mentioned had happened?

Bleu took another step towards Fuery.

The darker male responded by drawing his black blade and snarling at Bleu. Hartt stepped in front of his comrade, partially shielding him with his body and placing his hand over Fuery's to stay his blade.

"Do you not recognise whose company you are in?" Bleu said and Fuery's black gaze flickered to Loren. "Do you not recognise your prince?"

Fuery's eyes narrowed and he snarled through his fangs, black-sounding words in a tongue Anais didn't know.

Bleu's expression turned dark and dangerous. "Your prince is standing in this very room, not roaming Hell bent on bloodshed and destruction. That wretched male is not your prince."

"Watch your tongue, Bleu!" Loren snapped.

Bleu lowered his head and pressed his right hand to his chest. "My apologies, my prince."

Loke groaned and twitched, and everyone's eyes leaped to him. Anais stroked his brow, her heart aching with a need to help him. They were close, she could feel it. He was growing stronger. He just needed a little more from her.

"It's okay," she whispered and smoothed her fingers across his forehead and then feathered them down his cheek. "We'll have you back in Hell soon, safe in your cave."

"Cave?" Bleu frowned at Loke.

"The male is dragon." Loren returned his focus to Loke, placing his hands back on Anais's neck and on Loke's chest. "I will speak with him about the sword and your mission when he is well again."

Bleu nodded.

"Harbin?" Hartt grabbed hold of Fuery's wrist and the man lowered his black gaze to it, his eyebrow rising as he stared at Hartt's hand.

"I might be a while. Go on without me. I need to finish my mission and then I'll meet you," Harbin said.

Hartt nodded, cast one last look back towards Bleu where he now stood in front of his sister with Kyter at his side, and disappeared in a flash of silvery light.

Bleu muttered something in the lyrical language of the elves as he gave Harbin the evil eye and Loren responded.

Cavanaugh growled, baring huge canines, and moved in front of his sibling.

"Enough. No more fighting." Kyter scrubbed a hand down his face, his golden gaze filled with weariness.

The elf female stroked his arm and he frowned at her and then his face softened and he lifted his hand and caressed her cheek. She smiled and Kyter's gaze darkened, but not with a need for violence this time. There was hunger in it, desire that made Anais ache to have Loke look at her that way again, even when she feared he never would after everything she had done.

Kyter dragged the woman through the back door of the club and jealousy coiled in Anais's heart, fraying her temper again.

"Can you all get the hell out of here now so I can focus?" Anais barked and everyone looked at her. "I'm trying to save someone's life."

Cavanaugh looked down at his boots, tunnelled his fingers through his silver hair, and then lifted his gaze back to meet hers. "I'm sorry."

He caught Harbin's arm and led him into the back of the club.

Bleu cast her an apologetic look, and then glanced towards Sable and Thorne. His violet gaze turned troubled, an edge of hurt in it.

"Return home, Bleu. I will be there soon," Loren said and the elf nodded and disappeared.

Sweet silence fell.

Anais locked all of her focus on Loke and fell swiftly into the trance state. She lost track of time as energy flowed between her, Loke and Loren, a connection that felt like a living thing to her.

It made her veins pulse, a wave of heat travelling through her body with each beat, washing up from her toes to her head. A deeper awareness grew inside her, a sensation that she was connected to an incredible power, and she floated within it, drifting as light as a feather in the hazy pale glow that engulfed her.

Loren's hand left the back of her neck and the connection shattered, bringing the dimly lit club and Loke back into view. Her knees gave out and Loren caught her under her arms and lifted her into his, cradling her against his chest as if she weighed nothing.

"You have done all you can," he said. "Now both of you must rest."

Rest sounded good.

Anais clung to consciousness long enough to take one last look at Loke, hoping she had given enough of her life to save him but not so much that she wouldn't wake from the warm arms of sleep that were already wrapped around her and pulling her down into the darkness.

He slipped out of focus and sleep took her.

CHAPTER 25

The air smelled different. Loke breathed deep of it and frowned as it no longer burned his lungs. They easily expanded in a fluid movement, their silence rousing him further from sleep when he had grown used to them rattling and wheezing. Strength coursed through him and he was aware of it for the first time.

Aware that he had been weak and now he was strong again.

He slowly flexed his fingers against the soft material cushioning his tired body, pulling it into his fists. The aches were gone too. The burning in his bones that had left him feeling they were turning to ash.

What had happened to him?

He wasn't back in Hell. He knew that much. He wasn't in the Archangel facility either. He was somewhere new and unfamiliar.

Loke groaned as he tried to open his eyes and they stung despite the low level of lighting in the room. Perhaps he wasn't back to full strength after all, but he wasn't being drained of his energy by the mortal world either. Something had happened that had given him back his strength and had stopped it from fading away again.

Whatever that something was, it had left him feeling different.

He opened his eyes again and they burned less this time, allowing him to take in his surroundings. A room with wooden furniture and a soft bed. He looked down the length of his body at his bare feet where they hung off the end of the bed. His blue leather trousers almost matched the colour of the sheets beneath him.

Loke drew in another deep breath and used his senses to pick through the smells. There were others in the building with him. Immortals. He could smell shifters, elves, and the wretched demon who had knocked him out.

He could smell Anais.

He singled her out, using his senses to track her as she moved around somewhere below him. His heart stung and he rubbed his chest, trying to soothe it as the constant voice at the back of his mind began to taunt him again, reminding him of everything she had done.

The demon might have been the one who had knocked him out but it was Anais who had brought him to the mortal world and had placed him into the nefarious hands of her masters.

Anger curled through him, making him restless and driving him from the bed. He sat up and swung his legs over the edge of it, and paused as his head turned and the room spun around him. He pulled down another breath and stared straight ahead at a wooden set of drawers as he waited for the dizzy spell to pass.

The door to his right opened and Anais stood there, the brighter light of the corridor casting her into shadow. Her blonde hair hung around her slender shoulders, threads of it clinging to her black t-shirt. That black t-shirt blended seamlessly into her dark trousers, making her appear more like a wraith than something real.

Loke hung his head and grasped the edges of the mattress with both hands, anchoring himself to the bed when all he wanted to do was stand and cross the room to her, and pull her into his arms and feel that she was indeed real. The part of himself that was having difficulty handling what she had done rebelled against those softer desires, replacing them with a need to lash out at her.

He turned his face towards her.

She held her hands up. "Don't speak. I need to say something."

Loke nodded, curious to know what was on her mind.

"I'm sorry about what happened. I know it doesn't change anything, and I shouldn't have let them take you like that. It isn't what I wanted, but it all happened so quickly and I didn't have time to think." She paused and cast her gaze down at her boots. "Or maybe I did... I was muddled and part of me wanted to go back... and Sable said that Archangel only wanted information about the dragons so we could rescue the others. I was an idiot to believe them... and Sable feels pretty awful about it too because they duped her as well. If I had known they were going to put you in a cell like that... put you through tests and... if I had known that you couldn't be in this world without being in danger... I'm sorry. I really am."

He could feel her hurt flowing through him and it cooled his anger enough that he could look at her with clearer eyes and a more forgiving heart. She had placed him into the hands of Archangel, but she had also rescued him from them, placing herself in great danger and no doubt damaging her relationship with them.

"What did you want?" He rose onto his feet and she lifted her gaze to meet his.

The dark circles beneath her eyes alarmed him and he had moved a step closer and had raised his hand with the intention of touching her pale cheek before he even realised what he was doing. He halted and held her blue gaze instead, waiting to hear her answer.

Anais looked off to her right. "I don't know."

Her expression turned troubled and he could feel the conflict within her. She hadn't only hurt him. She had hurt herself too. He could hear it in the tremulous beat of her heart and smell it in her scent. She was nervous around him. Guilty. Afraid. Not of him, but of what he might say or do. She was afraid he would lash out at her verbally to inflict pain on her and punish her for what she had done.

The darker part of himself believed she deserved such retribution, but the rest of his heart squashed it out of existence because what was done was done and nothing they said or did would change it. He was stronger now, somehow able to cope with being in the mortal realm, and his life was no longer in danger.

He refused to hold a grudge when she had believed that he would be treated in a better manner than he had been. She hadn't betrayed him or intentionally placed him in danger. If he had been more honest with her about his species and why he had never been to the mortal realm, she would have known he couldn't survive in her world and she never would have allowed her friend to take him from his cave.

He knew that in his heart.

A heart that loved her.

A heart that feared for her.

"I had another vision." He let that confession slip out as a whisper but she reacted as if he had shouted it, her head jerking up and her eyes shooting wide as she stared right at him, her heart hammering in his ears.

"What did you see?" Her voice was weak, each word trembling on her lips.

"I saw you die," he whispered and took another step towards her when she swallowed hard and paled further. He couldn't shake the vision this time or how it made him feel. Afraid. Weak. Frustrated. He wanted to protect her but he couldn't. No matter what he did, the vision only changed slightly. "The location was different, but the shadowy figure and the outcome remained the same."

She dropped her gaze to the strip of floor between them, her fair eyebrows furrowing as she clenched her fists at her sides.

A deep need to comfort her filled him, but he remained where he was, struggling with his feelings as he looked at her. His little Amazon. She looked so weak now and afraid, and it pulled at him, strengthening his need to protect her.

"I thought that since I took you from the battlefield, I would have created a big enough interference in events to stop them… I had thought your fate would change." He barely held himself back when she wrapped her arms around herself. "I will protect you, Anais."

Her head lifted and her eyes leaped to meet his. "Why?"

He could understand her confusion, because part of him was also confused. He swore he had been muddled from the moment he had met her, never knowing whether he was coming or going, or what he was feeling. He no longer felt like the master of his own body. Something had seized control of him the second he had set eyes on her in the midst of that battle.

Possibly his heart.

He should have been angry with her, but the need to shield her from whatever dark future awaited her overshadowed that feeling. His love for her was too strong to deny. It was too powerful to be weakened or destroyed by the things that had happened. It was a love that would never fade. It would never die. It was eternal.

Forever.

He didn't have the courage to tell her those things though, not when he was unsure of how she felt about him. The look in her eyes, the soft edge of need, told him that she wanted to hear them but he couldn't lay his heart on the line.

Not when he had been carefully guarding it for six thousand years.

"The elves have agreed to take you back to your home." Those quiet words cut at his heart and they seemed to lash at her too.

Lines bracketed her mouth as she tried to smile and he decided that he didn't like seeing her this way. Defeated. He preferred the female warrior he had met on the battlefield. The one who had been confident and courageous. Strong. Sure of herself. Was she feeling the same way as he was, suddenly unsure of herself and uncertain of her feelings and everything else?

Before meeting her, he had been as sure of himself as she had been, certain of his future. He had known what lay ahead of him and the direction his life would take. Everything had been set in stone and she had shattered it.

She had turned his life upside down, but he wouldn't change anything that had happened. Well, maybe the past few days, but never the rest of it. He didn't want to go back to that life, that monotonous existence.

He didn't want them to part, and that was exactly what she was saying was about to happen.

The elves would take him home.

Without her.

She would remain here, in the mortal realm, far beyond his reach.

Forever.

Not if he had his way.

He was going to fight her on it.

He was going to fight for her.

Loke closed the distance between them. "I would like to meet these elves."

She tilted her head back and looked up into his eyes, her blue ones reflecting the pain he felt in his heart, and nodded.

He allowed her to lead him from the room and down a set of metal steps into a pale expansive room. He wasn't sure where they were and it was on his mind to ask her as they crossed the room to a door, but then she opened that door and he stepped into the next dimly-lit black-walled room.

The room from his vision.

His blood turned to icy sludge in his veins and he quickly took in the large room, and the occupants of it. The demon and the elf male. Which one would be the one who killed her?

His heart set off at a pace and he stormed towards the two males. The dark-haired elf eyed him with suspicion and called his black armour, replacing his tunic and trousers with it, and arming himself with sharp black claws.

Talons.

As he had seen in his vision.

Loke snarled at the male, baring his fangs, and prepared himself to attack.

"Loke." Anais was between them in a flash, blocking his way to the elf male.

The russet-brown-haired demon's eyes glowed red and his broad bare chest heaved with each hard breath he took as his dark leathery wings emerged and his horns curled around to flare forwards into twin deadly points on either side of his face. The elf used Loke's temporary impediment to his advantage, calling a black blade to his hand and backing off a step to gain some space.

The black-haired female he knew as Sable looked ready to join the two males in fighting him.

Loke growled, grabbed Anais by her arm and shoved her behind him. His claws grew longer as he faced off against the demon and the elf, his focus fixed on them so they couldn't attack unnoticed. He bared his fangs again and kept Anais tucked close to his back, shielding her with his body as he tried to calculate which of the two males was the one in his vision.

The elf was the prime suspect. He had the right build and the talons.

"What are you doing?" Anais tried to get past him.

He moved with her, his eyes constantly locked on the elf's violet ones. He was still weaker than usual, and the elf was old and powerful, a prince of his kind. The chances of him surviving a fight against the male, especially when the demon and the huntress looked ready to assist him, were slim but it wouldn't stop Loke.

He would protect Anais, no matter what.

"Explain yourself." The elf took a step towards him.

Loke roared and lashed out at him, swiping with his claws. The elf leaped backwards to evade his blow and glared at him.

"Loke, calm down!" Anais grabbed his left arm and pulled on it, but he stood firm, refusing to give the elf an opening in which he could attack. "He wants to help you."

He wanted to kill Anais.

Loke felt sure of it.

This was the male he had seen in his most recent vision, the one who would cause her death.

But ultimately, it would be the elf prince who died this night.

Loke wouldn't allow the male near her. He would kill the elf before he had a chance to hurt his little Amazon.

He broke free of Anais's hold and launched himself at the elf. They clashed hard but the elf made no move to attack him. He grabbed Loke and grappled with him, and Loke snarled as he realised the male intended to restrain him. He brought his right arm up hard, looping it over the elf's one and twisting out of his grip. He drew his arm back, his gaze narrowed on the elf and his focus on taking the male down before he could incapacitate him.

The elf released his other arm and Loke grinned as he saw his victory playing out in front of him, all because the elf refused to fight him and would only defend.

He would eliminate this threat to Anais and she would finally be safe.

He went to launch his fist at the male with every drop of strength he had in his body, a hunger to strike the elf down in order to protect his mate driving him and filling him with a dark craving for violence and bloodshed.

Anais grabbed his arm and he turned on her with a snarl.

And stopped dead as he caught sight of himself in the mirror beyond the black bar.

His eyes glowed bright blue, shining vividly in the low light, and his nails were like talons, his hand raised to grab her shoulder and push her to safety.

It was his vision.

A shiver went through him, as cold as ice but burning like fire, and he couldn't breathe as it all fell into place.

He had seen that image now staring back at him. A male lifting a hand to her, his talons poised to strike her down.

Him.

He had seen himself.

He was the one who would ultimately cause her death.

That was the reason he had seen her die in his cave. Why he had seen her die in this room.

That was the reason he couldn't see the person who did it, because he didn't want to see it. He didn't want to kill her, but he would.

And he didn't know what to do.

It wasn't that he would kill her right now, but that it would happen at some point, and the sickening heavy feeling inside his chest told him that he knew when that point would be.

The need to claim her as his mate burned in his blood and she wasn't strong enough to survive mating with a dragon.

And he wasn't strong enough to deny his need to do it.

"Loke, what's wrong?" she whispered.

He released her and staggered backwards, shaking his head as he stared at her through wide eyes, sick to his stomach as his heart shattered in his chest.

"I have to leave… now… I have to go." Loke looked from her to the elf male, the one who apparently wanted to help him get back home.

There was a knowing look in the male's violet eyes. Those eyes seemed to see straight through him, leaving no part of him untouched. The elf prince knew what was happening, even if Anais couldn't see it.

"We can go," she said.

Loke's eyes leaped back to her and the pain in his chest only grew worse as he realised that she wanted to return to Hell with him. He had been wrong. She wanted to be with him. Gods, the fates were cruel. All he wanted was Anais, but he could never trust himself with her.

He shook his head and her face fell, her hurt swift to race through him and worsen his own agony.

He kept backing away from her, even when all he wanted to do was pull her into his arms and swear he would find a way they could be together. He couldn't risk it. The need to claim her as his mate was already strong and he had already come close to initiating a bonding several times. If he took her back with him, if he stayed with her, it was only a matter of time before he lost his mind to the need to mate and ended up killing her.

"The vision," he whispered when her blue eyes implored him to explain why he was hurting her and distancing himself. "I just saw it again."

She took a step towards him and held her right hand out to him, her need for him to take it shining in her eyes and lacing her feelings. Gods, he wanted to give her what she needed, but he couldn't.

It was killing him.

He shook his head again and fear touched with pain and sorrow crossed her face.

She took another harder step towards him. "It's just a vision."

He held his hands up and she stopped. "It was not a vision this time. It was the vision made real. I saw what I had witnessed in my dreams. I saw myself."

She began to shake her head and her fair eyebrows furrowed.

"What are you saying?" she snapped, her voice thick with emotion that told him she knew exactly what he was saying but she didn't want to believe it.

He didn't want to believe it either, not even when all the evidence pointed to it being true.

"It is me. I am the one who will kill you."

The silence in the room grew heavy with tension and he could feel everyone's eyes on him but he didn't take his off Anais.

"No." She folded her arms across her chest and frowned at him. "I won't believe that."

He wished he could say the same thing with as much conviction as she had, but it wasn't about believing. It was the truth. It was fact. Nothing could change it.

"I have to go, Little Amazon," he whispered and clenched his fists at his sides to stop himself from reaching out to her and clinging to her as he wanted to. "I need to do this. I must protect you. It was always about protecting you... saving you. I did not think it would come down to protecting you from myself though."

"We can work it out." She took another step towards him, her eyebrows furrowing again and tears swimming in her eyes as her pain grew stronger, beginning to eclipse his own. Gods, he didn't want to hurt her. When she looked at him like that, he wanted to pull her into his embrace and take all her pain away. She shook her head. "Don't do this, Loke. We can figure out a way around it or to make it not happen."

"I cannot... will not place you in danger. I have to leave you." His voice hitched as his throat closed and the aching in his heart grew fiercer, ripping him apart from the inside. Six thousand years of life and now he felt as if he was dying, all because a little mortal female had made him truly feel alive for the first time. The thought of existing without her destroyed him, but he would do it if it meant knowing that she was safe. He coughed to clear his throat but his words still came out hoarse and strained, raspy with emotion. "Please do not make this any harder than it already is for me."

She kept shaking her head, the pain in her eyes colliding with fire, anger that he could feel in her and he deserved. He was hurting her, and it made him feel like a bastard, but if he had to wound her in order to drive her away and save her life, he would do it.

"You're my mate," she said it so resolutely that he halted, his feet frozen in place by her announcement and the steely look in her blue eyes that challenged him to deny it.

He couldn't.

Not when every fibre of his being was constantly screaming that she was his and he needed to mate with her to bind them together for eternity.

"You are my mate," he whispered and held his hand up when she went to speak. "I know it deep in my blood… but I also know what that means. Mating is dangerous for dragons. It is not unheard of for a male to accidentally kill their female during the bonding process. We lose control and are consumed by our instincts."

He started backing away from her again, maintaining the distance between them as she strode towards him.

"I will not put you through that, Anais," he said, his voice loud in the silent room. "I will not be responsible for your death."

His voice cracked on the last word and he couldn't take it anymore. He threw a look at the elf prince and the male barely nodded, accepting his silent plea for help.

Loke looked back at Anais, drinking in the sight of her and putting her beauty to memory. A memory that he would carry with him always and use as a balm for his broken heart in the cold centuries that lay ahead of him.

He allowed her to finally close the distance between them, tears lining his eyes as he kept them on hers. Her pain mingled with his and his heart broke all over again as she halted in front of him and they balanced on the brink of snapping the slender thread that tied their souls together.

His little Amazon.

He had found the true meaning of life in her, a life filled with incredible beauty and emotion, with purpose and warmth. All of it shared with another. His soul mate. His one fated female.

He didn't want to give all that up.

He held her gaze and whispered to her in the dragon tongue, "You are my eternal mate… and I wish with all of my heart that things could be different for us. I wish I did not have to give you up, because I am in love with you, and I always will be. There will never be another female for me. There will only be you. Forever."

He raised a trembling hand and touched her cheek, using the pad of his thumb to brush away a tear that had fallen. It killed him. He wanted to kiss her one last time, but he feared it would break him completely.

Loke settled his fingers against her face and found the strength deep within him. He was willing to risk it in order to take this one last memory of her with him.

One he would cherish forever.

His lips would never touch another.

He had been made for her, and he would always stay true to her.

He dipped his head and kissed her, and it utterly destroyed him, ripping him to shreds and leaving him trembling, his lips shaking against hers as he fell apart.

He needed her in his arms and he needed to never let her go.

He reached for her and the elf prince caught his wrist, spun him away from her and darkness swallowed him.

The black valley of the dragons stretched below him, cold wind buffeting him as he stood on the mountainside with the elf at his side.

Home.

It seemed so cold and empty now.

"It was a courageous thing you did to let her go." The elf prince released him and Loke shut down the part of him that wanted to beg the male to take him back, because his home wasn't here. His home was wherever Anais was. The male looked at him and sighed. "But courage is not always the answer. You love her and she loves you."

He didn't want to hear that. He turned away from the black-haired male but the elf didn't leave.

"She gave part of herself to heal you and bring you back in touch with nature through my connection to it. That was the reason you were able to live in that world without it killing you." The male's voice was low and quiet, but Loke felt as if he had shouted each word as they hit him and he realised the danger she had placed herself in for his sake. "She sacrificed a fragment of her life force to save you."

Loke closed his eyes and gritted his teeth. He knew what the elf was telling him, and he knew that Anais had no clue about what the male had done. He didn't think that the elf would have explained every little detail. The male had been meddling. He had known Anais's feelings for him, and his for her, and he had known what would happen if she gave part of herself.

He had known it would bind them together.

No matter how far apart they were, Loke would always feel her. He pressed a hand to his bare chest and sensed a faint glimmer of hurt and her despair through the connection that linked him to her. She would always be a part of him, and he a part of her. They would never be apart.

They would never stop wanting each other.

The elf had cursed them to drift through their lives feeling as if part of them was missing.

Loke hung his head and his bare shoulders heaved as he sighed. "What would you have me do? A dragon mating is too dangerous. She would not survive it."

"I know of dragons." The prince came around in front of him on the ledge, his back to the dark scenery stretching around them. He suited this forbidding place more than his verdant kingdom, his black armour making him look as if he had been made to live in the darkness of this land. His fangs flashed between his lips as he spoke. "I know of the great strength of your species and how that part of you makes you dangerous… but I also know that you love her. Love is a powerful force in itself. Love makes you want to protect her and keep her safe, enough to sacrifice what you had. Perhaps love can give you the strength to find a way to hold back the most dangerous part of yourself."

"Perhaps it could, but it would be a fool's venture to even risk it." Loke looked away from the prince, settling his gaze on the distant mountains in the direction of his cave.

A cave that would forever remind him of Anais.

"I am no fool, Elf, and I will not risk Anais like that." He flicked a glance back at the male.

The prince blew out his breath, an exasperated edge to his handsome face and violet eyes.

"I will leave that for you to decide… but consider the alternative. The next five decades or so aching for the female you left behind, and the next five millennia filled with regret." The prince weathered Loke's glare and the warning growl that curled from his lips. "I would speak with you soon about dragons… one in particular we are hunting. A dragon who attacked my realm and stole something precious from me."

Loke nodded, his heart pounding for a different reason as he sent a prayer to his gods that Taryn was safe.

"Think about what I said." The elf disappeared before he could respond, leaving Loke high on the mountain.

Alone.

Gods, he had never felt so alone.

His heart clung to the strained connection between him and Anais, and the need to see her again was already unbearable. He wasn't sure how he was going to last the next fifty years without her, let alone the next five thousand.

But he had to do it.

It was the only way to protect her and stop him from killing her.

Or was it?

CHAPTER 26

Anais stood on the flat rooftop of the old elegant sandstone building that had been her home for almost a decade but no longer felt like it. She felt out of place among the hunters that called it home now, even when the heads of the organisation had given her leave to remain as part of it, at least until there had been a full investigation into what had happened the night Loke had escaped. Those in Archangel who had been her friends now looked at her with suspicious eyes—the same way they looked at Sable whenever her back was turned. It was as if they had betrayed Archangel and those hunters by falling in love with their fated mates, when that wasn't the case at all.

Both she and Sable still burned with a desire to help the humans and non-humans who wanted to live in peace with each other.

In fact, her desire to help both sides in their fight against the immortals who meant them harm had grown stronger than ever.

Her gaze scanned the rooftops of London stretching around her, taking in the panorama of a thousand warm lights puncturing the inky darkness and throwing a glow up into the air.

She wanted to hold back the darkness just as those lights did.

She had taken to coming to the roof every night after she had finished her work. She liked the silence and welcomed the cool crisp air and being alone with her thoughts. Those thoughts always ran along the same lines.

Loke.

It had been five days since he had left her in Underworld with her heart in pieces and that heart still ached whenever she thought about him. She knew that he had left her in order to protect her, but that didn't mean it had hurt her any less. It didn't make it easier for her to handle and she wasn't sure she would ever overcome the pain he had caused her. It seemed to live like a constant thing within her, refusing to ease even in the slightest. She carried her pain wherever she went—into meetings, into battle, and onto this rooftop.

Sometimes, she swore the pain wasn't hers, not entirely anyway.

Sometimes, she swore she could feel Loke's presence.

Her eyes tracked a plane as it cut low across the clear sky, lights flashing as it headed straight towards London Heathrow.

Loke might have placed a barrier between them that was difficult for her to overcome, but that didn't mean she was going to give up on him. She knew from Sable that when an immortal found their fated one that they were compelled to mate with them and seal their bond, but she wished it didn't have to be that way if that was the only reason Loke had left her. The thought of never seeing him again hurt too much for her to bear.

She stared off into the distant darkness. London looked so bleak and cold to her now, a desolate place.

Because Loke was gone.

She hadn't realised how much light and warmth he had brought into her life until he had teleported out of it.

"I thought I'd find you here." Sable's voice cut through the quiet hum of the night and Anais looked over her shoulder at the black-haired huntress. She blended into the darkness with her black t-shirt, leather trousers and knee-high boots. "Still moping?"

Anais scowled at her. "I'm not moping."

"I bet he's doing the same." Sable halted beside her and looked off into the distance. "It's typical of men from his world. They don't have a bloody clue how strong Archangel huntresses are. Thorne was the same. He treated me as if I was some precious little princess who couldn't fend for herself."

"What did you do to change his mind?" Anais wanted to know, because she had seen Thorne when he had been like that, and she had also witnessed Thorne as a demon who showed Sable a hefty amount of respect and near-constantly praised her strength.

"I made it clear that I was a strong, independent woman who wasn't afraid to unleash some whoop-ass on him if he dared to belittle me." Sable placed her right hand on Anais's shoulder and squeezed it as she smiled brightly. "We can find a way to make Loke pay for being so bloody annoyingly chivalrous. Don't worry. You know where Loren dropped him?"

Anais sighed. "He's probably gone back to his cave."

Sable's smile widened. "You know, he's probably the first man I've met who can actually say he really has a man-cave."

Anais almost smiled. She might have if in that moment she hadn't experienced a sudden sensation of being empty, as if a piece of her was missing. The unsettling sensation eased and she frowned as she wondered what was wrong with her. Was it just the result of missing Loke and talking about him?

"Just say the word and Thorne will give you a lift. Contact me on my mobile if you need me." Sable released her and began walking back towards the stairs.

"Where are you going?" She had thought Sable was done with her work for the night but the huntress seemed to have other plans.

Sable looked back at her, an edge of darkness in her golden eyes. "I have to talk with an angel about a problem I feel I'm going to have with that Echelon angel. I need more info about my bloodline, because I have the feeling he's going to be one persistent bastard."

Anais did manage to smile now. "Your problems make mine look like nothing."

Sable shrugged. "Give me battles and enemies any day of the week. It's love that really knows how to hit you hard and kick you when you're already on your arse. The trick is to stand up, dust yourself off, and go out there and give it a swift kick in the balls until it falls into line."

Anais frowned. "You are speaking metaphorically now... or am I meant to go and find Loke and kick him where it hurts again?"

"Again?" Sable grinned. "That's my girl. Call when you've made up your mind... okay?"

"Okay." Anais nodded. "I just need some time to get my head on straight and think about what I want."

Sable's expression softened as she backed towards the metal stairs. "It's a big decision... but it could be worse. You could be half-angel, married to a demon king, trying to balance running a realm with protecting the world."

Anais couldn't stop herself from chuckling at that, even when she wasn't laughing on the inside. She waved Sable away and went back to staring at the city, feeling the pressing weight of her options on her shoulders as she tried to decide what to do.

Loke couldn't survive in her world and he couldn't teleport as Thorne and Loren could, so he couldn't transfer her between Hell and London. If she was going to be with him, she had to give up everything.

But it might just be a sacrifice she was willing to make to be with the man she had fallen in love with.

The distant sound of alarms sent a jolt of adrenaline burning through her and she turned on her heel and bolted towards the stairs that led down into the building. She took them two at a time and drew her sword as she reached the bottom and burst into a corridor on the top floor. Red lights flashed as the sirens screeched, hurting her ears.

She took a moment to get her bearings and then grabbed a man as he ran past. "What's happening?"

"Some non-human just landed in the cafeteria."

It was probably Thorne looking for Sable. He always caused a ruckus when he showed up unannounced in the cafeteria. But what if it wasn't?

She followed the man as he sprinted down the corridor, leaving her behind as he caught up with a group of hunters. The hunter quarters were on this side of the building, meaning the way into the cafeteria from this direction would be blocked by the number of men and women trying to get into it to face the non-human.

Anais banked right at the first junction, breaking away from the group and following a long corridor that ran the length of the building and would bring her down on the other side of the cafeteria. Fewer hunters would hit it from the direction she had chosen, meaning she could see what had landed in it and could get in on the action if it wasn't Thorne and was an attack.

She ran past the first set of stairs on her right and took the second down to the next floor, following it as it bent back on itself halfway, and banked right again, sprinting as fast as she could down the empty corridor. As predicted, everyone was coming at the cafeteria from the same direction. Score for her, since her patrol had been quiet. She might get to work off some tension tonight after all.

Anais leaped the wall around the next set of stairs and landed awkwardly on the steps below. She lost her grip on her sword as her bones ached from the hard landing, stumbled down the remaining steps and slammed straight into someone. Her cheeks blazed as she took them down with her in a heap and landed on top of them.

"Damn, I'm sorry." She shoved herself up, her eyes leaping to the face of the man who had provided a nice cushion for her fall, and froze as she met stunning aquamarine eyes. "Loke?"

He grinned at her and she almost pinched herself to see whether she had knocked herself out as a result of her fall and was dreaming. It wasn't possible.

She scrambled off him and he slowly got to his bare feet and grimaced as he stretched, making every honed muscle of his torso flex. She was definitely unconscious and dreaming. He looked far more delicious and gorgeous than she remembered. He stooped and picked up her sword, appraised it with an amused smile, and then held it out to her.

"What are you doing here?" She took the sword and the weight of it felt real enough.

Maybe she wasn't dreaming.

Loke grabbed her wrist and began dragging her up the stairs she had fallen down, his long blue-leather-clad legs taking them two at a time and making her have to do the same to keep up with him.

"I am abducting you." His rich deep voice stirred warmth inside her and she could only stare at the back of his head as she absorbed what he had said.

He had come for her.

A chill swept through her, raising the hairs on her arms and the back of her neck, and a laugh bubbled up her throat and tumbled from her lips.

Loke paused at the top of the steps and looked back at her. "You seem unwell. Did the fall injure you? I tried to land beneath you but perhaps I did not manage it well enough to stop you from hurting yourself. You came at me quite unexpectedly. I tracked your scent and the feel of you on my senses, but I had not expected you to launch into my arms like that."

"I fell." She wished she hadn't said that when his blue eyes brightened with amusement.

He had been under the impression she had thrown herself at him on seeing him, and it certainly painted her in a better light than the truth that she had been a clumsy oaf.

"You must be more careful, Little Amazon, there is only one of you and you are irreplaceable."

Those words melted her heart and she threw herself at him this time, looping her arms around his neck and dragging him down for a kiss. He growled against her lips, wrapped his arms around her waist and pulled her flush against him as he kissed her. She heated to a thousand degrees and melted into a puddle as he mastered her mouth, his passion flowing through her and speaking of his need for her. His desire.

He really had come back for her.

She shoved away from him and held him at arm's length as he tried to pull her back into his arms. When she locked her elbows to resist him, he stopped trying and frowned at her, his mouth flattening into a grim line of displeasure.

"How are you here? Why are you here? You can't be here!" She might have been speaking too fast because his frown took on a confused edge and he just stared at her. Her fingers tensed against his bare chest. "You can't be in the mortal realm. It's too dangerous for you… you'll die. You have to go back."

He nodded. "I intend to, but there is something I must do first."

The way desire darkened his blue eyes and heated her inside said that what he had in mind was wicked and possibly time-consuming.

"You don't have time. You'll get sick again and I don't want that to happen. I don't know how you got here, but we have to get you back to Hell. We can talk there." She pressed against his chest but he didn't move.

He was a solid wall of muscle and strength, unmoveable.

That gave her pause.

He wasn't burning up, sick or trembling and weak.

Loke smiled and heat flooded her again, leaving her trembling and weak. "Tell me something, Little Amazon, did the elf prince explain what would happen as a consequence of you giving part of your life in order to save mine?"

She wracked her brain but couldn't find an answer to that question. There was every chance that Loren might have explained some things, but she only remembered him explaining how to save Loke. He hadn't mentioned any consequences.

She shook her head.

Loke's handsome face shifted in a way that made her feel he had known that and having her confirm it had irritated him. "I will have words with him about it when I next speak with him."

"Was there a consequence?" She looked up into his eyes and sought the answer from them. They smiled at her, soothing her fears and showing her that the consequence he had spoken of wasn't going to be a bad one.

At least not in his opinion.

"We are bound, Little Amazon. The piece of your life you gave to me has tied us together. I could feel you when I was in Hell."

She nodded now, amazement filling her as she realised that the reason she had always felt as if Loke was somewhere close to her was because she was bound to him. They were connected to each other.

"The consequences of what you did reaches deeper than merely binding us together though." Loke planted his hands on her hips and slowly drew her closer to him, his gaze on hers the whole time. "It has given me a link to this world, one that allows me to be here without endangering myself. I cannot shift, and I am weaker, but I will not die in this world."

Anais had difficulty taking that in and what it meant.

Loke could be in the mortal realm without it killing him, and that meant he could visit her and she could continue her work with Archangel, at least for now.

Her heart stopped soaring and plummeted as she realised that it hadn't really changed anything.

The banishment that meant he couldn't survive in the mortal realm wasn't the reason he had left her.

"But the visions," she whispered and his face softened as he lifted his right hand and brushed his knuckles across her cheek.

"I thought about what the prince told me after he had taken me back to Hell, and I have found a way to stop the vision from coming to pass." His blue gaze tracked his fingers as he stroked her cheek and she sensed the nerves in him, a trickle of fear that ran through her too.

Whatever he had discovered, he feared how she would react to it.

"Tell me," she whispered and caught his hand, stopping him from caressing her. He opened his hand and pressed his palm to her cheek, and she held it there as she drowned in the endless depths of his blue eyes and the love they held for her.

"I am weaker in this world and I cannot shift. My dragon instincts are suppressed, but not extinguished. I still feel a need to mate with you and it still compels me to go through with it, but it is not as fierce as it is when we were in Hell." His voice trembled the tiniest amount and she wanted to smile at how afraid he was of saying things straight to her.

His fear was ungrounded.

She wasn't going to reject him.

Because she wanted what he was offering to her.

"I want to be your mate, Loke."

His eyes shot wide and he stared at her in stunned silence.

Anais giggled. "That's what you're asking, isn't it? You want to mate with me in this world, where you feel more in control."

He nodded.

Swallowed hard.

"You will be my mate?"

It was a ridiculous question, but one she knew he needed to hear her answer so he could believe it.

"Yes."

Loke grinned, his gaze fell to her lips and he went to pull her into his arms.

The sound of crossbows clicking as they were loaded froze both of them to the spot and Anais edged her eyes beyond Loke to the hunters stood there, aware that there were more blocking the other end of the corridor and the stairs behind her too.

She had been so caught up in seeing Loke again and the thought they might finally be able to be together that she had forgotten he had caused a mass panic and everyone had been hunting for him.

"This has to be the first time I've seen a captive come back after escaping."

Anais grimaced as Mark's, the head of the hunter department, voice cut through the wailing of the alarms. How the hell were they going to get out of this one?

Loke set her away from him, turned to face the sharply dressed fair-haired man where he stood in front of three male hunters, and narrowed his blue eyes on him. Anais looked between them as their eyes locked in silent combat and the tension in the air rose. She wasn't sure what Loke was going to do.

Mark had close to a dozen hunters backing him up. She would fight with Loke if it came down to it, but her dreams of being able to continue as a hunter for Archangel would die in that same moment.

Loke finally dragged his eyes away from Mark and settled them on her, and she couldn't stop herself from looking up at him, even when she knew he would see the conflict in her. She wanted to be with Loke, but she had a job to do here too, a mission that meant a lot to her and she wasn't ready to leave it all behind. Not yet. She wanted to be his mate, and eventually she would leave Archangel to be with him permanently, but she needed time to adjust and needed to fulfil her mission here.

A hint of a smile curved the corners of his lips and he looked back at the head of the hunters and said the last thing she had expected to hear, but it was something she knew he was doing for her, because he loved her and he wanted her to be happy.

And that meant the world to her.

"I have come to offer a deal."

CHAPTER 27

Loke hadn't expected things to take the turns that they had after he had flown to the elf kingdom to seek an audience with the prince. He'd had to face down an army of dark elves all determined to be the one who speared his chest with their weapon, and he had thought that would be his greatest obstacle in his challenge to reach Anais.

He had been mistaken.

He hadn't anticipated the elf prince agreeing to teleport him to the mortal realm and then dropping him in the middle of what had appeared to be Archangel's eating hall and wishing him good luck. The wretched male had grinned at him as he had teleported away, leaving him to face the hunters alone when he could have easily helped him by making his presence known. They knew Prince Loren. They would have put down their weapons if he had asked it of them.

But the male had wanted to test his resolve.

Loke knew that and it was the only reason he wasn't going to track the wretch down and teach him a lesson when he returned to Hell.

He would prove to the prince that he was determined to fight for Anais and win her as his mate.

Loke also hadn't anticipated running into Anais when he had been tracking her movements within the building while outrunning the hunters who also wanted to be the one to spear his chest with their weapon. It seemed elves and humans were no different. They both saw a dragon and wanted to slay it.

Saint George had a lot to answer for.

The last thing that Loke hadn't anticipated?

Striking a deal with a man who appeared to be a leader among the hunters.

But he had seen the look in Anais's eyes and knew in his heart that her position and her mission with Archangel meant a lot to her, and therefore it meant a lot to him. He wanted her as his mate, but he didn't want to jeopardise her happiness in order to achieve that. She had a life in the mortal realm and family too, and she would always want to spend part of her time in this world. He had come to terms with that over the days they had been apart.

That was the reason he was now standing in the office of a sandy-haired male who looked at him as if he was expecting Loke to breathe fire whenever he spoke or sprout horns and wings.

The male leaned his backside against a wide oak desk and folded his arms across his chest, causing the sleeves of his black suit to tighten over his muscles. Even in his weakened state, Loke was far stronger than the male, but the hunter had a glint in his grey eyes, a coldness that made it clear that he would fight Loke regardless of the difference in their strength if he didn't like what Loke was about to propose.

Loke took a step towards him and Anais shuffled restlessly where she stood near an unlit fire pit dug into the wall. The mortal world was filled with distractions that Loke wanted to explore now that he could survive in it, but he managed to keep his focus on his business with the male and off every fascinating object in the room.

"I did not return so you could incarcerate me again," Loke said, wanting that out in the open and made as clear as possible before he started. "I would not consider it. It appears I am able to retain enough strength when in this world now to do a great deal of damage to any who might be foolish enough to attempt to restrain me."

The male nodded.

"I am come for my mate." Loke frowned when the male's dark eyes left him and shifted to his left, towards Anais where she lingered near the fireplace. Loke could feel her embarrassment as the male scrutinised her, and he was on the verge of growling at him when the male did the right thing and took his eyes off Loke's mate. "I am not leaving without her, but I am not taking her from you either. She will remain as one of your hunters, and in exchange for your kindness and understanding in this matter, I invite your *scientists* to meet with me in Hell where I will… show them my dragon."

"Loke," Anais whispered with concern and disbelief lacing her soft voice and he held his hand up to silence her.

"I will not subject myself to any form of studying, but I will do all that is necessary to provide your people with a better understanding of my species, including the fact that we are not a threat to mortals or this world." Loke held the male's grey gaze.

There was a flicker of warmth in it now, a note of intrigue and interest that gave Loke hope.

"Very well. I will make the arrangements at my end and I'm sure the research division will be pleased to hear they will have their chance—"

"Olivia will lead the team," Anais interjected and the male flicked her a glare.

Loke growled at him, flashing a hint of sharp teeth as anger blasted through him and they shifted. The male backed down, schooling his features and settling his gaze back on Loke.

"Olivia will lead the team," Loke said, his tone brooking no argument from the male. "If she is not present when your people arrive at the agreed time and location, I will change my mind about not being a threat to mortals in this world."

"It isn't wise to threaten Archangel." The male lowered his hands to his sides and gripped the edge of the desk.

Loke narrowed his gaze on him. "It is not wise to threaten my mate."

The hunter looked as if he wanted to glance at Anais again, but sensibly kept his focus locked on Loke instead. "Olivia will lead the team of scientists. You will help us understand more about dragon physiology and your realm in Hell, but also the reason dragons cannot live in this world and why you can. Anais will retain her position within Archangel. Agreed?"

Loke nodded. "Agreed. I will also assist your hunters in saving their kin from the dragons and Anais and the one called Sable will lead that team."

The male nodded.

Loke held his hand out to Anais and she took hold of it. He gave one last warning look at her superior, turned and quickly led her from the room.

"You're insane," Anais hissed and he looked down at her as he shifted his hand in hers, interlinking their fingers.

"Perhaps, but it seemed like the only solution to our mutual problem. I want you as my mate, Anais, and I am willing to do whatever it takes for that to happen." He pulled her with him down through the building, sniffing occasionally and tracking the scents of immortals.

"Where are we going?" Anais looked around them as they reached an underground level.

"The cellblock. I require something from it."

He felt her frown at him.

"You're not going to break someone out are you, because it might not go down well. I got into a lot of trouble when I broke you out." She was serious and very much wrong about his reasons for returning to a place he never wanted to set foot in again.

"No. I am going to steal something... other than you." He tugged her along when she began to slow and ignored her glare. She wouldn't be annoyed with him wanting to steal something else from Archangel too when she saw what it was and knew his reasons for taking it. He shrugged. "I am a dragon. We are drawn to shiny objects."

The item he had seen had been very shiny and it was the solution to a problem that still stood between them, even though he was weaker in this realm and his dragon instincts were quieter.

When he reached the cellblock, he kept going straight rather than turning left down the stairs towards the cells. He stopped in the room he had seen when the guards had been dragging him back to his cell and glanced at Anais.

She stood just behind him, her blue eyes wide and her mouth hanging open.

It snapped shut and she shifted her eyes to him. "This is what you're going to steal?"

Loke nodded.

And picked up one of the sets of thick silver manacles.

They were heavy in his hand and cold against his skin, and the thought of being shackled unsettled him, but it was necessary and he would put himself through it if it meant he wouldn't hurt Anais during their mating.

He would hand control of it over to her.

A fierce blush burned her cheeks.

She was beautiful.

He held the restraints out to her and she just stared at them. "We will need a place in this world where I can be bound to something solid with these."

Her blush deepened. "It's not as if I have thick steel pipes or something like that just running through my room, you know? I really haven't got a clue where we could go that does... oh... well... I have seen one place that might work."

"Where?" He didn't like the way her fear rose, surging through him too.

"That nightclub."

"The one where I had a vision." Loke's stomach dropped into his feet. He didn't want to take Anais back there. It was too dangerous. He had seen her die in that place.

"I know what you're thinking. What if you take me back there and it all goes horribly wrong? It's the only place I know where there are places... private places... that we can do this. It doesn't exactly thrill me either... but I want to do this, Loke. I want to be your mate and I'm willing to risk it." The fierce look in her eyes, the determination that he could feel in her, backed up her words.

He looked down at the shackles. They were strong and he was weak right now. If they bound him to something equally as strong, he wouldn't be able to hurt Anais. She would be able to escape him if he lost control. She wanted to be his mate, and he wanted to be hers.

She was right.

It was worth the risk.

But only because the shackles minimised that risk until it was so small that he didn't fear for her life.

The nightclub had strong immortals residing in it. If he lost control, they would be able to handle him and take him down. Anais would be safest there.

He nodded. "Lead the way to this nightclub."

She pulled on his hand, leading him up through the building. The manacles clanked with each step he took, holding his attention together with the fear steadily building inside him, until Anais led him out into the night.

He released her hand and slowly walked past her, marvelling at the dark sky.

Dazzling sparkling white and coloured pinpricks punctuated it.

"They're called stars."

He swallowed hard and couldn't take his eyes off them. "My mother told me about stars. She learned of them from her mother. I did not expect them to be so beautiful."

Anais laughed. "They're drowned out by the lights of the city. You should see what they look like from the countryside where it's darker and there's less light pollution."

He dropped his head and fixed his gaze on her. "We can do that?"

She nodded and smiled warmly. "Later. I thought you had other plans?"

He did, but he was also a dragon, easily distracted by the things that fascinated or were new to him. So much in this world was new and it was almost too much to take in as he swept his gaze around them. Every building looked different. There were rectangular slabs of pale stone beneath his bare feet. Mechanical beasts prowled around with people inside of them and bright glowing white eyes that illuminated their path.

A loud roar came from overhead and Loke ducked down and snarled, baring his fangs at the giant metal beast that cut across the sky.

"A dragon," he whispered in awe and straightened.

Anais chuckled again. "It's a plane."

"A plane?" He watched it as it soared into the distance. "Does it live and breathe?"

She laughed. "Hell, no. It's a method of transport for people. Like the cars. We like to fly too, but we don't have wings."

Mortals had made dragons to carry them around the world. Incredible.

Anais cleared her throat, reached out and took the shackles from him, stealing his attention back to her. "Perhaps the quicker we get you to Underworld, the better. I swear I'll take you exploring and explain everything you want to know, but after we seal this deal."

She stole every last shred of his focus as she stepped up to him, placed her free hand against his bare chest and tiptoed for a kiss.

He bent his head and claimed her lips as he wrapped his arms around her, pulling her against him and supporting her. She moaned and he forgot about his desire to explore the mortal world.

The desire to explore every inch of her was even more pressing and infinitely more exciting.

Her lips brushed across his, tearing a low moan from his throat as he gathered her closer and lost himself in the warm soft feel of her in his arms and her mouth on his.

Gods, he needed her.

Now.

He scooped her up into his arms and began running.

"It's that way." Anais pointed and he backtracked and sprinted down the narrow alley between the buildings on his left.

She clung to his shoulders, bouncing in his arms with each long stride as he ran towards their destination as quickly as his feet could carry him. He longed for his wings and the ability to shift, even when he knew that the sight of a flying man or a dragon would cause widespread panic and Archangel would be severely unimpressed, and possibly extremely angry with him. He just wanted to get Anais to Underworld as quickly as possible.

He needed to claim her as his mate.

The fierce hunger for her had returned the moment their lips had touched, filling him with an urgent need to sink his fangs into her throat and bind them as one forever. His teeth sharpened at only the thought and he growled through them as he sprinted faster, following her instructions and battling his growing need to mate with her.

The scent of desire rolling off her wasn't helping matters.

He could feel her need pumping through him and his every male instinct demanded that he satisfy it, giving her what she desired. He wasn't sure how much longer he could resist his own need to kiss her and touch her.

Every inch of her was pure temptation. Her black trousers hugged her long legs and her t-shirt was tight across her breasts. Gods, he wanted to kiss and lick her all over until she was begging for him to fill her and take her.

"There!" Anais shouted and he lifted his head from her jiggling breasts and spotted the colourful sign of the nightclub ahead of him.

He skidded to a halt, his eyes locked on the sign, awestruck by the sight of it. It glowed, illuminating the area around it on the dark wall and the people below it. Amazing. Was this and the other lights he had seen the result of electricity? Were they all powered by the things Anais had called batteries?

Anais slapped his cheek. "Focus."

He shook his head to do just that and headed for the door below the sign.

He didn't wait when the man at the door shouted for him to. He shoved his way into the bustling building and scanned the crowd, searching for the immortals he had smelled during his last visit.

There were far more immortals in the club than he had anticipated. The last time he had been here, it had been empty save for a few people. Now it was filled to bursting point and it was so loud it hurt his ears.

Anais pulled herself up in his arms, bringing her breasts close to his face and ripping a groan from his throat.

She pointed towards the bar area. "The guy with the sandy hair in the white shirt."

Loke's gaze darted over everyone in that area until he found the one she meant. The fair-haired shifter stood at the far end of the bar, talking to a black-haired female. Loke pushed through the crowd, clinging to Anais when people jostled and bumped him, and breathed out a sigh of relief when he reached the shifter.

The male turned curious golden eyes on him and Anais. "Said he was your mate."

Loke could almost feel the heat of her blush on his skin.

"I don't suppose we can borrow your back room?" She held the cuffs up and the shifter chortled.

"Be my guest. I know an uncontrollable urge when I smell one and you guys are throwing off all kinds of pheromones." He waved towards the door that led into the rear of the nightclub. "Just be sure to let me know when you're done and I'll have a bottle of champagne ready."

"Kyter," the female admonished, and the male lifted his shoulders in a shameless shrug.

"I remember how badly I wanted to mate with you," Kyter purred and the woman blushed and cast her gaze down at the bar. "Gods, you're beautiful."

"Shut up." She pushed him in the shoulder.

"I have one thing I must ask of you too," Loke said, needing to seize the shifter's attention and secure his promise before the male got carried away in flirting with his mate.

The male nodded. "Name it."

"If I lose control, knock me out and keep Anais safe for me." Loke ignored the soft huff from Anais, keeping his eyes on the male.

The shifter frowned and then eventually nodded. "No problem… but try not to lose control… because although you seem like a nice guy, I have no desire to see your junk."

Loke wasn't sure what that meant but he nodded anyway. The male grinned and lifted a panel beside him, exited the bar and walked to the door. He did something with the device mounted on it and opened it for them. Loke thanked him with another nod and carried Anais through the door.

"You do know he was talking about your man bits?" Anais whispered.

Loke nodded. He did now, anyway. The shifter didn't have to worry. Loke had little desire to show that private part of himself to the male. He was going to do his best to retain control, because he loved Anais and wanted to be her mate. He wanted to put an end to his terrible visions of her and set them on a path towards a brighter future where they could be together without fear.

He followed her directions up the metal staircase to the left of the large pale room, heading back towards the room where he had awakened. It wasn't the one she had thought about. She pressed him to keep going when they reached it and they ended up in a different sort of room. This one had a table in the middle of it, a pale wooden floor, and cupboards.

"It's a kitchen," Anais said and there was an apologetic note in her voice. "But look."

She pointed directly ahead of them.

Thick metal pipes ran up the wall there, strong enough to resist him if he lost control. His heart lifted at the sight of them but his hunger for Anais also soared, already pushing at his control. She seemed to sense it as she slowly turned her face to look into his eyes, her own dark with desire, with need that called to him.

He growled and went to kiss her. She pushed out of his arms and disappeared from the room, returning just as he was about to hunt her down, her arms laden with blankets.

His thoughtful little Amazon.

She busied herself with making a nest for them and he shut the door. The sound of it closing caused her to still halfway through arranging a pillow near the pipes.

Loke stalked towards her, his heart drumming heavily in his chest, every inch of him filled with a need to touch her.

She straightened and slowly turned to face him. Her gaze raked over him, setting him on fire as it travelled over his body and the hunger in her eyes deepened, speaking of how much she desired him. He growled again and she lifted her eyes back to his.

Gods, he wanted to touch and kiss her for a while before he let her restrain him, but he couldn't risk it. He would have an eternity to take things slowly with her and indulge his every hunger. Right now, he needed to mate with her and make that eternity happen.

He grabbed the shackles and locked one over his right wrist. The metal was cold, tight and hard against his skin, but the discomfort would be worth it and he was sure he would lose awareness of the cuffs once he got his first taste of her.

She stepped aside and watched him as he sat on the blankets and threaded the other end of the restraints and the chain behind the pipes. They were hot to the touch, but dragons were resistant to heat. They wouldn't harm him.

Loke pulled down a deep breath to steady himself and obliterate his nerves, and lay on his back. Anais kneeled beside him, her sweet scent filling his senses, and secured his other wrist. He tugged on the restraints and they didn't give, not even when he used all of his limited strength.

The thought that he could mate with her without fearing hurting her, that he could lose control and she would be safe, had all of his dragon instincts hurtling to the fore.

He snarled and tried to grab her, hungry for his first taste of her. The chain snapped against the pipes and jerked his hands back. He fought them, growling as he tried to break free so he could reach his little mortal.

His fated female.

Her voice broke through the buzzing in his mind. "Loke."

She was calling for him.

He stilled and stared at her. His heart. His everything.

She knelt beside him. A benevolent angel who had blessed him with her love.

The female who had been made for him alone.

He groaned when she grabbed the hem of her t-shirt and pulled it off. Her breasts were bare beneath it, their dusky peaks calling to him and filling him with a hunger to taste them. He tipped his chin up, beckoning her closer and silently telling her what he needed. She resisted him, rising to her feet instead, and kicked off her boots. He was about to growl at her when she silenced him by stripping off her trousers and then her black underwear.

Glorious.

She stood before him nude and beautiful, but not naked.

Around her neck hung the pendant he have given her. She had kept it. Her right hand rose to it and she fingered the teardrop diamonds, a smile on her rosy lips.

"You look as if you thought I'd pawn it or throw it away." Her smile grew, teasing him. "Never, Loke. It's precious to me."

"As you are precious to me." He jerked his chin again. "Come, Little Amazon… you are killing me. I need you."

The scent of her desire in the air grew stronger and her eyes darkened a full shade as her pupils widened with arousal. He groaned and breathed deep of her, savouring her need for him as his need for her pushed him closer to the edge.

She kneeled beside him again and ran her hands down his chest, her gaze on his the whole time. Her fingers traced the contours of his muscles and the way her eyes grew even darker empowered him and made him want to roar. His female liked his body. He would give it to her.

He groaned when she reached his blue leathers and began unfastening the lacing. His cock pulsed eagerly, each one paining him. He was too hard, too hungry for her. He felt as if he might burst.

Cool air washed over his aching length and then warm satin stroked him and he rolled his eyes closed and flexed his hips, driving himself into the soft circle of her fingers as she caressed him. It was too much. He grunted and thrust, losing himself in the pleasure that rolled through him in response. His teeth sank into his lower lip and he frowned as she tightened her grip on him. Gods.

He snarled as her hand left him, his eyes shooting open to pin her with a glare that would relay his displeasure. All of his anger melted in an instant as she threw her leg over him, planted her hands on his bare chest and lowered her hips. Her wet heat scalded him, pinning his shaft between them, and every inch of him tensed as he grasped the chain between his shackles, seeking a way of anchoring himself as he feared he might float away on the wave of bliss that crashed over him.

She moaned and he lost himself in watching the pleasure flitting across her face as she rocked on him, rubbing herself on his cock.

Her golden hair spilled around her shoulders like a veil of sunlight. His little mortal. She was everything in this world that he lacked in his. She was sunlight and blue skies. She was beauty. She was softness and warmth. She completed him.

He growled again as she rocked on him and his need for her collided with the flimsy barrier around his primal instincts. His nails lengthened into claws and his teeth all sharpened, becoming twin rows of tiny fangs. Her eyes widened and then narrowed, and he stilled right down to his breathing as she leaned over him, lifting herself off his length, and kissed him.

He carefully kissed her back, afraid of cutting her with his teeth. Her tongue stroked his fangs and he groaned, shuddering as bliss rocked him. He couldn't take it. He needed to be inside her. He needed to sink the fangs she was caressing with her tongue into her throat as he claimed her.

His feral snarl seemed to convey those needs to her and he tensed and jerked as she reached between them and settled one hand around his length. She kissed him harder, a brief clashing of their lips that filled his mouth with the intoxicating taste of her blood, and then leaned back.

Loke moaned in time with her as the head of his cock nudged into her sheath and he clutched the pipes, clinging to them as she eased onto him, slowly taking him into her hot wet core. He trembled and bit his lower lip, drawing his own blood as she rose off him and sank down onto his length. She was so hot and tight, gripping him fiercely. She rotated her hips and his instincts roared back to the fore.

He snarled and rocked his hips upwards, driving into her, ripping a loud bark of pleasure from her lips as she dug her nails into his chest. She flicked her eyes open and locked them on his. Her hands shifted to his hips and she pressed them down hard as she fought him for control. He wanted to bite her. He needed to mark her as his.

It was all he could think about as she rode his cock, bliss dancing across her face with every meeting of their hips, her hands pinning him and holding him at her mercy. Gods, she could ride him straight to Hell and he wouldn't care as long as it felt this good. He groaned and tipped his head back, banging it against the pipes as he tried to handle the overload of pleasure that ripped through him. It was too much.

His love for her tempered his dragon instincts, but it didn't hold them back. They broke through, shattering his control and unleashing the primal need to mate with her. He rocked his hips in time with her, driving into her tight sheath, tearing moan after moan from her sweet lips. His mate.

She would be his.

He stared at her as he pulled on his shackles, fighting them in order to reach her. He would reach her. He needed to sink his fangs into her throat and mark her. He needed to claim her. Nothing would stop him. Not chains and steel. Not her. He arched his back and growled as he pulled on the chain, unleashing every drop of his strength into his attempt to break free.

Warm hands pressed against his chest.

Soft breath puffed across his lips.

He stilled and stared at her where she hovered above him, her golden hair spilling down to caress his chest.

Her blue eyes shone with understanding and he couldn't breathe as she reached her right hand over the back of her head, caught the fall of her hair on her left side, and drew it away from her throat, exposing it for him.

She leaned closer. "Bite me, Loke. Claim me."

His heart gave one hard beat.

And then he lurched up and sank his fangs into the subtle curve of her neck.

She cried out, her body tightening around his, and he wanted to hold her gently even as his every instinct said to grasp her tightly and never let her go.

She was his now. He battled his darker instincts, fighting against them as the first drop of her blood touched his tongue. She had given herself to him, and he was blessed by her love for him and what she had done, and he would do everything in his power to make their mating as special for her as it was for him.

He rocked his hips slowly, keeping each thrust controlled and measured, a deep stroke of his cock that would give her pleasure as he drank from her vein. She moaned, the sound music to his ears, and relaxed against him. The taste of her was divine, but he refused to let it intoxicate him. He clung to the tattered shreds of his control, determined to make this a moment they would both remember fondly.

Anais moaned and started moving on him, building the pleasure within him, sending him soaring as the connection between them began to open and grow stronger, forging the bond between them. She clutched his shoulders and her breath tickled his ear as he thrust into her, countering her movements, taking her as deeply as he could while retaining his hold on her with his mouth.

Pressure built within him as her emotions ran through him, as clear as his own, and he knew they had formed the bond between them and brought it close to completion. He convinced himself to release her and she pushed herself up, tearing a groan from his throat as he sank deeper inside her.

She needed his blood now.

He sank his teeth into his lower lip, cutting it open for her. Her eyes fell there and narrowed, a hungry edge filling them, desire that he knew she had little control over and that he hoped wasn't frightening her. She didn't feel afraid. She felt as hazy and intoxicated as he did, filled with the pleasure of their mating and hungry for more.

Anais leaned over him again and captured his lips in a fierce kiss that ripped a moan from him. She delved her tongue between his lips, tangling it with his as she rocked on him, taking him up to Heaven and beyond that realm. She tightened around him and he could feel she was close, on the precipice as he was.

She moved back and sucked his lower lip into her mouth, pulling on it and drawing his blood from him.

It was a blur after that.

The moment she swallowed, her head shot up and she cried out, her body quivering around his and her heat scalding him. He grunted and pleasure blasted through him, a combination of hers and his own as her climax drew his from him. He fell apart as she clung to him, his whole body shaking as his cock pulsed, shooting hot jets of seed into her, and couldn't control his hips as they thrust shallowly in time with each groan that left his lips.

Anais stayed rigid and tensed above him, breathless moans escaping her as his body pulsed within hers, and then slowly sank down against his chest. She pressed her hands to his pectorals and her cheek to the spot over his heart, and he breathed hard as he struggled to bring himself down and acclimatise to being able to feel everything that she was.

He could feel her pleasure flowing through her and her happiness.

He could feel her love for him.

And he knew she could feel his for her.

He went to wrap his arms around her and growled as he met with resistance and remembered he was shackled.

But it had been worth it.

Because she was his mate now, bound to him forever, and the dragon instincts that had possessed him and tried to control him were already receding, satisfied by the bond that existed between them.

She lifted her head and kissed him, and he sighed against her lips, causing her to draw back and frown at him.

He rattled his manacles, hinting at her freeing him, but she only smiled at him.

She leaned back over him and kissed him again, and whispered against his lips. "I'm not done with you yet."

He groaned as his body responded to that, hunger for her surging through the haze of his climax to drive it back and reignite his need for her.

"When will you be done with me?" He meant it as a way of asking when she would release him but her slow smile stole his heart together with the twinkle in her eyes.

"Never." She brushed her fingers across his cheek and leaned in to kiss him.

Never.

He liked the sound of that.

He had feared he had found his mate only to have cruel fate steal her from him. He had feared that he would be forced to face forever alone.

But now he had his beautiful mate and they would never be alone again. They would always have each other.

He had stolen many things in his life as a dragon, all of them beautiful to a degree, but he had never stolen anything as precious as his little Amazon that night he had taken her from the battle.

And he had never had anything stolen from him.

Dragons fiercely guarded that which they owned.

Anais had done the impossible and had taken a dragon's most precious possession.

She had stolen his heart.

The End

ABOUT THE AUTHOR

Felicity Heaton is a New York Times and USA Today best-selling author who writes passionate paranormal romance books. In her books she creates detailed worlds, twisting plots, mind-blowing action, intense emotion and heart-stopping romances with leading men that vary from dark deadly vampires to sexy shape-shifters and wicked werewolves, to sinful angels and hot demons!

If you're a fan of paranormal romance authors Lara Adrian, J R Ward, Sherrilyn Kenyon, Gena Showalter, Larissa Ione and Christine Feehan then you will enjoy her books too.

If you love your angels a little dark and wicked, the best-selling Her Angel series is for you. If you like strong, powerful, and dark vampires then try the Vampires Realm series or any of her stand-alone vampire romance books. If you're looking for vampire romances that are sinful, passionate and erotic then try the best-selling Vampire Erotic Theatre series. Or if you prefer huge detailed worlds filled with hot-blooded alpha males in every species, from elves to demons to dragons to shifters and angels, then take a look at the new Eternal Mates series.

If you have enjoyed this story, please take a moment to contact the author at **author@felicityheaton.co.uk** or to post a review of the book online

Connect with Felicity:
Website – http://www.felicityheaton.co.uk
Blog – http://www.felicityheaton.co.uk/blog/
Twitter – http://twitter.com/felicityheaton
Facebook – http://www.facebook.com/felicityheaton
Goodreads – http://www.goodreads.com/felicityheaton
Mailing List – http://www.felicityheaton.co.uk/newsletter.php

FIND OUT MORE ABOUT HER BOOKS AT:
http://www.felicityheaton.co.uk

Made in the USA
Columbia, SC
08 December 2019